Dreams of Chaos: Book 1

by

Ashley Chappell

Discover Other titles by Chappell:

Dreams of Chaos Series
Alice Will
Tilt
A God of Gods
A Mother of Gods (Spring 2019)

Other Titles
Of War and Taters
The Firefly Paradox

View samples, news, and extras at
http://www.ashleychappellbooks.com/

Praise for Chappell

"It's smart, it's funny, it's sad, it's action-packed... It's like Harry Potter with a divine twist!"
- Elizabeth Seckman, author of the *Coulter Men* Series

"It's a rollicking adventure with nail-biting suspense tempered with humor."
- Tom Hooten, author of *Hollytime*

"What I will say is that when this book is good, which is 96.3% of the time... it is damn good."
- Dennis P. Sharpe, author of *The Coming Storm Trilogy*

To Steven, for his love and inspiration,
My Mother, for her enduring faith,
My Father, that this gift may find him in the stars.

FOREWORD

Journals are, to a writer, deeply personal things. The moment we put our first thoughts on their pages they become a piece of our souls. My own favorite brown leather journal is also where I always turn to give my fledgling ideas flesh; I have shaped entire worlds between its covers before pushing them out into the world. That book (whose cover is still hanging on by sheer miracle) became my confidant, my talisman, my security blanket, and eventually my inspiration for Alice and her own journal. When I first started brainstorming her story in its pages, I thought I was going to be telling a story about a little girl whose journal was enchanted with the ability to transform the world around her into her most secret desires. I thought it would be a story about the dangers inherent in actually getting what we want and in learning to temper our desires with the needs of others.

In a way, it still is.

But eventually, it was writing in my journal that changed me instead of the other way around.

Now *Alice Will* is also about laughing at ourselves and the empty traditions we value without knowing why. It's about taking stock in our instincts before we let our fickle brains over-rationalize us out of the right choice. It's about learning the hard way that maturity, at any age, is no match for experience. And finally, it's about remembering that the right thing to do is *still* the right thing to do when no one is looking.

I hope you enjoy the adventure and the new universe that grew out of a sentimental attachment to a pile of bound stationery (that also happens to contain a large and scribbly part of my soul).

PROLOGUE

Religion is a by-product of living in a world brimming with gods. And a by-product of religion – though it's really more of an occupational hazard – is the Apocalypse. Following this formula, each of the many religions of the flat world of Aevum spawned their own expectations for the end of the world, but, given that the end of the world was also the end of the believers, no one was still around to say "I told you so" when the end actually came. The only religion that came close to what really happened was the Nihilese belief that one day the world would simply fall out of reality and ultimately never have existed in the first place. Not one of them ever suspected that the world would end by being swallowed by the imagination of a child.

See that child here: A frail thing, hurting, sad, and alone, making her way through a blizzard with barely a drop of moonlight piercing the snow. This snow is the kind that gangs up on the way down and forms snowballs filled with ice shrapnel.

Now see her here: Crawling quickly under the boughs of Grandfather Tree, the giant fir that had been by the river longer than even the village. Digging beneath the needles with frozen fingers, then finding the tattered book she so loved. The shadow of the word 'Journal' is across the front cover of the book, barely visible as the gold leafing had long ago peeled away. Squinting in the muted light filtering through the snow-encased limbs, she rereads her last entry before creating a new one. The entry was happy, it was beautiful, and it sounded like it had been a perfect day for any six year-old girl.

It was just a shame that it had been nothing like her real day. It never was.

CHAPTER 1

"What... what the...? Oh, gross!" Trotter went from deeply asleep and dreaming to awake and revolted in under two seconds. Waking up to a cat's paw shoved against your lips will usually have that effect.

"Prowler, that's disgusting," she said as she tried to wipe her mouth with her sleeve even though it probably wasn't much cleaner. "What's wrong with you?"

The cat, a sleek gray-blue creature, narrowed his eyes at her and pretended to suddenly find her less interesting than the bit of trash in his paw.

"Seriously, why would you even do that? Other cats gently nuzzle their people awake, you know. And I know you've been out all day so gods only know where that paw's been." She tried to spit.

Prowler sniffed and turned his back to her. It's well established that cats demand gratitude for every gesture they make toward their owner, from dragging in fresh kills to considerately covering their poo in the cat box. If this gratitude is not tendered then you simply cease to exist as a part of the world which interests them.

Trotter left her bed with a stretch and Prowler connived to keep his back to her as she crossed the room while still trying to pretend that he hadn't noticed her existence. It was the same effect you get from the pictures with eyes that seem to follow you everywhere you go, only in reverse. She patted the pouting cat on the head as she walked behind him and was hissed at before he returned to the careful study of his paw.

"So I guess this isn't the part where you're going to apologize for waking me up with whatever new disease you walked through? Just thought I'd check," she added when he glared back in response.

She shoved the makeshift curtain aside and the purples, pinks, and reds of another amazing sunset over the picturesque harbor of Sarano poured into the room.

"Crap! It's almost sunset already. I'll miss the Market!"

"Oh, now she gets it!" Prowler wheeled around and faced her with a harassed air. "I simply try to wake her up before she's late and I get nothing but grief for it."

Cats are natural masters of the haughty stare, but Prowler had the advantage of having had much longer than the average cat to take the art from mere mastery to sheer perfection. About one hundred and eighty years longer, in fact.

"Is that what this is about?" Trotter sighed. He was temperamental, but Prowler was still the best friend she had. "I'm sorry. Thank you, Prowler, for waking me up in time for the Market. But don't you think there might be better ways of waking me up next time maybe? Like telling me to wake up rather than sticking your paw in my mouth?"

He twitched his tail. "I tried. But you couldn't hear me over the racket you were making. And considering that you've been snoring for the past two hours, you're lucky I waited until now to put my paw in your mouth. Actually, as loud as you were, you're lucky it was just my paw."

"I don't snore," Trotter mumbled.

Prowler leaped up into the windowsill beside her and continued, effectively accepting her apology while by no means acknowledging it. "Anyway, I ran into Miro earlier this afternoon. She said she'd have everything on your list ready when you got there tonight."

Not surprising, even though Trotter hadn't even given Miro her list yet. Miro always knew everything. No matter what you asked her, she always had it, and usually included what you were going to ask her for before you ever asked. It was a little unnerving sometimes.

She slid the first clothes she found on the floor over her sleeping gown and reached for her brush, closing her hand on empty air. It was usually on the crates she'd stacked up under the mirror, but it wasn't there now. A glance around the warehouse loft found plenty of junk from wood scraps to iron chunks to broken tools, but no hairbrush.

"Prowler, have you seen my brush anywhere?"

"It wouldn't be brown with a tortoise shell handle by any chance, would it?" He asked with contrived innocence.

"You know it would be. It's the only brush I have. Now why don't you tell me where it is?"

When he didn't answer straight away her eyes searched lower to the ground. Sure enough, there it was a few inches above the floor adhered to the wall on a sticky wad of gloop. It was filled suspiciously with blue-gray hairs.

"Are you kidding me? How did you even do that without thumbs?"

"Thumbs? Ha!" He laughed contemptibly. "The day I miss having thumbs is the day I quit living this feline existence. Claws are so much more utilitarian. Besides, if you brushed me more often I wouldn't have to resort to such drastic measures. Thumbs! Who needs thumbs, anyway?" He muttered to himself before returning to the licking of his paw.

Trotter gave him an apprising look and glanced from the wall back to him. "You glued your paw to the wall, didn't you? That's why you've been licking it so much."

"That's ridiculous!" He sneered defiantly. She continued to look sternly at him and waited patiently while his defiant sneer melted into a dejected sulk. "Ok," he conceded, "but it was only for a minute. I'd like to see you do as well given the circumstances. Besides, it's not like you need a brush. Just make you hair to do what you want it to do."

"It never works out like I picture it," she said, a whine creeping into her voice. It was true, though. No matter what glamorous style she imagined for her hair to weave itself into she always ended up looking like she'd been attacked by a failed beautician turned circus costumer.

"What do you expect? You're only fourteen. Most demi-gods spend years practicing to get the hang of their powers, and you refuse to try half the time. These things take practice and patience. No better time than now, as they say."

"Alright, fine." She started to concentrate and realized she was still being watched. "I can't do it with you looking!" Prowler rolled his eyes and turned his back to her. It was so embarrassing to be watched, especially when you weren't even very good at magic to begin with. She focused and pictured her hair growing longer and sleeker, the mousy brown turning itself into a luxurious chestnut brown and piling itself on top of her head in the elaborate fashion of the day. She opened her eyes and looked at Prowler.

"Well?" She asked hesitantly.

Cat expressions are usually hard to read, but this one was clearly full of shock. "Oh my. Do you still have that hat, perhaps? You know, the really, really big one?"

She glanced at the mirror across from her and for just a moment thought a large fruit was looking back at her. "I'm never going to get the hang of this, am I? Some demi-god I am." She dropped onto the floor under the window and laid her head against the wall in defeat, her head coming to rest on the unnaturally cloud-like pillow of hair. Prowler dropped down next to her without a sound.

"Cheer up," he said as he laid his head down on her lap. "It's not really that bad. It's a bit too big and fluffy, but I'm sure no one will notice how orange it is. They may even think you're trying to start a trend. You'd be amazed at the types of things that catch on."

"Right. I'm sure someone out there is just dying for an excuse to try a hairdo that looks like a giant pumpkin."

The sounds of the seaport city of Sarano winding down the day filtered up to her window above the old doorknob factory. She could hear the rattling of the trundlers' carriages and their snorting old mares as the trundlers freshened the oil and lit each of the street lamps. When they finished, the street would be almost as bright as day and those who worked the night shift would take over the twilight city. Seaport cities never truly slept. Not when there was money to be made every hour of the day.

She gave up on restyling her hair. It had a stubborn mind of its own, so she'd be stuck with this until she woke up tomorrow.

"Alright, I guess we should get going." She gently picked Prowler up and set him on the floor beside her as she stood up, trying to smooth down her hair. He stretched and yawned dramatically.

"We? I was counting on a nap. I've been out all day long."

"I thought cats were practically nocturnal?"

"I'm sure alley cats and other such ragged beasts are, but I like to keep to higher standards."

"Well, you don't have to go, but I heard that Aggie Mimm is fixing her cheddar rat soufflé for the Night Market tonight. But if you're not interested," she trailed off, suggesting a possible future without the coveted soufflé.

"Dear, dear Aggie." His voice would have been silken to the touch. "The wench can do black magic in the kitchen with a nice plump rat. If only she were a cat," he said wistfully. He turned and headed toward the door, looking back to see if Trotter was behind him. "Aren't we leaving now? Don't forget your hat," he added with a fang-filled grin.

Trotter grimaced. "Even if I actually had a sense of humor that still wouldn't have been funny." She made one last attempt at forcing the cloud of hair back down before trying to tuck it unsuccessfully into a scarf. It wasn't much of an improvement. It now looked less like a pumpkin and more like a turban. She took one last look in the mirror and sighed.

"Oh well. At least Miro will have my shopping list already so maybe no one will even see me."

"One can only hope. Now let's go - I mustn't keep Aggie waiting!"

*****

The door to the inn opened and shut quickly. In weather like this it was practically a hanging offense to leave it open for long. Despite the haste with which it had been closed, the wind still seized the opportunity to deliver a blow to the raging fire in the hearth before being cast back outside. The flames and swirling ash resettled quickly and began anew the tedious work of spreading their heat back across the sitting room, but the cold gripped each body with icicle teeth while the fire fought to exorcise it.

The guests of the Tarbach Inn clutched at their cloaks, waiting for the cold to abate before returning to their beers and hot ciders. This storm was what they referred to as a Tartar Snow, meaning that you could see just as well outside if you smeared mayonnaise on your eyeballs. There were always guests at the inn in the winter. Some were delayed here all winter long if they didn't make the pass to the south before the snows walled them in. They were usually merchants or travelers seeking the famous lights of the northern sky, but the inn saw its fair share of soldiers and mercenaries, as well.

At some point in Drimbt's long history, the nobles discovered that the best way to keep the peasants from freezing to death was to keep them active. And the easiest way to keep them active, they'd also discovered, was fighting. The fighting, in turn, also provided the added benefit of thinning down the numbers a bit so there would never be too great a shortage of food. Drimbt had then divided itself into baronies which warred with each other almost constantly. The village of Klempt, which was famed for the hospitality of the Tarbach Inn, found itself in the Barony of Proustich.

The inn was not luxurious by any usual definition. However, it was always clean and full of food and warmth, both of which were luxuries in many households in Drimbt. The Drimmish were not an altogether talkative people, but the conversation at the inn this morning was scarce even by their standards. The quiet seemed awkward and forced, particularly near the lone man warming himself by the parlor fire. The other guests, casting furtive glances toward him when they dared, were crowding at the bar near the kitchen hearth where Frieda, the innkeeper's wife, was boiling a spicy stew of sausages, onion, and barley flour.

"Earl," one of the guests quietly addressed the innkeeper, "do you have any more of the rum for the cider?"

"Alice will get that for you, Mr. Porter. Alice!" Frieda turned from her stewpot and called for their servant. A little girl of six entered from upstairs where she had been dressing the beds. "Alice, get Mr. Porter some more rum, will you?"

Alice disappeared and reappeared with the quickness known only to children with a heavy clay jar of rum. It took both of her hands to carry it. Frieda flashed the girl an irritated look and took the jar from her hands to pour for Mr. Porter.

"I told him not to get one so young," she confided quietly to Mr. Porter. "I told him we'd spend all our time as nursemaids before she'd ever be any use to us."

"Well, you know how it is. You take what you can get at a decent price from the Auction." Due to the ever-present wars in Drimbt, there was never a food shortage, but there was also never a shortage of new widows and orphans, either. To solve the problem of guardianship for those unable to care for themselves, the baronies had instituted the auctions. Widows and orphans were then auctioned off as indentured servants until such time as they were able to marry, remarry, or otherwise provide for themselves.

"Still," Mr. Porter continued, "she seems to put her heart into whatever she does. I've had some as couldn't even stack a pile of wood, myself." He looked warmly into the face of Alice. She was a tiny thing even for her young age with locks of curling blonde hair and eyes the green of emeralds. She was filthy, but there was something beneath the grime that transfixed the observer.

"Don't let her fool you. As soon as she thinks we aren't looking she'll sneak off again to the river and hide there all night."

"But the girl doesn't even have any shoes on!"

"It doesn't stop her. It's as if she doesn't feel it," Frieda whispered conspiratorially.

Mr. Porter looked away from the small girl's smile feeling suddenly uncomfortable.

The commonest way to keep a servant from running away was to ensure that they had no shoes in which to run. Alice, as per tradition, had been provided with a small pair of leather thongs to protect her feet as minimally as possible. Feet that spent long unprotected in the snows around the village should have been lost.

"Frieda, where are the blasted beer mugs?" Earl was searching under the counter of the bar. "Alice will get them!" She turned an angry eye on Alice who ran to the kitchen. Beside the wash basin were a dozen ceramic beer mugs clean and dry. She began to gather them when out of the corner of her eye she spotted several strips of salted pork on the cutting board.

"Alice!" Frieda called from the front. Her patience was always fragile, but it came closer to terminal whenever the child was concerned.

Alice carried as many of the mugs as her arms could carry to Earl and kept her head down as she handed them to him. She ran back into the kitchen and returned with another arm load a minute later. After Earl took the last one from her she ducked under the bar and behind the cabinets where her bed of thin blankets and pillows was kept out of sight from the guests.

When she sat down, she pulled the salted pork she'd hidden under her dress and chewed on it slowly, savoring the juices. She was so, so hungry.

*****

Every city, no matter how wealthy, has those who are less fortunate. They have ghettos or slums where the impoverished are hidden from view of the wealthy so they can continue to pretend that the poor don't exist. Sarano was an exception to this rule. It no longer had slums. More to the point, the Chamber of Commerce didn't allow them. Instead of slums, there was just the area of the city where, on occasion, a person of lesser means might starve to death, a child die of sickness out of reach of a doctor, a hungry family huddle together for warmth, or an innocent bystander might accidentally get themselves mugged and/or killed. This is not an easy area in which to sell property to foreign investors. So, to solve the problem of poverty in the city of Sarano, the Chamber had wisely decided to refer to this area not as slums, but as the 'low-rent district.' The low-rent district consisted of a large block in the heart of four cross streets: Poorbetters Street, Kettle Black Alley, Churn Lane, and Bellows Street.

Trotter approached the low-rent district from the backside of Bellows St. This was where the blacksmiths sweated next to their fires day and night. The buildings on Bellows St. were always smudged with sooty stains, much like those who lived and worked there.

She glanced again at the setting sun.

"We're almost out of time, Prowler. I don't think we'll make it."

"Why not? You could be there in seconds if you weren't such a chicken, you know."

"You can forget that. I'm not walking through walls again." She picked up her pace and dodged around a cart. Prowler paused only long enough to hiss and startle the horses who then trod nervously on the foot of the carter. His whiskers twitched mischievously as he hurried away from the man's cursing. He, like most creatures barely over hoof high and with noses close to the road, hated horses.

"It's literally your god-given right! And it's the simplest thing to do if you'd only give it another try."

"I don't want to hear it! You weren't the one stuck with one leg in a wall for the better part of a day."

"I'm sure your father would help –"

"Leave him out of this." She said coldly. Prowler meant well, she knew. But it wasn't fair of him to keep bringing up her father. If he actually wanted to see her, then he could damn well come to her. Or at least even bother to ask her to come to him. The silence from him was the worst; even an 'Oh, sorry dear, late night in the godding business tonight. I'll try to make your birthday next year,' would be better than the heaps of nothing she received.

"Fine. All I'm saying is that you'll never improve if you don't practice. And you'll never make the market at this rate anyway."

She ignored him as she ducked down Kettle Black Alley and pushed at a seemingly empty place in the brick wall with all of her might just as the sun fell beneath the horizon. It remained, stubbornly, a solid brick wall.

"No!" She whined. "We were so close! We just barely missed the In-between." She laid her head against the wall.

"We? I could have made it in time if I hadn't been nice enough to wait for you. So much for my taste of Aggie's culinary genius," he added morosely.

The In-between was the one time of day that the door was open to the other side of Sarano. The gate opened at the moment the sun touched the horizon and closed at the moment that the flash died and the day became night. The wall on Kettle Black Alley was one of the few soft spots where the gates would open and allow entrance to those with magical blood. This other side of Sarano, this city behind a city, was called the Wedge. That was the real low-rent district that the Chamber of Commerce fortunately never had to try to sell to a potential trendy café owner. The Wedge was where those of non-human descent spent most of their time among a variety of magical beings.

The Wedge was also host to the Night Market. Though, don't be fooled - it wasn't so named because it was held at night. There was no difference between night and day in the Wedge. There were no stars, sun, or moon overhead to discern a difference, yet it was always bright there, lit with the eerie blue light of the lamps found all over the Wedge. You could bring matches from Sarano proper and they would still burn blue when you struck them. Trotter tried not to think about why. But the Night Market, creepy though it could be, was where she did her grocery shopping. There were just certain things that a growing demi-god needed that couldn't be found at your average fishmonger.

"Well? Are you coming or not?" There was laughter in the kind voice that greeted her. Trotter looked up to see Miro's silver-haired head sticking out of an expanding opening in the wall. Miro, the self-proclaimed queen of the Night Market, was one of the few people of the Wedge who could come and go as she pleased. Only the original citizens of Realm had this ability. Trotter had never asked her about this; as an original citizen it meant that Miro was as ancient as the gods themselves.

As the gate opened fully she stepped out of the portal and smiled at the girl and her cat. "I knew you were going to be late," she chided.

Flooded with relief, Trotter took Miro's dainty brown hand and followed the ancient woman from the twilight glow of Kettle Black Alley into the blue-lit alleys of the Wedge.

*****

Pale winter light and icy air flooded through the thin wooden slats of Alice's bedroom under the bar. She pushed her eye to the knothole through which she could observe the guests of the inn unseen. A soldier had entered. People were always kind to soldiers in Drimbt. Many of them had sons, brothers, or husbands who were also soldiers. Or, in most cases, had died as soldiers.

She watched as the soldier stooped by the guest at the fireplace and quietly exchanged a few words with him. She wondered why people were so intrigued in the man by the fire, watching him from the corners of their eyes, though they seemed too afraid to speak to him. To her eyes from under the bar he was a shock of gray and brown hair exposed above the chair back. From time to time, though, he coughed violently.

The soldier returned to the bar to speak with her master, leaving the older man in another coughing fit, and handed him a sack that smelled of fresh garlic.

"Landlord, the baron wishes me to inform you that there will be another guest for dinner tonight. The rest of the ingredients for the dinner he requested are there," he nodded to the sack, "and should readily accommodate the new guest."

"Yes, Captain, we'll see to it," Earl answered somberly, handing the sack to his wife to take to the kitchen. He chanced a glance at the fire. He hoped for the baron's sake that the unexpected guest was a doctor. The cough frequently took soldiers like that in the winter, and it just as frequently didn't give them back.

"Earl!" Frieda's head poked urgently around the corner of the kitchen. She had panic in her eyes. "Earl, come back here quickly!" She tried to soften her voice, too late to avoid attracting attention. Their voices could be heard in a low argument from the kitchen before they returned, Frieda pushing a sheepish Earl in front of her. He was tugging at his sleeves nervously.

"Er, Captain Carmony? A word with you, if I may, sir."

"What seems to be the trouble, Landlord?" Captain Carmony stayed put, enjoying his mug of beer at the bar.

"It would seem... I'm afraid..." Earl's eyes kept flicking from the captain at the bar to his baron at the fire. The baron hadn't moved or acknowledged that he'd heard anything. "The salted pork, I mean, there's some missing," he finished as quietly as he dared.

"Missing? You mean from the short time ago this morning that I brought it here to just now it has gone missing?" He chuckled. "They said it was their freshest, but I didn't think it was fresh enough to walk away," the captain answered disinterestedly to general laughter from the room.

Earl hung his head. Despite being one of the wealthiest residents of the village he knew where he stood with nobility. And that was at the bottom, waist deep, and holding the ladder for them to climb over him.

Frieda, however, suffered no such class shame. She pushed in front of him to speak. "It was Alice who did it! That little ingrate, that little monster! Alice, get out here! I know you're –"

"Alice who, please?"

Silence smothered the room. Even Frieda, whose penchant for whining was famous, was hushed. The voice had come from the chair by the fire. It was an old voice, but it had the tone of one who never had to ask permission to interrupt and expected an answer.

"I'm not sure, milord," answered his captain good-naturedly. "Perhaps the good landlord will tell us more of Alice."

"Alice is our servant, milord. She don't have a last name. We bought her at the auction as a baby and no one knew her name." Earl was trembling.

"I'd like to meet this Alice," the baron rumbled. "Child? You can come out now. I won't bite." He said gently.

Alice watched with her breath caught in her throat from under the bar. He had a kind voice, but she was still afraid of this man around whom everyone tread so carefully.

Earl kicked the bar. "You heard what he said. Get out here now, you little monster!"

The captain took Earl by the shoulder before he could kick the bar again.

"I'm sure that won't be necessary, Landlord."

Carmony knelt by the small door of the bar. "Hiding in here, are you, little Alice? I get the feeling you must be awfully hungry to eat that salty pork. It must have made you terribly thirsty. If you come out here I'll give you some cider." He signaled to Earl to pour a cup. Earl, avoiding the dirty looks from Frieda, brought it to him quickly.

Small scuffling sounds arose from the cabinet and a mop of golden curls appeared before the grime-smudged face of Alice appeared. He smiled at her and offered her the promised mug of cider which she drank greedily. Frieda started to protest, but stopped when she saw Earl glaring at her. He'd been expecting her to open her big mouth again.

"There now," Captain Carmony said to her. "Isn't that better?"

Alice nodded and looked to the chair by the fire.

"Bring her to me," the baron ordered, his voice warm despite the command.

The captain took Alice's hand and led her to the baron's side. His face was lined with years of worry, and the winters had taken their toll on his health. His skin was pallid, but his eyes burned like a man who had much to do before he rested. This was the face of a man who was not just a ruler, but a leader. Alice felt herself relax immediately in his presence. She'd never known a grandfather except from fairy tales, but if she had one she'd want him to look just like this man.

"So this is the infamous Alice, the great pork thief," the baron said with a smile. "My name is Baron von Proustich. Tell me, now, did you eat the pork from the kitchen, little one?"

Alice nodded eagerly and touched her stomach to show him how good it had been.

"She'll pay for that, she will!" Frieda finally broke her silence, despite Earl's frantic gestures to be silent. "Alice will go to the butcher to get more pork, milord."

"She will, will she?" The baron did not sound pleased. "It seems to me that all morning I've heard that Alice will do this, and Alice will do that, and that Alice will generally do everything. Except complain, that is. It seems to me that you should call her Alice Will."

Impervious to sarcasm, Frieda continued. "Well, she will, milord. We'll send Alice to the butcher right away to replace the pork she stole. We needed all three slices for –"

"Two," piped a small voice. Alice spoke seldom enough that her words were afforded the same silence given to the baron.

"What was that, child?" He prompted.

"Only two slices. I looked at the recipe in the kitchen, and it needs two slices of salted pork. I only took what was extra because I was so hungry."

Baron von Proustich looked more closely at Alice. Her wrists were mere twigs and her cheeks were gaunt with hollows dimpling in at her mouth. He was certain that if not for her dress he would be able to count her ribs.

"How old are you, Alice?"

"Six now, but I'll be seven next week they said."

"And you can read?"

"Yes, sir."

The captain looked to the innkeepers questioningly. It was rare enough for peasant children to be literate, but it was almost unheard of for a peasant girl to read at any age in Drimbt. As it was, Earl had haltingly read the recipe himself to Frieda earlier that morning.

"She taught herself, milord." Earl answered after an expectant pause.

"Taught herself? To read?" Asked the baron from his chair. His eyes remained fixed on Alice. It was hard to see, but mischief flitted across her face for just a moment before she could suppress a grin. She was obviously pleased with herself.

"Yes, sir. One day a guest read a story to her out of a book of fairy tales, you see. When he left, he gave her the book as a present. She decided that she wanted to be able to read it for herself, and the next day, well, she just could."

"Are you sure she hadn't just memorized the tales that the guest read to her? I'm sure it could appear that she might be reading, even if she were only reciting from memory," he asked incredulously.

"No, sir. You see, we had her read other things to us to prove it, and she read everything we gave her. Even the book of medicines we keep. She started addin' up guest bills for us, as well. Quicker 'an we ever could, at least."

"So not only can the child read on her own, but she can also add numbers? Astounding. Yet what's even more amazing is that you still treat her like a dog you can beat when she doesn't please you." The sound of a roomful of people holding their breath is louder than one might think. The baron was angry, and no one wanted to accidentally attract his attention. "Captain?"

"Yes, milord?"

"Please inform our landlords that we will have another guest for dinner tonight. Alice will be joining us since there is apparently still plenty of pork to go around."

"With pleasure, milord."

Alice was as stunned as everyone else in the room, if not more so. She'd never had dinner with people before. She was only allowed to eat what remained after the guests and the innkeepers had dined. Some nights, and her stomach grumbled angrily at the thought, there was nothing left at all. A look at the anger smoldering in Frieda's eyes told her that she would pay for this later. But, at least for now, she had found a friend. Her first one ever.

CHAPTER 2

Trotter squinted the tears out of her eyes. There was always a period of adjustment from Sarano to the dimmer blueness of the Wedge. The sudden difference in light always made her eyes water at first. Then, slowly, her eyes would become used to the blue flames that lit every house and street and her brain would begin to filter it until she could see the colors that were truly there, from the orange hair of the fairies to the yellow eyes of the shape shifters. The shape shifters could be anything they wanted to be, so long as what they wanted to be had yellow eyes. It was the only thing they couldn't change, and it was the reason they only shifted from their natural grey scales to human form to go into Sarano at night.

The streets of the wedge were crowded as usual this evening. They passed many people and creatures on their way and Miro greeted all of them, addressing them by name and inquiring about their families. She was always treated deferentially, as though she were every bit of the queen she proclaimed herself to be. She swept down the streets with a confidence that Trotter envied, and all who saw her seemed to feel better for having been near her. The tattered but still majestic robes that draped her were covered with long scarves that seemed to have a life of their own, the tasseled ends swishing occasionally as would a cat's tail in an echo of emotion.

A fairy that Trotter hadn't seen before, a young boy yet, only around seven feet of the fifteen feet he would be once full grown, stopped and stared down at her own shock of orange hair escaping from her scarf with his mouth open in surprise. Trotter hurriedly tucked it away again and was about to say something to him when his mother came behind him and scooped him up into her arms. She looked down upon the trio and smiled, making an apology for her baby before extending her leathery wings and flying over the dark cottages across the street.

The street looked very much like a village would in the night, if the roads were paved with black cobblestones and the cottages made of twisted wood in shades of gray and black. No grass grew here, there were no animals aside from the more exotic inhabitants, and the only trees tended to migrate from place to place in search of, well, let's just say most people feel better not knowing.

The other peculiarity about the Wedge, aside from its inhabitants, of course, was that there was never an echo. There might have been thousands of people and creatures milling the streets as far as Trotter knew, but you never heard anything except what was near enough to be seen. It was as though the darkness plucked the noise from the air, absorbing it into itself and dampening everything.

This made it all the easier for her to be startled when the imp laid his hand on her arm and pulled her toward him in the shadow of a particularly gnarled tree.

"Hey, get your hands off of me! Miro, help me!"

Trotter smacked at the imp and tried to pull out of his grasp, but his hands felt as strong and as gnarled as the branches of the tree above them. Prowler hissed and swiped at the imp, but one of the tree's roots pushed roughly above the surface and flicked him, sending him tumbling back to the road next to Miro.

"That's not funny!" He yelled as he rolled to a stop at her feet.

Miro was laughing. Her scarves joyfully flicking the air as she did so. "Jorg, don't be so rough with her. I think you've forgotten your manners."

"I apologize, mistress." The imp she addressed as Jorg responded with a voice that reminded Trotter of the whisper of wind through tree leaves. "I did not intend to be ungentle."

"Wait, you *know* him? Please make him let me go!"

"Trotter, Jorg here is a tree dweller. All tree dwellers are truth tellers. Have you ever met a truth teller before?"

"Is that like a fortune teller?" She twisted uncomfortably in his grasp and stifled the urge to gag when he pressed his pointed nose to her hair and sniffed deeply. His eyes were two tiny beads of black, his nose taking up most of his face. He might have been as tall as Trotter, were it not for his hunched and crooked back. Jorg seemed to be talking to himself as if contemplating her scent.

Miro laughed again. It was something she did often, as if everything around her was part of her own private joke. Her laugh had a pleasant musical quality, as though it were woven from silk and lullabies, and Trotter felt calmed by it.

"No, nothing like a fortune teller. Fortune tellers can only tell you what might happen to you one day. A truth teller can tell you what is happening and what has happened."

Trotter looked at the silver-haired woman for any trace of sarcasm. "I don't see how that's very helpful. I think I could do that for myself without having to be sniffed to death."

"I hear the irony in your voice, young one," Jorg whispered to her as he released her from his gnarled grasp, "but you may be surprised by what you think you know that you never knew, and what you always knew and thought you didn't know."

Trotter gritted her teeth. "That doesn't make sense," she growled, stifling the tingling sensation in her right index finger. That was her smiting finger, and it seemed to have a mind of its own these days, especially when someone annoyed her. Puberty was an especially rough age for people of the magical persuasion as it was also a time of a magical coming of age. She was more sensitive to even harmless silliness than ever, and especially to people who spoke in nonsensical riddles.

"Oh, but it does," Miro answered her. "What you know is what you see, and what you see isn't always the truth. Take yourself, for instance. What do you see when you look at yourself in the mirror?"

Trotter chewed on her lip. "I just see a girl. A girl with messy hair and an upturned nose. There isn't anything really to see." She kicked at the edge of one of the tree roots dejectedly. It kicked back.

This time it was Jorg's turn to laugh. "Just a girl! Oh my, just a girl, indeed." The rustling leaf quality to his voice only increased when he chuckled. "The daughter of Stoicese, the one God of Truth, Lord of the Canvas, thinks she's *just* a girl!"

"Leave him out of this," Trotter replied angrily. "He has nothing to do with me, got it?"

"Oh, but he had very much to do with you, my child. Else I don't think you'd be here now, would you?"

She gritted her teeth and tried to calm her smiting finger. If she'd been born to one of the other gods, maybe Brino, goddess of Love, or

Harpicedes, god of Music, she'd probably feel differently. She could have been unnaturally gifted with talents that most kids would kill for. But no, she'd been born to the god of truth. Her main godlike power seemed to be the annoying ability to point out logical flaws and inconsistencies. In fact, they grated on her like nails on a chalkboard. Sometimes having to live in the real world was like having a constant toothache. The human race might dip a toe in the puddles of truth once in a while, but they swam in the oceans of delusion. It was amazing the things that they could believe were true simply because they *wanted* them to be true.

She looked more closely at the tree dweller. At first she'd mistakenly thought that he was leaning against the tree. Now she realized he was actually a part of the tree, his body merging with the trunk below his waist. He noticed her gaze.

"Yes, you see true. We are one, the tree and I. I take my nourishment from him and in turn I protect him from those who would turn him into just another pile of firewood."

"Him?"

"Of course! He doesn't look like a girl, does he?" Jorg laughed raspily.

"That's just crazy! Trees are not boys or girls, they're just trees," she said defiantly. The tree quivered and for a moment Trotter thought it seemed offended. *I must be imagining it*, she thought.

Miro laid a reassuring hand on Trotter's shoulder. "I think that's enough. Prowler, take Trotter on to the Night Market and I'll be along shortly. Prowler?" She looked around for the missing feline.

Prowler's head emerged from where he had been cowering in a ditch across the street well out of reach of the tree roots. "I, um, I thought I saw a mouse over here. I might have been wrong, though," he added when he saw their cynical expressions.

"Come on, Sir Galahad. I'll protect you from the mean tree." Trotter turned once more to Jorg, who was watching her with a curious expression. "Goodbye. It was nice meeting you, I think." He bowed reverently as she turned to leave.

Miro watched until she and Prowler were out of sight. "So, my old friend, what did you see? What is her truth?"

Jorg shook his head sadly. The tree limbs heaved with the weight of his emotion. "In her mind she truly is only a girl. She has no idea how powerful she really is, and she resents what power she tries to use. She resents *him* most of all."

"Resentment is dangerous. It's the same poison that led to the war in the first place. Have we lost her so soon?"

"No, not yet. She is not even aware yet that she has a choice to make. We have not lost her if she has not made the choice."

Miro was thoughtful. Her forehead creased with concern. "Perhaps isolating her from the reach of Realm with only the cat as a guardian was not the wisest decision."

"It was the only decision. Even there she is still being watched too closely by others who do know her potential. They knew both of her parents."

"Jorg," Miro asked hesitantly, as though afraid of the answer. Her scarves twitched nervously. "What truly *is* her potential?"

"Don't you know? She could destroy us all with just a thought."

*****

Sitting at the right hand of the baron himself, Alice had dined like a princess. His other guests doted on her when he told them of her special gifts with words and numbers. They tested her first, and asked her to add random numbers and then to subtract them. One man, the one with the cynical leer, asked her to do multiplication. She'd never heard of that before and asked him to explain it to her. He did so reluctantly since he wasn't very comfortable with numbers himself, but the idea spread itself in front of her eyes as though she'd always known it.

"Why, that's easy!" She exclaimed.

"Easy?" The baron guffawed. "My dear, there's no need to show off. It's alright if you don't understand. I'm sure not many people do understand numbers that multiply themselves."

"But it really is simple, sir," she insisted. "It's like this: there are six of us at this table. If this room multiplied itself five times over then there would be thirty of us instead of just six. Do you see? The six of us added together five times over is thirty. It's *exactly* like addition, just done really fast."

The table had fallen quiet and remained that way until dessert, each man trying to add six five times over in their heads until they were quite sure she was right.

In an attempt to change the subject to something less unnerving, the baron proposed a toast to the inn itself and the fabulous beer that had been warming the party steadily all evening. The guests were all anxious to question Frieda about the nature of the famous brew that gave it such a hearty kick.

"Well," she finally gave in with great reluctance, "it's the dynamite, you see. One day when we were keggin' we grabbed a barrel that still had some of the dynamite residue that we use to open the passes instead of the proper beer barrel. We didn't realize 'til after we'd poured it for customers that it had been fermentin' in dynamite. But it went over so well, y'see, so we just decided to keep doin' it."

"Dynamite? We're drinking dynamite?" Choked one of the guests. A couple of others were hastily stabbing out cigars as far from their mugs as possible.

The baron laughed heartily before giving over to coughing. "Gentlemen, I'm sure if anyone had accidently exploded by drinking beer we'd have heard of it by now. Just don't relieve yourself too near a fire for a few days!"

All the while Alice avoided the icy glares from Frieda as she served the party in Alice's place. She knew her respite was over when dinner ended and the gentlemen soldiers and the baron retired. After she left the pot of boiling water with the baron for his bath she tried to hurry back to her bed under the bar before Earl or Frieda could catch her and punish her.

Her heart sank when she discovered it was already too late. When she reached the top of the stairs she found Frieda standing near the bottom waiting for her.

"Well? Aren't you coming down? Or do you think you might stay up there all night?" Frieda's arms were crossed and her voice dripped with the malice she wrung from every word. Alice waited for a moment, pondering her options before darting with the quickness of a rabbit past Frieda, but she hadn't been fast enough. Frieda's foot snapped out in front of her, a snake to her rabbit, and Alice tumbled down the last several stairs, twisting her ankle painfully.

"Maybe that will keep you from gettin' any more big ideas, you little witch. You'd better learn your place." Frieda spat on the stairs below her before turning toward her own bedroom, leaving Alice in a painful heap at the bottom, choking back her silent tears.

Now Alice was limping toward the safety of Grandfather Tree, ignoring the blinding snow falling all around her. Grandfather Tree shined like a beacon to her even if she couldn't see two inches in front of her face.

As she crawled under the comforting branches she tugged the candle stub and tinderbox to freedom from the folds of her thin coat. She wedged the candle among the pile of needles and spoke to the tree. "Don't worry" she whispered to the trembling branches. "I'll be careful with the flame."

She let the candle flame warm her frozen fingers before digging her journal out of its hiding place and beginning her newest entry.

"Today was a wonderful day!" She wrote. "This morning my grandfather came to visit me and brought some of my friends over. They threw a feast just for me and our servants waited on us hand and foot, bringing us every kind of delicious treat there is. We played games and I taught them about multulpulcation. They brought me presents for my birthday as it is only seven days away. We had such a wonderful time together and everybody laughed and had fun. We even had a warm apple tart for dessert and they put a candle in it just for me to wish upon. I wished for a new doll for my bedroom, and I think I may get one!"

And so she wrote, reliving the perfect day she'd never had.

Inside the inn, Frieda was pulling the bun out of her hair at her dressing table. She stopped, silent, and listened.

"Did you hear that?" She asked.

"Hear what?" Earl responded gruffly, almost asleep already.

"That noise. I thought I heard voices for a minute. Laughing, like at a party. And, yes, I think I smelled apples and cinnamon." The sounds were gone, but the smell lingered. She listened a bit longer, and then decided she'd imagined it as the scent of cinnamon faded at last.

*****

Truth telling is a gift that runs in families descended from the original seers of Realm. Even the merest of truth tellers can tell what a person is thinking and can see through the lies a person believes. But the wisest and most powerful truth tellers are prized for their ability to see the world as it is anywhere they wish to see it. The world lives in front of their eyes as though they were windows to infinite lives.

There is one such powerful truth teller here, in the darkness of a cave. He is the last of the only remaining line of pure truth teller blood, his last ancestor having died centuries ago and his only son murdered even longer ago. There would be no more truth tellers with his strength when he was gone. Even now he floated in a pool of dark water, his ancient bones too weak to support his meager weight. He was watching...

*****

The Night Market was, as always, quite rowdy. It was set off from the rest of the streets of the Wedge by tents and canopies purely for ambience. It wasn't as though the Wedge had any weather from which to protect the customers, but they did at least afford some small measure of privacy and marked the boundaries from one stall to another. Some of the items available in small jars lurking in the darkest corners of certain stalls of a particular reputation were more than simply exotic. Some of them were downright dangerous, or sometimes just embarrassing. These were the places where a zombie could find a replacement finger for one that had fallen off, or an enchantress could find virgin's blood for a love potion. There was even a powder that, despite its remarkable potency in curses and cures alike, has to be kept out of sunlight and buried in a marsh with a crow's feather in a leather pouch tied off by spider silk every third Tuesday to keep it from going critical and turning anyone within a five mile radius into swamp slugs.

In many of the stalls, however, were stew pots, brew pots, and urns filled with meals and drinks unique to the people of the Wedge. The beer here was brewed from the bitter tears of centaurs, whose tendency toward raging alcoholism was famous. This led to an incredibly strong beer that was most safely consumed from very small lead cups, wooden goblets inclining to burn when it was poured into them.

When Miro rejoined her, Trotter was sitting in Aggie Mimms' tent enjoying a piece of her celebrated cherry pork pie while Prowler was purring over a dish of her cheddar rat soufflé.

"A plate for you, too, milady?" A round and smiling Aggie offered to Miro as she sat down next to the girl.

"Not today, Ags. Right now I'm here for business." She winked at the jolly lady and laid a large cloth sack on the table next to Trotter. "Everything you wanted is in here and a couple of other things that you need, as well."

"You knew everything I wanted? Even the old broken horseshoe?" Trotter grinned.

"Now don't go thinking you can pull one over on me. I knew that was just to see if I was paying attention. So, no, I didn't get you a broken horseshoe. The cheese from Ostano that you love, the Wedge garlic, a loaf of never-ending bread, and the dried roast, I did get you, among other things. I also added in a hairbrush just before you arrived. I understand your old one met with foul play?" She turned a lopsided grin toward Prowler.

Oblivious to his part in the conversation, Prowler continued to devour his soufflé with relish. "It's so, mmm, so good," he mumbled with his mouth full.

"I don't know how you do it, but thank you. You said a couple of things that I need. What was the other thing aside from the brush?"

"Now that you're growing so fast your non-human side needs nourishment, too." She produced a bag which held several dried flowers. They were mostly white, but they changed colors where the light hit them in different ways, from a pale yellow to a vibrant green and then to a ruby red. When she laid them on the counter they turned to a mottled brown and blended so well as to be almost invisible. "These are chameleon violets from Realm. Take just a pinch at a time to brew a weak tea and they'll help your powers develop and make you stronger."

Trotter began to shake her head in protest. "Thanks all the same, but I really don't need —"

"Yes, you do," she cut her off. "Your powers are a part of you just as much as the heart in your chest. If your heart is not healthy," she chided her with a scolding tone and tapped her breastbone, "*you* are not healthy. It's the same with your powers. When they suffer, you suffer. Drink the tea, Trotter. You'll feel stronger and your powers will become stronger."

"I'm not sure I want them to be stronger. Every time I use them something goes horribly wrong. I can barely control my smiting finger as it is."

"That's because you still think of your powers as something separate from yourself. How many times can I try to explain? You breathe in magic constantly. If you aren't using it then you're losing control of it."

"What do you mean, losing control? I never *had* control to begin with."

Miro shook her head in near exasperation. "Of course not. You can't hold it in any more than you can hold water in a full cup that's still being filled. At some point it will have to leak out or it will gush out, and that's what happens when you do finally try to use it. It comes pouring out of you in a flood when all you want is a trickle because you've dammed so much of it up inside of you. You fear your powers because you think that they are stronger than you are and that's where you are so mistaken. Your powers draw their strength from you. Always from you. Practice using them, practice controlling the flow and you'll be very surprised at how easy it is."

"Yes, ma'am," she replied in defeat.

"Now, on to the business part. What will you give me in exchange for these items?"

Trotter began to pull a pouch from her pocket. It jingled with coins. "How much will you take for it?"

Miro waved her hand as though disgusted by the idea of touching the coins. "You know I won't take money. I want you to give me a gift." When she smiled Miro had an almost child-like quality.

"What kind of gift? I'm afraid I don't have much of value."

"You can give me anything in the world. Just call it into being, my dear."

"Oh, you mean magic, then." Trotter looked down at her half-eaten pie dejectedly. "I've never been able to make anything before. The last time I tried to make an apple I ended up with something like burnt apple sauce."

"Then you were trying too hard. You're trying to force it to happen when what you should be doing is imagining what you want and then just *letting* it happen. Look into my eyes and see what I need. Then take it from my mind. Try it now."

Trotter laid her fork down and tried to relax as she looked into Miro's eyes. Even Prowler looked up from his soufflé and watched with deep interest. He fought the urge to hide behind the counter; he'd been present at some of her previous attempts. Fortunately for him, the last of the green stripes in his fur had finally grown out.

Miro's deep blue eyes were patient and kind, the type that made a person feel as though they could fall into them. Suddenly Trotter realized that they reminded her of the sea.

That was when it happened.

The hissing tea kettle and the other sounds of Aggie's kitchen tent disappeared and were replaced by the sounds of a seashore. Not the sounds of the busy seaport of Sarano, but of the tranquil lapping of waves and the roar of a seashell pressed to her ear. She could even taste the salt in the air. The gulls screamed in the sky above, and below them she could even hear the gentle splashing of the eel skimming the surface of the water. Trotter plunged deeper, and then she could taste the brine on her lips and feel the school of silvery fish swimming all around her. The sea felt so crowded with life, as though it was pressing on every inch of her, but then she knew that this wasn't just *a* seashore. She was experiencing every seashore and every sea creature that ever existed.

"Well, now. That *is* interesting." Miro's voice broke her trance. Trotter snapped back to reality and noticed that Miro was staring at an item on the table with wide eyes. The sounds of waves faded off into the distance. The other patrons had stopped eating and were watching the pair nervously.

"What is it?" Trotter asked as Miro inspected the small shell. It was beautifully curved and pointed on the outside, and as she turned it over in her hands, the mother-of-pearl lining glinted magnificently in the blue lamplight.

"It's from my old home," Miro responded distantly, as though she were lost in memories. "You looked into my mind and brought this not just through the world, but through hundreds and hundreds of years." Her eyes focused on Trotter.

"I'm sorry, I didn't mean to do anything wrong. Maybe I can put it back?" She'd never felt so uncomfortable in her life. Her cheeks were burning with embarrassment and she could feel the eyes on her back.

"You did nothing wrong, nothing at all," Miro soothed her, rubbing her long fingers over Trotter's small hand. She had a hint of tears in the corners of her sea-blue eyes. "It's just that you surprised me. Something like this, moving something real from that far away, takes more power than simply creating a copy of the object you want. This is no ordinary sea shell, and it's no copy. I believe this was meant for you and not for me." She placed the shell in Trotter's hands.

"This is a summoning shell, and, well, I guess it's the last of its kind. All of these were destroyed by Erov, the god of the sea, in a jealous rage more years ago than most people can count."

Trotter closed her hand over the shell. It was surprisingly warm. "What does the shell summon?"

"Me," Miro responded sadly. "The very last one was used by a man I came to love dearly, and for that Erov destroyed the shells and cast me out of Realm."

"Because you fell in love?"

"Because I fell in love with someone other than him." Her scarves were uncharacteristically still, almost mournful as they huddled beneath her.

Before she could question Miro further, the ground beneath them began to shake. It began as the tiniest tremble, causing her fork to rattle and fall off of the plate before she realized it was happening. It grew into a rumble that knocked glasses off tables and toppled tents. Then it was simply over as quickly as it had started.

"What was that?" She asked a now fearful looking Miro. The shaking had come and gone before anyone had time to react, but now the muffled sounds of terror were spreading throughout the Night Market.

"It was a Wedgequake," she said, taking a moment to catch her breath and regain her composure. "It was only a tiny one, thank Chaos. There hasn't been a quake in centuries." She broke off distantly.

"Then what caused it?"

"The Wedge rests on the foundation of Aevum and if that shifts, we shift as well. It means that something small has been altered out there in the world where it shouldn't have."

Trotter looked around the wreck of the room and realized that where everyone had been staring at her out of curiosity before, they were now staring at her in horror.

"Miro, what's going on?"

Prowler answered for her. "I'm afraid they think you caused it."

*****

Across a sky painted the blue of gemstones, a brilliant red bird soared. It flew quickly, its talons flexing with tension as it ignored mice and other small birds as it traveled over the chaotic patchwork quilt of the land far beneath it. There was urgent business ahead of it.

Finally, it circled a castle with an impossibly tall spire the color of diamonds at sunset. At the top of the tower was a balcony where a grim man stood alone. It circled lower and lower and as it lighted on the stone floor beside the man its wings became red-skinned arms and its legs, though still hinged as a bird's, grew muscular and long to support what was now mostly a man. His eyes were still piercing and black, and his skin was the same red of his previously brilliant feathers. His hair swept back from his face, giving him the appearance of still rushing through the wind.

Despite his formidable appearance, he waited anxiously under the stare of the grim man awaiting him on the balcony.

"Then you felt it, too," he said to the hawk man. It was not a question.

The hawk man said nothing in response. The fear in his eyes was all the confirmation his master needed.

"Something is about to go very wrong. I can feel it, but I can't see it. Go and find it for me. Find where it is happening and whomever is doing it."

He watched as the hawk man nodded and leapt from the ledge, resuming his hawk shape as he fell and swooped away into the distance.

"By Chaos, please," he said aloud, "don't let it be my daughter."

CHAPTER 3

The ripples of the dark pool had finally subsided by the time the truth teller's screams quit echoing in the cave. The Wedgequake had barely disturbed his cave, but his mind was firmly a part of the fabric of the reality he watched; therefore, when the fabric was torn and a new seam inserted, his mind experienced the tear in an unspeakably physical way.

Footsteps pounded frantically into the room.

"Geldon, get him out of there!" A voice of authority barked to an unseen hand and the truth teller was hauled to the edge of the pool.

"It hurts!" He gasped and held his head with bony fingers. He was only dimly aware that someone was kneeling next to him.

"Calm down now," the man said, sounding uncharacteristically comforting. The kindness didn't taste right on his tongue and he restrained the urge to spit. "The quake is over. Tell me what you saw."

"Master," he replied, still gasping, "she has altered the world. One tiny piece of reality. So tiny, but so much pain it causes!"

"Bring him the tea," the master barked again at Geldon who, more than happy for the excuse to leave, rushed out, wiping his gray hands on his trousers. He found the truth teller creepy at the best of times, but never more so than when the twisted creature howled like he had during the quake.

The master waited as patiently as he could for the truth teller to recover himself. When the creature seemed calmer, he pressed.

"Who altered the world? Was it the girl? Was it Stoicese's daughter?"

"No. She was here at the Night Market when it happened. But there was something just before…" The truth teller rubbed at his head again. It had almost been yanked from his mind, but he'd seen it first. "Yes, that was it. She has a gift her father never learned. She summoned an artifact from a reality long ago. Not a copy, not something new, but the item itself."

"What item was this?"

"I… I can't see it now. But it was powerful. And it had been destroyed by the very god who created it. No one should have been able to retrieve it, but the girl pulled it across Chaos and time and has it now."

Geldon returned with a cup of chameleon violet tea. The master fed it to the truth teller, holding it to his mouth for him as his crooked hands could no longer grasp the cup. As the creature drank his breaths grew steadier and his shivering ceased. The master set the cup aside and let his thoughts develop, his claws clicking across the stone with the effort. For him, this was a slow and tedious process. His kind was used to relying on instinct alone.

"But this didn't cause the quake?" He asked.

"No." The truth teller's voice was stronger and deeper now. "There was another. Far from here, and only just coming into her powers. What she altered was small, and I think not on purpose, but it hid her from my sight."

"Another Changer? I didn't think any others existed. Can you find her again?"

"It would be impossible. She has now stepped away from reality and is somewhere in between. But there is another way. I sense that the girl demi-god and this girl are somehow connected. I believe that she will lead us to this World-Changer."

"I thought you couldn't predict the future?"

"I can only see what is true as of each moment that passes. And at the moment of the quake, they were both, in part, outside of reality. Only the demi-god returned."

"This item the demi-god retrieved, this magical artifact, could she do it again? Retrieve something else that had been lost?"

"Without a doubt, master. She grows stronger every day. Far stronger than she knows."

The master was thoughtful. This girl, this young *child*, could reach into the past and save what the gods themselves would destroy. Surely that would mean that she could easily reach out and find items that were merely hidden. And if items, could she also bring a person, or a lost god?

"Yes," the truth teller answered his thoughts. "Anything. Even a god," he said meaningfully.

"Then there is a way. Finally, after all this time, there is a way," the master said to himself. He turned to his servant. "Geldon, bring the child here. She has something we need."

When Geldon smiled, his yellow eyes glinted in the gloom.

*****

"How could I have caused that?" Trotter was shocked.

"I don't think you did," Miro answered her quietly, "but we should probably still leave. Quickly." She turned away to say something soothing to a frightened family near her at another table.

As Trotter pulled the coins from her purse to settle up with Aggie, a gruff voice addressed her from behind.

"Just what do you think you're doin'?"

She turned and looked for the voice and found nothing until it spoke again.

"You can't just go Changin' things like that! It ain't safe!"

This time she looked down and found the voice coming from near her feet. A gnome stood there indignantly and steaming slightly from the mound of hot pork pie that had apparently fallen on him during the quake.

"I'm sorry, but I didn't actually do anything. I didn't cause that."

"Ha! We all seen you do it. You reached somewhere you shouldna' and pulled that little trinket out and the whole place about comes down on our heads!"

"Harry, give it a rest, will you?" Miro rolled her eyes exaggeratedly as if unable to believe that she had to explain this to him. "She didn't Change anything. It was just a little conjuring trick. Do you really think a little seashell is going to tear the fabric of reality?" She asked him as a grade school teacher might ask a child if he really believed that stepping on cracks would break his mother's back.

He looked suddenly shamefaced as a glop of pie fell off of his head onto the floor. "No, I guess not. But it was awful strange how it happened like that. She's the only Changer allowed outside of Realm. If she ain't the one what made the Change, who did?"

Miro took Trotter by the shoulder and gently led her through the throng of people as she answered loudly to be sure everyone heard. "I'm not sure yet. But I can promise you that Trotter and I will find out."

This seemed to please everyone in the room with the exception of Trotter. "Me? How am I supp-"

"Shh!" Miro hissed in her ear. "I'll explain later. For now just smile and nod." Trotter obeyed and the two left the tent quickly.

Prowler stayed behind just long enough to gulp the last two bites of his cheddar rat soufflé and mumble a heartfelt 'thank you' to Aggie with his mouth full. As he turned to run after Miro and Trotter he heard a velvety and familiar, if not entirely welcome voice.

"Psst! Hey, Lap Cat!"

"Mmmpphh?" Prowler asked, trying to swallow his last bite. "Oh. Felicia. How lovely. Look, I'm in a hurry so I'm afraid we'll have to catch up later." Prowler started to strut away when the voice called him back.

"You'll want to hear this. It's about that pet girl you keep," Felicia called after him.

Prowler turned to face the speaker. She was an amber colored cat just a bit smaller than he was. She was long and muscular, though slightly dirty, and had a wild look in her eye. This one was dangerous. Practically feral. Unlike Prowler, Felicia had never been human before. Her previous owner, a lonely witch, enchanted the cat and gave her a voice for her company. Upon acquiring a keen mind and conversation skills, the cat promptly learned that the witch was a terrible bore and ran away as quickly as she could, making her way in the Wedge as an alley cat. Alleys in the Wedge, however, tended toward more exotic fare than your average rat. Fare with a larger than average number of legs and/or claws, for certain. She proudly wore the scars of her battles throughout her coat, and not a one of them diminished her charm as a strikingly beautiful creature.

She sidled closer to Prowler and stretched nonchalantly. "It's been a while, Lap Cat. You don't come around as often as you used to."

"Please don't call me that," he backed up nervously. "And I've been very busy lately."

The amber cat gave a chuckle that rippled. "Prowler, Prowler, as tame as ever, I see."

"Felicia, you said this was to do with Trotter. What do you know?"

"I hear things, you know. When a cat wanders near even the people around here aren't smart enough to stop talking."

"So what have you heard?" He asked less patiently.

"She has a watcher on her. The last pure truth teller, they say. He watches her day and night."

Prowler was shocked. "But why?"

"They watch for her to become useful. For her powers to develop enough to know if they will be able to use her. Unless I miss my guess," she circled him territorially while she spoke, "she just pulled one heck of a trick in there."

"You mean the summoning shell? What was so impressive about that?"

"Tsk, tsk," she shook her head at him. "For someone who used to be human you sure don't know how they think. That shell is powerful, and it was destroyed by a god. What if she brought back one of the really scary things that the gods destroyed? Say, the bell of Sherba whose toll killed all the first born of Gibro? Or the sword of Istandal with a strike that killed not only the warrior whose heart it pierced, but also his entire male line? If memory serves, you were at that battle, weren't you? Taking notes, I believe."

"Oh no," he said quietly, his tail twitching as he worked out the danger. "I have to tell Miro." Now nowhere will be far enough to hide her, he thought angrily.

Felicia stepped in front of him. "What? Without thanking me properly?" She nudged him with her nose.

One thing for which Prowler was eternally grateful to his fur was the masterful way it covered the blush rising hotly in his skin. "Felicia, we're from different worlds," he said. "It just can't work."

"That didn't bother you before," she answered suggestively as she turned to walk away. "Anyway, when you change your mind, you know how to find me. Until then, Lap Cat."

He resisted the urge to watch her walk away and ran in the direction Miro and Trotter had taken.

*****

Miro's warm and confident smile paved the way for their escape from the Night Market. Even as they passed words such as 'World-Changer', 'demi-god', 'dangerous', and worse filtered up to her ears from those watching her with suspicion. The wary looks made her uncomfortable, but the hissing of the grotesque spriggan, as musty as an old grave, made her draw closer behind Miro as they walked.

"Miro," she asked as they passed the final tent that signaled the market boundary, "what is it exactly that they think I did? Even if I had caused that quake, and I didn't, it was just a small one, wasn't it?"

"What people fear is seldom what's actually in front of them. Pictsies and gnomes still fear and mistrust each other over the atrocities their ancestors committed against one another more than five hundred years ago in the Diminutia War, despite living in as much harmony as anyone can for centuries since the truce. They don't fear what is, or even what might be. They don't have near enough imagination for that. They fear what *was*. That's what's happening right now. The people here aren't afraid of the little quake that just happened. They're afraid of the Reconstruction."

*****

The village of Klempt was, not surprisingly, quiet in the early frozen morning. Such animals as the village kept huddled closely together in their barns for warmth and barely made a sound. What was surprising about the peaceful morning, however, was the perfectly yellow sun rising in the perfectly clear sky. The blinding snow of the previous day had passed as quickly as it had arrived and left behind it the stillness of death. The only signs of life in the village were the curling smoke trails from the rooftops. That of the inn was spiced with the welcoming smell of bacon and several of its inhabitants were already busy preparing for the day.

At the hearth, Frieda was humming uncharacteristically as she stoked the fire even higher. Earl kept looking at her sideways while he stacked the day's firewood to thaw against the wall.

"What's got into you, woman?" He asked her as he threw the last piece to the top. "You've been makin' that blasted noise all morning," he said irritably. Frieda's speaking voice tended toward the nasal side, but her singing voice was reminiscent of an ill goat.

She stopped what she was doing and looked blank for a moment. "I'm not sure," she answered a little distantly. "I didn't think about it until you said that."

"Well, knock it off, will you? You'll scare the guests. They'll think we're skinnin' cats in here."

Alice wandered in from the kitchen, sleep and the remnants of dreams blurring in her eyes. There was a smudge of ash across her face as she'd made her bed next to the hot coals of the kitchen fire last night. Fires in the village never really went out in the winter. It was a matter of pride, not to mention survival, that you kept your fires hot enough to burn through the night and rage back into life with a fresh log in the morning.

"Good morning, Alice!" Frieda trilled happily. She nearly shoved her fist in her mouth when she realized she'd said it and looked to Earl with panic in her eyes.

Earl looked at her appraisingly. Sometimes the winter did that to people. They said it was something to do with not getting enough daylight. They said it turned a person's thoughts inward, and sometimes what they found there was too much for a mind to handle.

"Frieda," he soothed, "maybe you should go and have a lie down. Alice'll finish off the bacon and biscuits this time."

"Don't be silly. The child can barely tend a stew what with her daydreaming. I'm just not quite myself this mornin'." She looked warily to Alice who seemed to be oblivious to what had just transpired. She whispered to Earl, "If I didn't know better, I'd swear that child was puttin' thoughts in my head!"

"Hmmpf. That's ridiculous. They'd've told us if she was a witch and they'd've marked her, too. There ain't been one around here in ages so you can put that outta your mind." This was at least what he said. What he didn't add, and what he was wondering nervously, was how they would know if the girl was a witch if they didn't even know who her parents were.

Unaware of the conversation behind her, Alice began her morning task of pouring out water in small bowls to leave at each guest's door for washing. She carried them up one by one and laid two fresh candles by each door. At the Baron's door she laid something extra, however. From around her neck she pulled a necklace of twine with a pendant of a green stone she'd found the day before. The stone was almost heart-shaped and through what would be one of the upper lobes of the heart was a perfect hole through which she had pulled the piece of twine she'd taken from the log pile. It wasn't much, but it was the first gift she had ever given anyone. She took it in her hand and whispered to it.

"You bring him good health and keep him safe, alright?" Then she laid it reverently on top of the candles.

As she walked away she didn't notice the tiny glow that encompassed the stone for a brief moment before it faded back into, by all appearances, just a simple stone once more.

*****

For once, Trotter was grateful for the bright sunrise in Sarano and the screaming of the early gulls. They pulled her from an unrestful night filled with nightmare after nightmare. She dreamed of the Reconstruction as Miro had described it to her. It had been a war between the gods, she'd said, long before Realm had separated itself from the world of man. That was when the gods walked on Aevum among them and were worshipped in person. Each god had a kingdom, and in that kingdom held dominion over his or her believers in a fiercely physical way.

They used them as a king would use serfs; to build glorious monuments, to farm for them, to serve them, and even to sacrifice to them. They were fueled by belief. In some kingdoms, worship was compulsory and refusal meant pain or even death. But when the words became emptied of their meaning for the hatred of the whips that compelled them to pray, worship was no longer enough. Just as a greedy monarch will covet the riches of a neighboring kingdom, the gods began wars with each other in their jealousy over worship. Looking to expand their dominion and believers, they would strike at each other with the only weapon they had.

Reality.

Gods are not mired in reality in the same way that artists are not mired in their paintings. An artist is, however, affected when his masterpiece is threatened. This was the threat that the gods used against each other. Lives were twisted, humans were turned into creatures, creatures were turned into humans, and Aevum itself was even ripped apart and reassembled, putting lakes and mountains where they had never been before. Many of the magical creatures that existed today owed their creation to the Reconstruction. Even the Prawn Mountain, so named because the unlikely bulbous top resembles the carapace and legs of a prawn, was created in this chaotic time.

During this war, a loving family could go to bed after wishing everyone a good night and awake in new houses with new lives and no memory of ever having been a family. Some did not awake at all, or some awoke as terrible creatures. Towns and villages were plagued with dragons and trolls, people were tormented by illness, and always, the world was different every day. The world could change so quickly that a home on the plains could be plummeting off the side of a mountain cliff or sinking underneath the ocean before the ground had even finished shifting. The only thing that was consistent during this time was the fear. The quaking ground signaled that change was coming again, and the only thing to do was fear the blind and indifferent rage of the jealous gods to whom they were barely more than livestock.

Such were Trotter's dreams through the night. Miro's words were still fresh in her mind. The Reconstruction had been a living hell for those alive at the time. The story of the Reconstruction was one that every child of the Wedge and Aevum alike heard as a rite of passage, and because of this it had become more folklore than anything. But what it also represented was the story of how the world as she knew it came to be.

A truce was not forged until some of the gods realized the irreparable harm the mortals would suffer if the war continued. The wiser of the gods who had been long against the war called for a separation of the gods and man. They created the realm of the gods and called it Realm, because gods, among other things, have no imagination. Realm was a new layer of reality never more than a breath's thickness from mankind. The multitudes of magical creatures and magical humans left behind as casualties of the war found themselves in a world where mankind did not welcome them warmly, the confused memories of the Reconstruction being too fresh, and thus the Wedge was created in the tiny space between Realm and reality of Aevum, opening only into Sarano, as the refuge of the magical. The Wedge became the only intersection between Realm and Aevum as the denizens of the Wedge could enter either world they liked, but the gods could never leave Realm again.

With this separation, mankind flourished once again and the gods, while many still had believers and temples, were sometimes forgotten. In light of this, the gods began to specialize. The Accord of Realm had already decided that only one god, the one who'd shown the most restraint in the Reconstruction, would hold dominion over reality. Stoicese, constant and unwavering in his values, became the god of Truth, which encompassed all of reality. Erov took dominion of the sea, Kaito of the winds, Vadin of the storms, Sylvia of the forests, and so on, until there was a god dedicated to every attribute, element, or trade available. Specialization, the gods discovered, offered worship and a reprieve from extinction. If you are the goddess of music your name is being honored anywhere a song is rendered with skill by a musician, whether they truly believed or not.

Mankind picked up and moved on, and as the centuries passed the Reconstruction was relegated to the ranks of mythology, though partly out of denial. If it were held as history, then it would be something real, which meant it would be something that might happen again. It was easier for a human mind to believe in tooth fairies than it was in something as horrible as the Reconstruction. It was also easier to laugh at the geologists who swore that in some places Aevum was older than in others because, of course, that just couldn't be right.

Only those who dwelt in the Wedge and were citizens of Realm were aware of it as being history. Few alive outside of the gods themselves could remember the horrors of it, but there was an inherited fear of that tremble. And an inherited instinct that told them that it wouldn't be the only one.

The latter instinct had been correct. As Miro opened the gate to let Trotter back into Sarano the ground trembled again, this time uprooting a tree across the street that flopped miserably as it tried to right itself on its roots.

"Go!" Miro had nearly shoved her through the gate. Prowler remained behind in the shaking Wedge with Miro. "Get some rest and stay low tonight. I'll come see you tomorrow." She shut the gate quickly, leaving Trotter feeling unstable as she stepped from quaking ground to solid ground. The sound of thunder that accompanied the Wedgequake ceased as the gate closed and all she was left with were the night sounds of Sarano's low-rent district.

In her dreams, the ground never stopped shaking and Sarano was burning.

CHAPTER 4

Far north of the warm seaside breeze of Sarano, Baron von Proustich opened his eyes. The mornings hurt the worst. Before the fire was stoked and the hot broth had soothed his chest, his every breath burned like daggers of fire and ice. A cough began lightly and then grew into a strangling spasm that shook his body violently. The pain was everywhere now, and the Baron was growing more certain each time he closed his eyes at night that it would be the last. Sometimes, when he awoke to the crippling pain, he wished it had been.

What kind of a leader is a man who must be helped from bed every morning? His weakness plagued him. It wasn't the appearance of weakness that bothered him; he well knew that his adversary, the Baron Fierfen, was in no better shape than he. What bothered him was that he was not able to stand in front of his own men – and, all too often, boys – and speak to them himself. While he and his retinue were camped within the comforting walls of the Inn for the baron's health, his soldiers were freezing in camps with hastily made barracks that stood up to the Drimmish winds no better than rice paper. In his younger years he would have camped with his men and shared the same fate as they. Since his only son was killed in battle, however, his fate became a pressing concern to the entire barony, particularly those of his officers that were already maneuvering for more power. Without an heir, his death would mean chaos for his army and it would be all too easy for Baron Fierfen to tear it apart and commit it to the same wholesale misery that passed for everyday life in the wretch's own barony. Starvation, crime, impossible taxation, and murder were staples of life in every village that owed fealty to Baron Fierfen.

It was a fate that Baron von Proustich was not willing to allow to fall upon his own barony, so when his faithful captain insisted upon moving him from the camp to the Tarbach Inn for the worst of the winter, his arguments against it were half-hearted at best.

There was a knock at the door. The baron was grateful to hear it. Carmony must have been lingering near enough to the door to hear the baron's cough, the tell-tale sign that he was awake.

"Come in," he rasped.

The captain entered carrying a tray with a steaming bowl of broth and the water left by Alice earlier that morning. He laid the tray beside the bed and without fuss or fanfare assisted the baron in sitting up, wrapping the blanket firmly around the man's shoulders before he hurried to stoke the fire.

As the baron reached for his broth, something else caught his eye. "What's this?" He asked, holding up a small necklace of twine.

Captain Carmony smiled congenially from the fireplace. "I believe milord has an admirer," he answered. "It was wound around the candles when I picked them up with the water. She may be a bit young for you, though," he chuckled.

The captain laughed naturally. It was one of the things that drew the baron to him and why he'd kept him as his closest attendee, despite having officers with more experience and higher rank. Drimmish men were usually severe, drawn, and humorless, yet the captain found humor and enjoyment during even the worst of times. When the baron asked him about this, his response was that he would laugh until he died and would probably even die laughing. Life itself, breathing, living, experiencing, and having a chance to fight back at the evils of the world was reason enough to smile. And so the baron quickly found a place for him in his retinue. The captain reminded him that where there was life, there was hope and there was a reason to fight.

He fingered the trinket thoughtfully as he sipped his broth. "Dear little Alice. What a remarkable child."

"Remarkable, indeed. Remarkable enough that she almost frightens me," Carmony responded. When he saw the baron's inquisitive look he continued, "Please don't ask me to explain that because I'm not sure if I can. It's just a strange feeling I get around her, as if what I'm seeing isn't really there."

"I think I know what you mean. Still, children her age can be quite odd. I'm sure it's nothing out of the ordinary, despite her unusual skill."

"I'm sure you are correct, sir. Would you like me to take that dirty thing away?"

"This?" The baron studied the necklace. "No, no. In fact, I think I'll wear it for a while. It wouldn't do to be ungracious about it." He slipped it over his neck, much to the captain's surprise.

"As you wish, milord. I do have some good news for you. The blizzard is completely gone. I spoke to the village wisewoman this morning and she seems certain that the snows will be gone for a week or more. The innkeeper assured me that she's never wrong about the weather."

"That means we'll be able to move the army finally to a more suitable camp closer to Fierfen's lines. We should move before he has the same idea and we end up nose to nose with each other. Tell the innkeeper that we are grateful for his hospitality and that we will be taking our leave today."

"I anticipated your wishes, sir, and let him know that this might be the case. He ordered the girl to feed and prepare your horse."

"Alice?" The baron was shocked. "That war horse is more than three times her height and likely to step on her without even knowing it. And if I know that bastard of a horse he'll probably even be aiming for her." The baron started to rise from the bed. "We have to stop her –"

His strength gave out and the captain caught him as he started to stumble. "Don't worry, sir. I argued as much with the landlord and he suggested I go with her to see for myself. Pericles actually kneeled down for her to place his blankets upon his back." He shook his head, searching for an explanation that would make sense. "She speaks to him and I swear it's as if he understands her."

"Stranger and stranger," the baron muttered.

"I think she'll be rather sad to see you go. Actually, she may be in denial. When I told her that we would be leaving today she told me that we couldn't possibly leave because of the snow. She tried to convince me that the blizzard was just about to start."

"The poor child. I'll be sure to tell her goodbye before we leave. She deserves better than what she has here." As he'd struggled to stand, the necklace had slipped beneath his nightshirt and now hung against his chest. Absently, giving it the barest of attention, he noticed that it was almost hot against his weary skin.

*****

With tears stinging in her eyes, Alice struggled to the base of Grandfather Tree. She'd left Frieda yelling for her and ran as quickly as she could across the snow. Leaving? How could they? She'd only just made friends for the first time in her life and there, in the barn, the captain told her that they would be leaving her today. She'd waited until he'd gone upstairs with the broth and ran to the only place that would make her feel whole again.

She dug her tattered journal out from under the tree and wrote furiously on the first blank page she could find.

"Grandfather is planning to leave today." A tear fell and blotted the charcoal line on the page. "But I want him to stay for my birthday. The snow is moving in again and it looks like the blizzard may come back and I don't want him to be traveling if that happens. He should stay here for another week and see what the weather is like then. We can play together and read stories and he can tell me what my mother was like when she was a little girl like me. The snow is coming soon; I can see it even now. It will be heavier and whiter than ever before and it will cover the whole village. Grandfather can't travel in this kind of weather. We'll have fun together while he's here. I'm lucky to have a grandfather as kind as he."

She put her diary away in her secret pouch under its bed of moldering needles. Feeling better now, Alice crawled back out from her safe-haven and headed back to the inn under a sky that was growing increasingly gray.

*****

Baron von Proustich stood by the fire, warming his hands. The captain was pleased to see his master moving around so well this morning and remarked upon it.

"I do feel stronger today, somehow," he agreed with the captain. "The landlady's broth warmed me like a potion this morning. I must remember to pay her my complements before we leave."

"And I'll see if we can take some extra along for the trip."

This time it was the baron's turn to laugh. He took a deep breath and was pleased when the expected fit of coughing didn't come. "This will be a good day," he said warmly. He walked more steadily than in days over to the huge wooden shutters of the room's only window with a desire to see the morning light. The shutters, still crusted with ice, yielded only after he pounded on them to shake them loose. When he pulled them open he gasped as the frigid wind struck him full in the face.

"Captain, I thought you said the day was clear?"

"Indeed I did, milord. The sky is as blue as can be."

"I think you should take another look."

Confused, the captain left the baron's luggage half-packed as he joined him at the window.

"That's not possible! The storm would have had to have come out of nowhere. There wasn't a single cloud in the sky!" They looked at the ground outside the inn and other villagers were gathered in the square, staring at the darkening sky in like-minded astonishment as the clouds continued to build. There was thunder in the distance. That was rare during a snowstorm here. Many of them had left their houses for the first time in days in anticipation of the clear weather and as the spell of shock broke they began hurrying back to their homes to stoke their fires and secure their shutters. The village wisewoman was ambling around in between them in a panic as the first heavy flakes were falling.

"It's not real!" She screamed. "It's not supposed to be snowing, it's not real!"

Her reaction clearly disturbed the other villagers. One of them put his arm over her shoulders to calm her and led her back to her cottage. The captain looked away from this and shrugged helplessly at the baron.

"I guess I'll go and tell the innkeeper that we'll be staying after all. I don't understand it. I just don't." He pulled the wooden shutters back together and sealed them tightly.

"Maybe next time you should get your weather report from little Alice," the baron replied grimly.

*****

When the ball bounced against the wall, off the floor, and back into Trotter's hand for around the 439th time Prowler made his move. As it left her hand again he sprang from the bed and snatched it from the air, sinking all four of his claws deep into the soft sides of the spongy leather ball before it could strike the wall. As he quickly discovered, cats with both sets of claws gripping a ball do not land on their feet. Prowler and ball came tumbling down in a pile crumpled at Trotter's side.

She looked down at the mound of disgruntled feline.

"Don't speak to me yet," came the muffled voice from the pile. Prowler rolled over and viciously shook the ball from his claws, using his back paw to extract the final one. It deflated sadly as the magic escaped it with a whine.

"I didn't think a cat would chase a ball. Especially an enchanted cat."

"I wasn't chasing it! I was killing it for my own sanity. If you'd bounced that ball one more time I think I might have given up one of my lives right then and there."

"Well what am I supposed to do? I don't have anything to do at all up here." She huffed theatrically and laid her head back against the bed. She was sitting on the floor now staring up at the window. "I wonder what's going on down at the docks?" She asked.

"Don't even think about it. I promised Miro we'd stay here and wait for her. There were more quakes last night before I left."

"But that was in the Wedge, not here! Sarano is perfectly safe. I don't see why we can't just go for a walk."

"Sarano is only safe at the moment. The quakes start in the Wedge because it's only built on top of reality. It's like a barometer for magical activity. Nowhere in the real world will be safe if this keeps up."

"Prowler," she turned and faced the cat almost nose to nose, "what did you tell Miro after I left? Why did she want you to stay behind?"

His ears flattened in discomfort. "I don't know what you're talking about. I went back for more of Aggie's soufflé."

"You're lying."

"I am not!"

"You are, too. You always wrinkle your nose when you lie."

"I do not!"

"You do. In fact, you're doing it right now. Go take a look." She pointed to the mirror in the corner. Prowler, predictable in his vanity, ran to the mirror and studied himself closely.

"See? I'm not wrinkling my nose at all," he announced proudly as Trotter quickly lowered the crate over his head. He stared at her through the wooden slats that comprised his makeshift prison. "You little sneak," he said, not believing how easily he'd let her trick him.

Trotter slid a saucer of milk and another with dried bacon rind through the slats for him. "Don't be mad at me. I'll bring you back something really yummy from the dock, ok?"

"You may as well bring me a tombstone. Miro's going to kill me over this, you know. And it's going to take some time because I still have at least seven lives left!"

"Don't be so dramatic. I'll explain it to her if she gets mad," she answered as she brushed her hair out with her brand new brush.

"Trotter, I'm deadly serious. It's not safe for you right now!"

"Really? Does that mean you're going to tell me what's going on?" She asked defiantly.

"You're being watched," he replied in defeat.

"Watched by who?"

"By whom. And I can't tell you that because I don't know yet. Miro is trying to find out."

"Well, it seems to me that if I'm being watched I shouldn't just be sitting here in one place and making it easy for them. Now, are you going to come with me or are you going to sit in the crate all afternoon? You never like the fish I choose for you so you might as well just come with me. It's your choice."

Prowler slumped. "Some guard cat I am. Alright, we'll go for just a little while. But stay close to me, don't talk to anyone, and we have to come back when I say, promise?"

Trotter's fingers surreptitiously crossed themselves behind her back. "Promise!"

She lifted the crate off of him and headed toward the door triumphantly.

"Dead cat walking," he sighed to himself as he followed her out into the busy streets of Sarano.

*****

There is a universal law which naturalists and scientists have yet to discover that supplies that anywhere people gather or pass through, someone will arrive to sell them things. It is due in large part to the tremendous attractive force between the street creature known as a vendor and the gold residing in the pockets of anyone who isn't them. This is why Trotter and Prowler were able to purchase and devour two fresh steamed cods, a sampling of shrimp, fried caramel snaps, banana pastries, and a very large syrupy fruit drink made with fizzy water, all within just a few blocks of the old factory they called home. Trotter was just finishing off a deliciously sticky taffy dainty when they reached the foot of Poorbetters St. and a new sign caught her eye.

"Hey, look! The boys have a new store."

"I heard about that. Apparently a child in the west side started asking too many questions about one of the gadgets and the parents got suspicious. So, they packed up shop, changed the name a little, and here they are. Good choice, too. People around here aren't into asking questions."

The store ahead of them had a sign that advertised "Pratt, Pratts, Potts, and Pot: Items of Technific Wonder." Though the quartet had moved around quite a bit they were always simple to find by those who knew them. The store in the illustrious west end of Sarano had been called "Pat, Pratt, Pots, and Potter," and the store before that had been of another similar variation. The reason for their constant moving was that after a while people would catch on to who they really were and chunks of brick would invariably be hurled through their window at best or, at worst, flaming bottles would be thrown in the night. Yet this didn't deter the young men whose names were actually Pratt, Pratt, Pratt, and Pratt.

Pratt was, or Pratts were, if you will, a mage. Early in his life he discovered that he had a natural aptitude for magical inventions and also discovered that he had far too many ideas and inventions to create than he could do alone in one lifetime. His solution was as simple as it was impossibly insane. Rather than attempt to find another mage to work with, he decided that he worked better by himself, so that is exactly what he chose to do. Using a little-known loophole in Scatcatter's Infundibulum Dispersal, he cast a small net in time and caught himself from one second in the future. With the help of his slightly future self, he repeated the process two more times until Pratt was certain he had enough help for his creations. The only drawback was that he tended to fall into a four second loop in his conversations with other people. Therefore, only two Pratts worked in the front of the store at any time while the other two worked feverishly in the workshop constructing toys that were part magical and part mechanical.

It was generally held among the public that yes, magic existed and yes, it's quite handy to have around when someone gets ill or the dragons get frisky again, but it's not really *proper*, is it? And so it was that they tended to become uncomfortable around practitioners of magic. When groups of uncomfortable people gather together they typically become a group of angry people quite quickly if for no other reason than it seemed to be fashionable at the time.

Magic, unfortunately, was never fashionable in the trendy and modern city of Sarano. It signaled a time when people, chiefly people with money, were not in control and put them largely in mind of pitchforks and torches. It was tolerated, however, in the same way that mice are tolerated to exist so long as they did not appear in one's kitchen.

The Pratts made beautiful toys and timesaving inventions that could practically prepare and cook an entire meal if the buyer had enough gold to spend. However, in order to entice an affluent citizen to purchase one of their magical goods they'd had to be creative, and even a little devious. Pratt, one or all of them, came up with the name 'technifical' to describe the creations and called himself, themselves, an engineer. Since everyone knew that nobody could understand an engineer anyway they seldom asked them what technifical meant. If a brave or morbidly curious soul did ask, then they would be ambushed with terms like reversible inverse momentum, floppy circuits, limited infinite quantities, and quantifiable unknowns until the listener gave up and went away pale, shaken, and confused.

Still, from time to time an enterprising mind would dissect one of their wonders and discover that where they'd expected to find clockwork was nothing but seemingly sparkly air or sometimes even a flapping butterfly. Then the Pratts would have to pack up their store and move yet again. It no longer bothered them, actually. It was a matter of pride that they were never in one place long enough for the property tax bill to arrive.

The newest incarnation of their store stood in front of Trotter with the promise of at least one thing: it would alleviate an entire morning's worth of boredom in one stop.

"Let's go in for a visit," she said, swallowing the last of her taffy.

"Not this time. We need to get back and wait for Miro."

"Oh, come on, it's right on the way! It won't take long." She jogged toward the door.

"You promised!" Prowler called behind her.

"What? I can't hear you. You should speak up when you're so far away," she taunted as the door to the shop began to close behind her. Prowler darted through before it could shut on his tail.

"Five minutes. Then we really have to go. I'm getting a bad feeling right down to my whiskers now."

"Don't be such a fraidy cat." The buzzing of toys and gizmos filled her ears as soon as she stepped through the door. As she wandered down an aisle a small rodent sized toy zipped in front of her, pausing only long enough to squeak a tinny apology before hurrying along. In the corner a toy bird was flapping from wall to wall while a life-like toy frog hopped into her hands. It had a small key turning in its back, but she knew it was only for show. That key turned nothing at all and would never need winding. What it *did* do was make it look less magical and therefore more acceptable to the parents of proper children with pockets full of gold.

"Hello? Pratts? That's odd," she said as no one responded. Finally she heard a pattering of footsteps hurrying from the back of the store.

"Trotter! How good to see you!"

"Trotter! How good to see you!"

The length of time between the echoes generally gave you a good idea of which Pratts you had in front of you. As a rule, they tried to keep a minimum of two seconds apart when dealing with the public and tried to keep to short statements. She could only assume that she'd just been greeted by either Pratts One and Three or Pratts Two and Four. And for some reason one of them seemed a little nervous today.

"What do you think of our new store?"

Trotter, out of habit, was waiting for the echo. When it didn't come she noticed that the other Pratt, the one she'd mentally dubbed Nervous Pratt, seemed at a loss. His eyes also seemed to be pleading with her to answer the question.

"Oh, um, it's lovely. I think it's bigger than the store you had on the west end, isn't it?"

"Oh, it is! And the workshop is so much bigger if you'd like to see -" Nervous Pratt stopped speaking under the glare of the other Pratt.

Again, the echo didn't come. "I've never heard you not repeating each other. How are you doing that? It's almost as if you're different people."

Nervous Pratt squeaked a bit and looked at the floor, his fingers knotting themselves in his clasped hands. The Other Pratt smiled disarmingly at her.

"I'm glad you noticed. We've been practicing. We're so good at it now we practically *are* different people."

Prowler sniffed the air and twitched his tail. "Trotter, it's time to go. I've got a bad feeling in here," he whispered from the ground. Prowler hadn't yet grasped the psychology of a teenager. The only way to ensure that a teenager will do something is to expressly forbid them from doing it in the first place.

Trotter bent down to pet him and whisper back surreptitiously. "You're doing it again. You're such a chicken."

"I'm a cat! It's called instinct."

She rolled her eyes as she stood back up to address the Pratts. "It looks like you've made a lot of new toys. Do you have any more of the Following Balls? Mine met with a little accident this morning," she added with a glare at Prowler. For the uncoordinated, the Following Ball was a minor miracle. No matter where you threw it or what it struck, it would always return to the hand from which it left.

"Following Balls?" The Other Pratt began to ask before glancing at a subtly nodding Nervous Pratt who was still staring at the floor. "Oh! Of *course*, Following Balls. We do have some of those," he said with a dismissive flick of his hand, "but if you'll come with me we have something *much* better than those."

He briefly tangled with an immobile Nervous Pratt as he turned toward the back of the store. "In the back? Remember the new toy?" He said to him, shoving him ahead of him. He turned and cast his disarming smile again back at Trotter. "He forgets sometimes, you know."

"He forgets? But he's you, isn't he?"

"Ah, see? I told you we've been practicing!" He said with a self-satisfied grin and led her toward the back.

"Trotter, please?" Prowler grabbed her pants leg with his paw and looked up at her pleadingly.

"It's okay; I'm with you on this one." The Pratts were starting to give her the creeps. Especially the Other Pratt. Her visits with the Pratts were usually fun and filled with exotic new creations. She'd spent afternoons in awe just watching them build toy after toy or tool after tool. One could see an idea spark in the mind of one of them and after a very few words with the other three and a few scribbles on paper watch as an entirely new tool for peeling potatoes begins to come to life before turning into Pratt's Technific Automatical Backscratcher and Exfoliation Device - Also for Use with Potatoes.

It was always fascinating watching them work together. But the point was, they were *together* on everything, always. That was what made them work. So why would they be practicing being different? Something was wrong.

"Actually, I probably need to be going. I forgot I've got something stewing in the pot at home. Thanks, though." She started to turn to leave when she was suddenly aware of a hand on her shoulder pulling her not-so-gently toward the back of the shop. Prowler hissed beside her.

"Don't be silly!" The Other Pratt boomed. "You can't leave without seeing this." He pulled her faster toward the workshop.

"Hey!" She tried twisting out of his grasp, which only made him pull harder. When they were within sight of the workshop Nervous Pratt darted through the door, and as it swung back she saw the other Pratts. All three of them, in fact, tied and gagged in the floor of the workshop. Nervous Pratt must be the only one he kept free, she realized.

Prowler had seen it, too. He leapt onto a shelf and onto the Other Pratt's shoulder, wrapping his claws around his face and tearing at his eyes as he howled like an alley cat.

"Run, Trotter! Get out of here!"

Other Pratt was quickly becoming not a Pratt at all. His skin became gray, his body lengthened by more than a foot, and his eyes became a luminous yellow. With one quick move he tore Prowler from his shoulder and hurled him into a closet across the room. The door slammed shut with a wave of the monster's hand, cutting off Prowler's yelp of pain.

Trotter stared at him, too afraid to move. "What are you?" She backed away into a shelf. "Your eyes... shape shifters can't change their eyes!"

"Well, as I said. I've been practicing." He was leering and smug now. He moved toward her to drag her back to the workshop.

"Stop it!" She screamed and threw her hands up into an exaggerated spell-casting position. To her surprise, he looked anxious as to what she might do next. She decided to take advantage of this. "If you come any closer I'll turn you into a wart on a frog's butt!"

He paused for a moment and blinked his yellow eyes. Then he broke into a sharp-toothed grin. "I must be losing my edge. I almost believed you, little demi-god. Now be a good girl and come with me before I lose my temper."

As he reached for her again she reached as deeply as she dared into that well of magic she'd worked so hard at controlling and thought 'frog' at him as hard as she could. He flinched backward as a few sparks danced around her fingertips and a slightly smoky smell filled the air. Then it seemed to be over. He laughed as he grabbed her arm again.

"Pathetic. And yet they think you're the key to restoring Laramak."

Before she could ask what he meant, a large and warty toad fell from the ceiling and struck him on the shoulder. Then another stuck him in the face as he looked up to see what had happened. More and more fell like a throaty, warty rain until he found himself up to his knees in toads. He dropped her arm to shield his head as they fell. His struggles to move away from the onslaught ended with disgustingly squishy sounds as the growing pile cascaded to trap his feet again with each step. Even those that fell away tended to hop back onto the pile of their own accord.

Trotter took her chance and ran for the closet where he'd locked Prowler. She tugged at it with all of her strength but it wouldn't budge.

"Prowler, I can't get it open!"

"Just go! I'll be fine in here." He cried feebly under the door.

"I'm not leaving you!"

"Do you have Miro's shell?"

"I think so," she felt in her pocket and pulled it out. It was as cold as the sea bottom. "Yes! I have it here."

"Use it!

"How?" She turned and looked over her shoulder as the shape shifter growled triumphantly. He'd grown to more than twice his previous size and was stepping over the pile, looking for her. The rain of frogs still followed him, but it could no longer keep up with his immense size.

"Just hold it and call for her. It knows what to do!"

She held the shell in her hands firmly and rubbed it. "Miro, if you can hear me, I need your help! Please!"

Trotter shrieked as the now giant shape shifter grabbed her bodily with one hand. As he held her up to the ceiling his fingers lengthened and hardened, closing together at the tip until his hand became a cage around her. A cage with bars of bone.

"If you try another little trick like that again I will crush every bone in your body, do you hear me, you little brat?" He spat the word.

"And if you try that I will feed you to giant squids at the bottom of the ocean." Miro's voice came from behind him just as one giant tentacle snaked around his neck and two others around his arms. One of them squeezed his cage hand until the bones holding Trotter cracked and broke, causing him to howl in pain. Trotter fell to the ground as the cage turned back into a hand, now too mangled to hold onto her. She pushed past him to safety behind Miro and gasped at what she saw.

Miro, still stunningly beautiful, was also terrible to see. She was supported by tremendous trunk-like tentacles that carried her around the room gracefully, and smaller yet still frightfully strong tentacles were wrestling with the shape shifter as he struggled to find a shape that could slip her many-fingered grip. In her strong grasp he bounced from shelf to shelf, sending toys and gadgets flying, some running away of their own accord. There was a frenzy of fur, teeth, talons, bone, feathers, and scales as he sought a suitable form with which to fight her, screaming insults and curses at her all the while. She had no less than five tentacles holding him, and his own attempt at a similar shape only confused the situation. He was nowhere near as strong as she was.

As the creature's howls of pain worsened and his fighting lessened, Trotter realized that Miro had been chanting quietly all the while. Finally he faded into a mere shadow of the monster he'd been and quit moving entirely. The creature was now no taller than Trotter, and possibly even shorter. The gray skin had been replaced by a covering of loose white flesh with vines and long grasses hanging beard-like from its face. Moss grew in scattered clumps from its body. If she'd seen it laying in a field she would have thought it was no more than a mossy stump. It stood unmoving and unseeing in front of them. The only thing left of the original creature was the luminous glow in its yellow eyes. Miro waved her hand in front of its eyes and smiled, pleased with her work.

"There," she said. When Trotter turned her eyes back to Miro, she was once more the woman known since she was a baby. All smiles and shimmering silver hair, her tentacles gone and replaced by her ever-moving scarves once again.

"What was that thing? And what did you do to him?" Trotter asked, her mind still trying to convince herself that Miro had been anything but just a woman only moments ago. It had all happened so fast.

"I bound him. This wretch is a leshy. There aren't many of them around anymore, thank Chaos. Leshies are adept shape shifters but they are also demons, and that means they are still bound to the laws of Realm. Demons are required to serve any master who can bind them with strength and the proper spell," her face darkened, "but there should be very few outside of the gods themselves who still know the words to use. That language died long, long ago."

Miro twisted the doorknob in her seemingly dainty hand and it groaned under the pressure. It snapped away from the wood and the door fell open. Prowler walked out warily, blinking in the light. There was terror in his eyes as he sought out Miro. "The demon mentioned restoring Laramak. They couldn't, could they?"

Her eyes rested uncertainly on Trotter for a moment. "I don't know yet. I still don't even know who's making the Changes, but it's definitely not in Sarano. There are rumors, but they seem to be born more out of fear and stupidity than truth," she shook her head sadly. "Even Jorg can't see where the truth begins. Each Wedgequake drives him madder and madder. For him it's like having his mind cleaved into two halves that aren't on speaking terms."

"Is it really happening again?" He asked. Miro nodded, her shoulders tensing.

"You're talking about another Reconstruction, aren't you?" Trotter asked.

"Yes. Another Reconstruction is beginning, but this time it isn't the gods. The truth tellers are at a loss and Stoicese may well be the only one left who can see what or who is causing it."

She turned and took Trotter by both shoulders. "It's time for you to meet your father."

CHAPTER 5

The clouds piled above Klempt thicker and higher than the snow-laden country of Drimbt had ever seen. They swirled toward the village from every corner of the region known as the Ice Bowl, forming a gigantic frozen eye over the village from miles around.

Far above the icy cloud line of the blizzard, a red speck circled the eye cautiously. As a creation of Stoicese, the red hawk had the gift of truth telling and what his piercing eyes saw in front of him was not what his mind's eye, the eye for seeing the truth, told him should be there.

To his mind's eye, it was a clear and sunny day over Klempt, perfect for soaring and hunting. Unfortunately, the winds buffeting his wings told him that the cyclonic blizzard was certainly there, whether it was real or not. The hawk pinned his wings to his sides and plummeted through the whirling clouds to the village below.

When he emerged beneath the clouds and spotted the blanketed village his eyes fell upon a little girl standing practically barefoot in the snow, seemingly oblivious to the storm all around her. His eyes were the only proof he had that she was there; in his mind there was nothing but a white path leading to the river where she stood defiantly watching him as he landed in the snow-laden bough of a fir tree near her. She approached the tree where he landed.

"You're in Grandfather Tree, you know. He doesn't like it when birds try to nest in him."

The hawk cocked his head on its side, curious at this strange child. It seemed that she'd been waiting for him. He fluffed his feathers and called to her with a shrill cry.

"Name?"

"Alice. My name is Alice Will," she said proudly, her mouth frowning angrily, "and you don't belong here. You will go away now!"

The red hawk was soaring above the clouds and almost to Realm again before he realized he'd left the giant fir tree.

In a place that was both impossibly far and only a whisper away from the snow-covered mountains of Drimbt, a wretched creature watched through the eyes of the hawk from his pool in the darkness and saw what had transpired. Its face twisted slowly into a smile as it recalled the small face framed by golden ringlets as she sent the hawk away.

"I see you now, little Alice Will," it laughed.

*****

Despite the fire raging in the giant hearth, the dining hall was nearly frigid. It was sparsely decorated, the few tapestries remaining from the previous owner having nearly rotted from neglect. The castle was the same in every room; the walls were dark stone and every corner was choked with grime and cobwebs. What furniture there was crumbled from disuse, the upholstery turning to dust and the wood flaking with dry rot. It contained thirteen bedrooms, none of which were used. The master did not sleep, and his servants slept in the dungeon.

This place was not a home. It was a monument, a place of waiting.

Even the dining hall existed as merely a function of necessity; the long table where the master devoured his meal was the only piece of maintained furniture in the room. It was lined from end to end with meat. Little of it was cooked, and what was cooked was nearer to rare. The rest of it was raw, and not always fresh. A cloying scent hung in the air over the table. It smelled of iron, and of the hunt. To the hunted, it would have smelled exactly like death.

The master tossed a few bones from his plate to the two dogs tied near the blue fire raging behind him. The word 'dog' used here is only an attempt to describe these beasts in a familiar way. It applies nearly as well as the word hot describes a sea of lava. They were canine in the sense of the word, but they were canine distilled. These were not pets, not guards; they existed only for the hunt. Charcoal black eyes set in sleek black faces spoke of a mixture of both restraint and strength coiled into an almost visceral patience. They waited for the word from their master that would release them for the chase as an arrow from an over-taut bow.

Before the footsteps even approached the entrance to the hall both dogs turned their eyes toward the door and growled lowly to alert their master.

"What do you want?" He asked as the nervous servant hesitated at the doorway. It was always dangerous to interrupt the lord during his meals.

"I apologize, Master, but the truth teller said to tell you he's found the other World Changer. It's a young girl, sir, in Drimbt."

"How young?" He tossed another handful of bones over his shoulder to the hounds. The servant watched in horror as they disappeared. Despite having jaws that could have snapped them like twigs, the bones were swallowed whole. One of them looked up at the servant and licked its lips as if to indicate that it could perform the very same trick with his head if it so chose. "I asked how young," the master reminded the terrified man.

"Perhaps six or seven, the truth teller says. She's very strong, but he thinks she might be lonely."

His master laid the remainder of the still warm quail aside on his plate and turned thoughtful. There was blood glistening in streamlets around the edges of his mouth. He dabbed at his face with a napkin and smiled as he rose from the table. The servant stepped back from his master more quickly than he'd intended, and the ropes that loosely bound his ankles caused him to topple backwards.

"A lonely little girl, you say?" He laughed, tossing his plate with a crash toward his beasts who eagerly awaited the rest of the quail. With his other hand he grasped the servant by the shoulder and hauled him to his feet, inhaling the scent of the man's mingled sweat and fear. "Let's send Arriman to meet her, then. I'm sure they'll get along like a house on fire until she can meet Lord Laramak."

*****

Some stories are told to celebrate memories. Some stories are told to transform them. Sometimes a story describes something so terrible that people need to forget the horrific events that entailed the original story and so, over time, the story gains a hero, a new twist, or even a happy ending. It isn't long in the retelling that the terrible memory is no longer a memory at all, and becomes no more real than a child's fairy tale.

The story of Laramak was just such a tale.

During the dark time of the Reconstruction there were many gods of war. Each held dominion over the various attributes. Tercius held dominion over strategy and tactics, Wymbala over courage and bravery, Pak inspired the songs of the warriors, and so on. Lord Laramak, as he preferred to be called, held dominion over those who died in battle. He thrived on bloodshed, violence, and the horrors of war, and he grew more powerful with every life given in combat. His kingdom was a dark and bloody place where the sun blazed hot and red, and his castle filled the horizon with jagged towers like claws reaching from the ground. Below the twisted castle, the gruesome wendigos stalked the lands and feasted after every battle. The sight of the wendigo haunted the nightmares of those few who survived Laramak's onslaught.

It was Laramak who created the berserkers, the terrifying and mad-eyed soldiers who rushed to battle with only their teeth and clawed hands as weapons. What made them most terrifying was that they were humans one moment, and the next they were snarling creatures driven mad with rage by Laramak for the sheer joy of watching the chaos and death they spread. When at war with the gods of nearby kingdoms, he would send a tide of blood-lusting berserkers into their villages. They would scour the kingdom of life, leaving piles of mangled bodies and burnt villages in their wake. They knew no fear, no pain, no hunger, and did not tire. They wanted only to kill again and again.

As per the ever-changing nature of stories, the story of Laramak is now told as follows:

During the time of changes, a blacksmith lived with his two sons in the kingdom of Stoicese near the black shadows of the Stain Mountains where Laramak sat on his throne. The blacksmith's skill in the forge was unmatched, his steel stronger and his swords sharper than in any other kingdom. Still, the villagers feared for the blacksmith and his family. It was all too often they had lost loved ones who had ventured too near the edge of Laramak's kingdom and never been seen again. The blacksmith laughed at their fears and showed them proudly the swords and armor he'd made for his boys. Each sword would slice through the thickest armor and cut a tree in half with a single strike. Their own armor was as thin as paper, but would withstand a blow from a sledgehammer or any other sword in the world.

"Stoicese will protect us," the blacksmith said, "and if he cannot, my armor surely will! With it my boys are as strong as Laramak himself."

From his throne high above them, Laramak watched angrily as the blacksmith and his family scoffed at his power.

It wasn't long before Laramak spotted the blacksmith's sons hunting together at the edge of the shadow lands that marked the boundary. The villagers seldom hunted here in fear of Laramak, so the deer, fowl, and rabbits that thrived in these lands were fat and plentiful. In his arrogance he sent a single berserker after them. The boys laughed as they saw the beast running after them, the mouth foaming and bloody.

"Is that the best he can do?" One of the sons laughed as they shot him down with the steel-tipped arrows his father had forged.

Laramak was furious. He scooped some clay from the ground and spoke madness into it as he molded it. The roughly shaped lump he set back down grew into the most terrible beast he'd ever created. It had the torso of a horse with six legs, each ending in claws and talons. The chest was protected with plates of living stone and each of its four arms ended in clubs, swords, and mauls. Its head was more teeth than flesh. All said, the beast stood nearly as tall as two men.

"Make War," Laramak breathed into it and set it after the blacksmith's boys.

John, the younger of the boys, had killed three rabbits already and was holding them quietly while his brother, Ralston, sighted a deer along his arrow and released. As he watched, his prey was snatched off of the ground before his arrow even reached it. Laramak's beast tore the deer to pieces and started toward the boys with the clear intent of doing the same to them.

"John," Ralston called to his brother, "let's play Mirrors with this one, yeah?" The boys played Mirrors when they hunted the giant bears from Laramak's land that sometimes terrorized their village. They rushed each side of the beast identically to confuse them, leaving them torn between attack and defend until the beasts could do nothing but stand and be run through with their swords.

John laughed and followed Ralston's lead. The boys ran in an arcing circle around the flank of the beast before it could reach them. It stumbled wildly; Laramak had given it six legs that were powerful for tearing and crushing, but they were too complicated to run with. At a signal, the boys charged the beast from both sides and, to Laramak's fury, their father's steel ran right through the creature's stone plating and sliced the body in half. The boys were gleefully trussing up their kill to carry back to the village when Laramak approached them disguised as another hunter in the shadow land.

"What a fine kill you have there! How is it that you kill the fiercest creatures that the mighty Lord Laramak creates without getting even so much as a scratch on yourselves?"

The boys were filled with pride at the recognition of their skill. "It's our father's steel, you see." said Ralston as he banged upon his chest. "Nothing can get through the armor that our father makes. His is the hottest forge in the land and makes the steel stronger and harder than even Laramak himself."

"Is that so," said Laramak in his disguise, biting back a snarl at the insult. "Why, there must be something that can cut through your armor.

Does it really have no weaknesses?"

"Only one," said John, approaching the hunter and hefting his sword proudly. "Only our father's finest swords are strong enough to pierce it, but we two are the only ones who carry them."

"With these weapons you can kill any of Laramak's beasts but you can only be killed by each other?" Laramak asked John who nodded with confidence. "In that case," Laramak dropped his disguise and breathed into John's ear, "Make War."

Laramak turned to Ralston who watched in horror as his younger brother twisted into one of Laramak's mad-eyed berserkers. "You've insulted me, blacksmith's son. You've killed my creatures and dared to challenge me. You're strong, certainly, but let's see if you're strong enough to kill your own brother." Laramak laughed as he returned to his castle at the top of the Stain Mountains. He continued laughing as he watched the battle rage from his throne, John mad for Ralston's blood and Ralston trying to defend himself while not harming his brother.

Finally, as Ralston tired, he knew he could defend himself no longer. His brother, now lost forever as one of Laramak's berserkers, would never tire and would move on to the village to fight and kill until he died. Ralston cried out in rage as he finally ran his own brother through with their father's finest sword. When John was still with death, he carried his brother's body back to the forge and tearfully told his father what had happened.

Angry and heartbroken, the blacksmith took his son's body to the castle of Stoicese and begged his help in avenging his son. Stoicese looked kindly on the blacksmith and his family and, though he could not intervene directly, gave the man a single black key.

The blacksmith returned home and told the villagers that he'd been given a miracle by Stoicese. He spent the next two days alone in his forge with Ralston and John's body and the fires of his forge blazed night and day. On the third day he left the forge shouting that the miracle had worked, that John was alive and well in the forge and together they would hunt again in Laramak's lands without fear. To honor Stoicese and the miracle the villagers then had a feast, which the blacksmith said John wouldn't be able to attend because he was still healing.

Word of the celebration for the blacksmith's miracle reached Laramak's ears in the highest spire of his castle. He was enraged that Stoicese would interfere and decided to go and see the miracle for himself.

Dressed in his most terrifying armor of the darkest nightmare and adorned in battle axes, bones, and skulls of those who'd died in his name, Laramak strode angrily into the village and demanded the blacksmith show him John's body.

"Alright, but we'll have to go to my forge. He's been there all day," the blacksmith said. He set out for his forge with the war god beside him. To be that close to Laramak meant to hear the cries of those who died violently. They whispered from the skulls on his belt. Ralston walked behind them a short distance away, glad that his brother's skull was not on that belt to torment him with his cries again.

When they reached the forge, the fire was indeed still burning hot within. The blacksmith stood aside at the door and gestured to Laramak. "After you, Lord Laramak. I can hear John even now."

"Show me," Laramak demanded, untrusting. "You will go in first so I can watch you. The boy will wait here."

"As you wish," the blacksmith agreed. He turned to Ralston and nodded sadly before entering the door to his forge with Laramak following behind him. Once inside Laramak spotted John sitting at the table with a mug in his hand and rushed toward him angrily, grabbing him by the collar and shaking him.

"How dare you live again!" He shouted at the unresponsive boy. As the mug of beer fell from John's limp hand Laramak realized that he'd been tricked and John was still long dead. As he turned around he saw the blacksmith had already closed the door behind himself.

"Wherever it will be, we three will be going together," said the blacksmith as Laramak charged him with his axe. He died satisfied with his revenge.

When the door closed behind his father and Laramak, Ralston had rushed forward and inserted the black key from Stoicese into the lock. As he turned it in the lock, the key blazed hotter in his hands until he could no long bear to touch it. He heard Laramak scream in rage as the key melted and flowed like quicksilver into the lock. The forge began to glow, burning hotter and hotter until the very stones began to melt and pour into the building itself, killing everything within it. Stone, steel, and wood twisted with flames tinged blue and white until the once proud forge was a pool of molten steel and lava seeping into the ground. When the heat died away, all that remained behind was that lock.

Ralston wept for his brother and father as he recalled the words of Stoicese in his castle. "Take care when you use this key. It will fit any lock, but whatever it locks can never be opened again."

The villagers cheered and proclaimed the blacksmith and his family heroes as the shadows lifted away from the borderlands and Laramak's castle crumbled to bits. It is said that the lock itself still exists in that village today where it is kept under guard at the bottom of a deep well, covered to stifle the sounds of Laramak's ghost screaming from the keyhole.

This, at least, is the story of Laramak as it is now told in fairy tales. As will happen with fairy tales, only parts of the story bear any resemblance to the truth as it actually happened. There was a key, there was a lock, and there was a blacksmith. But there are no heroes in the true story. Neither does Laramak's ghost lie trapped in a keyhole. This is mostly because gods cannot be killed and can never die. In reality, he is still sitting behind the door that trapped him.

He is waiting for it to open again.

*****

Trotter hugged her knees close to her body as she waited for Miro on the cool sands by the many-colored piers of Sarano watching the masts of the small yachts bobbing hypnotically. The beach was tranquil here at the sailing marina, nothing like the flurry of commotion at the deeper harbor of the busy seaport. It was serene and peaceful, and sitting on these sands being warmed by the sun she felt calmer than she would have thought possible after being attacked by a shape-shifting demon and learning that the world as she knew it was on the verge of ending.

A seagull landed near her and watched her expectantly.

"Food? Food? Fish?" he cried piercingly at her, hopping closer to her.

"Push off," she said sullenly, casually tossing a pebble in its direction.

It turned toward Prowler with hopeful eyes. "Fish? Mate?" It asked suggestively.

"You are not just barking up the wrong tree but the wrong evolutionary ladder, bird-brain." He made a half-hearted lunge at the bird, which launched itself into the air with cries that, for a seagull, amounted to a hearty cursing.

This would have normally left Trotter gasping for breath with laughter, but now she only sighed. Nothing could inspire an imagination to nightmarish heights like waiting helplessly. Miro was taking the demon to a place far beneath the lapping waves of the ocean for safekeeping.

Trotter liked the idea of tons of water between her and the horrible creature.

"How long has she been under now?" Trotter asked, her eyes still fixed on the spot where Miro had disappeared beneath the waves. There was something about the horizon that was bothering her, but she couldn't quite place her finger on it. It almost made her eyes water.

"Maybe twenty minutes," Prowler answered. "Don't worry, she'll be back soon."

Trotter rubbed her eyes vigorously and tried to focus on the area past the harbor.

"Why is it so foggy today? It hasn't rained all week."

"Fog?" Prowler asked incredulously and looked from Trotter to the harbor and back again when realization seemed to dawn on him. "You're still looking with your eyes, aren't you?"

"What else would I look with?" She rolled her eyes at him.

"Ok, smarty pants. Try something for me. Keep looking out toward the ocean but let your eyes relax and blur over. Then keep looking past the blur and see what's there. Got it?"

"Fine, whatever." She focused her eyes and then looked further until her eyes were blurry. Then she let them drift a little further, and –

"Oh my gods!" She dived toward the ground and tried to hang on to the sand. "Are we going to fall off? What happened to the fog?" She stared in horror at the new image in front of her.

"There never was any fog. You were seeing two things at once. Your eyes were seeing one thing while your mind saw what was really there and the images overlapped. Where the images began to disagree I imagine you just saw fog." Prowler sighed. "I wish I could just see fog."

"Doesn't anybody else see this? Why are they still sailing out toward it?"

"They only see what they think they should see. You could take them right to the edge and show them that the world ended just past the harbor and they still wouldn't believe you. It's because it's not real yet. But it's getting closer to reality," he added with worry in his voice.

She couldn't tear her eyes away from the jagged edge of the scene in front of her. It looked as though someone had taken a picture of the harbor and torn it apart, cleaving the horizon clean away. There was simply *nothing* beyond the second buoy in the harbor. The water didn't fall off the edge and it wasn't blackness beyond. It was simply blank. The blankness was more terrifying than anything else she could imagine.

"What happens to the boats that sail past it? Where do they go?"

"I imagine they go on out to the sea and have a good day of sailing."

"But the sea isn't there!"

"Yes it is. We're just looking at a different reality than they are. The sea is still there right in front of us. But the reality we're looking at is gaining strength and soon it really *won't* be there anymore. A new reality is forming and it doesn't look like Sarano is a part of it."

Nearer to the shore Miro's silver head emerged from the water. There was a brief flashing of tentacles around her as they settled into her familiar scarves and she stepped onto the beach. After twenty minutes at the bottom of the ocean she wasn't even dripping. In her hand she held a staff that Trotter had never seen her carry before. From its pointed tip it coiled up and around and curved its way to the top where a fish adorned the end. The fish itself looked so life-like that it seemed to have been frozen in the moment of capture and was still struggling to free itself. The entire staff was in her trademark mother of pearl, the light glancing off of it in enchanting rainbows. It was a staff fit for a queen.

She held it in front of her as she approached the pair on the beach. Trotter was still staring at the edge of the world in front of them. Miro followed Trotter's eyes.

"She's seen it, hasn't she?" Prowler nodded. Miro peered again at the edge and looked panicked. "Oh no! She's reinforcing it! Trotter? Listen to me. Look at the ocean, not the edge. The edge isn't really there. You have to see the ocean, do you hear me?" Trotter shook her head slowly. Eventually the fog began replacing the edge and she could see the boats far off that only a moment ago had seemed to sail off the edge of the world.

"It's so horrible," she shuddered.

"It's nothing compared with what Laramak would do. Come on," Miro extended her hand and helped the shaken Trotter to her feet.

With no ceremony whatsoever, she turned and stabbed the staff into the ground. As she did so the fish frozen at the end of the staff jerked into fitful life as it squirmed and gasped for air at the top of its prison. From her own mouth Miro produced a small pearl which she in turn placed into the mouth of the fish before stepping away from the staff. The fish was now as still as it had been before, refrozen in its struggle, but the staff seemed lighter and less real now. It had become almost transparent, and the light around it seemed to swell and part.

"Walk past the staff and into the light. You'll be safe in Realm with your father."

"You can't come with me, can you?"

Miro shook her head sadly. "No. But I'm sending you with two messages. One for Erov, and one for your father." She placed two small objects in Trotter's hand as she spoke. "They'll know what they mean."

"How do I find Erov?"

"I have a feeling that when he hears you're in Realm he'll find you."

As Trotter reached for the staff Miro had one last word of advice. "Be very careful of whom you speak to, but when you see Paraben tell him you'll be needing my old staff."

Miro's voice faded away with the seagulls as Sarano dissolved in front of Trotter.

*****

Prowler was about to enter the gate to Realm behind Trotter when he suddenly found himself hanging by his scruff in the air in front of Miro.

"That's really uncomfortable, you know," he said sullenly.

"I wanted to be sure you heard me."

"There are other ways of getting my attention. 'Hey, Prowler' usually works just fine."

"But this is so much more effective." She set him back down on the sand in front of her and squatted down on her own haunches, smoothing his fur for him. "I learned something from the leshy just now. It seems that the watcher is working for the Last Wendigo."

"That's impossible! He's been imprisoned in the castle for centuries!" Prowler shuddered hard. The wendigo was a creature born from the nightmare of Laramak's reign. It was more fearsome than the berserkers for the single fact that while the berserkers attacked blindly and without reason, the wendigos were calculating and evil. They lived for the sheer joy of the hunting and feasting on flesh, but they would also feast on the kills of the berserkers in the villages they slaughtered. Those who escaped the villages that were attacked by Laramak's armies would never return for fear of seeing what the wendigos did to the remains of their loved ones.

"He can't leave the castle, true, but he can still call the demons to serve him. I'm sure he was the one who sent the leshy after her. That means there will be more coming. Whether or not she can really bring back the key to Laramak's door, the Last Wendigo seems to believe that she can. He won't stop until he has her, Prowler."

His ears flattened against the top of his head. "What do we do?"

"She'll be safe in Realm for as long as she's there."

"And when we leave?"

She brought her own face closer to Prowler. "Then I'm counting on you. I've done what I can for her from here but I can't go any farther. So help me, if you let one hair on her head even get a split end I'll turn you back into a human!" Death threats meant little to a creature with nine lives. Being returned to his sad life as a weak and awkward human, however, was a low blow.

He slunk toward the gate with a new weight on his shoulders.

"Lovely. The fate of all mankind rests on the protective abilities of a house cat. Why me?"

"Because I can't go and you're the only other one who knows why we've been protecting her for so long. And since cats are also sensitive to shifts in reality that makes you the best candidate three times over. Face it, Prowler. You have to protect her. If you fail, there won't be anything left to protect when Laramak is through with his revenge."

"This is just great," he muttered to himself irritably as he left Miro and Sarano behind. "Now if Laramak turns out to actually be a giant mouse the world might be saved after all."

CHAPTER 6

Baron von Proustich waited patiently while Captain Carmony latched the final brocade to his formal uniform. It had been months since he'd last felt well enough to bear the weight of the full regalia. Come to that, it had been months since he'd felt like dressing at all.

"There, milord." The captain stepped back from the baron with an appraising smile. "You look like you're about to ride into battle."

The baron laughed heartily. "Don't tempt me. If this blasted blizzard would let up I feel like I could make Fierfen regret the day he was born. Actually, what I know I feel like right now is a large plate of ham steak with goose eggs and fried potatoes and dumplings. Go downstairs and tell the innkeepers I'll be down shortly for my breakfast."

Captain Carmony left the room with a broad, if bewildered, smile. The rest of the baron's retinue had been preparing for his death since the cough first seized his lungs at the start of winter. The captain, sick at the thought of any of the leeches in his high command getting their greedy, groping hands on the barony, was doing everything in his power to keep the man alive. Seeing him with a vigorous appetite for the first time in weeks gave him heart.

He was still elated when he turned the corner at the bottom of the stairs and nearly ran into something evil and terrifying. He was about to yell when a friendly voice spoke straight into his brain.

"Hi! I'm a little boy. A harmless, sweet little boy and you want to like me."

And Captain Carmony suddenly felt foolish at being startled by this little boy. At least, he was almost certain it was a little boy. It had ears that were a little bit too pointed for human and he had a nagging feeling that every time he tried to turn his eyes away he saw a suggestion of a tail. But still, he knew it had to be a little boy.

"I'm sorry if I startled you, little boy," he said with some difficulty. "I'm Captain Carmony. What's your name?"

"Me?" Its teeth flashed when it spoke. "You can call me Arriman."

*****

Prowler collided with Trotter's leg as he came through the gateway. She was completely mesmerized and didn't even notice Prowler's yowl of surprise. The gate deposited the two of them on the Cliffs of Ingressa, which gave them a full view of the chaotic patch-work quilt that is the realm of the gods. It was not a beautiful place in the aesthetic sense of the word; it was stunning and exquisite in its eccentricity, but it was no more beautiful than a plate of melted crayons. As they were accustomed to having their own kingdoms when they were among humans, they also had their own kingdoms here in Realm. Each god or goddess created a kingdom strictly to his or her liking, and most gods probably think 'artistic restraint' is some form of risqué performance art.

This is where it should be mentioned again that gods have no imagination and therefore reached for the grandiose as a replacement for actual taste. The kingdoms tended toward garish and kitschy and grew gaudier almost daily with the profound sense of competition that is inherent to the psyche of a god. If your neighbors built a summer castle with purple spires that spout flames, why not just build a golden mountain on your front lawn that spouts a constant stream of blue lightning and green lava?

It was this reasoning that made the view of Realm laid out before Trotter and Prowler look like a hellish diorama created jointly by Dr. Seuss and M. C. Escher. What at first seemed like a small garden that must be nearby turned out to be a huge garden of monstrously oversized flowers several miles away. She could even see the individual petal on one of the roses as it fell from the flower, nearly collapsing one of the castle walls beneath it. Nearer to them, a yellow fur-covered blimp the size of a house belched its way across the sky below the cliff, stopping only to graze the vines clinging to the cliff sides which sprouted gas-filled melons the size of beach balls. As she looked at the ground below, she found a large ferret in a jaunty sailor's hat steering a canoe carved from a giant pea pod across the forest bed below. Even the grass, which could only be described as chartreuse, seemed to be lapping at the edge of the cliff like waves.

"I think that staring at the edge of the world was easier than staring at this," she said. "I always pictured Realm as someplace beautiful and elegant where the gods would recline in robes and have grapes peeled for them. There should be columns and statues and things. But this place makes my eyeballs hurt."

"The ancient Carathanians always painted them as apolaustic and noble creatures of taste and grace, and over time that's the only way people really pictured the gods. Ironic, isn't it? They'd think all of those columns and olive branches are pretty boring, let alone lying around all day eating healthy. Two ton sunflowers and waterfalls filled with wine, now *that's* what a god would call style."

The only thing spoiling the effect, or at least distracting from it, was the large sign at the edge of the path leading down the side of the cliff. It was a map of all of Realm with the deities and their respective kingdoms labeled. The sign itself was glowing with all of the territories in different colors. Near the top was a drawn hand pointing to a particular spot on the map with the words "YOU ARE HERE" flashing at her.

"What exactly is this thing?"

"They call it an 'over-active map.' In theory, you'd press the kingdom you want to find and be transported down to it. Unfortunately, it never works right and I have no idea where it might really send us."

"So how do we get down?" The only path leading off of the cliff would have made a mountain goat need a change of shorts.

"Ah, therein lies the problem. We have to select one of them at least to get down there. Around here, that's less like a game of eenie, meenie, miney, moe and more like a game of Drimmish Roulette. Some gods are less friendly to drop in on than others, and when a god doesn't want to be friendly you'll be lucky to walk out with just a few scorches. Come to that, you'll be lucky to walk out at all."

"There has to be a better way." Trotter stared at the map until she found the kingdom belonging to Stoicese between the kingdoms of Ursula, the bear goddess, and Rhombus, the patron god of jewelers. Rhombus didn't sound bad, but she had visions of vicious, ravenous bears prowling Ursula's kingdom. Suddenly her eyes were drawn down to the bottom corner of the sign where a flashing button proclaimed "Press ME for help!"

"Hey! What about this one?"

"What about what - No, don't push that!" Prowler yelled too late. Trotter was already pushing the button. He ducked his head under his paws and waited for the inevitable horrors that come from randomly pushing buttons.

A sudden screeing, as of a tape being re-wound, was followed by an onslaught of cheery but tinny march music. Two small sparklers emerged from the top of the sign and waved excitedly in the air as the larger fireworks exploded too closely above them to be anything other than terrifying. Trotter joined Prowler on the ground as the sparks rained down on them. The confusion died away finally as the music ground to a sudden halt and the sparklers were zipped back into the sign once more.

"Great arrows of Avis! Why do you even bother asking what the button is if you're just going to push it anyway?" Prowler batted at his cheek to put out the smoldering whisker.

"Give me a break, it's just a button! And what was that all about?" Trotter asked, still coughing from the smoke.

A peevish voice answered her. "Around here it's known as making an entrance. No wonder you had to ask for help." If a voice had eyes to roll, this one had an eye roll like a double barrel back flip.

"But I didn't ask anyone for help," Trotter said uncertainly.

"You pushed the button, didn't you?" She nodded and Prowler groaned. "Well then, you asked for help and now you've got it. I'm Barry Metric, Senior Engineer and Variable Geography Expert, at your service. If you didn't actually need help then you will be sent a bill from the Engineers' Guild for the very expensive fireworks you just wasted. And you'll have to sign a form stating that you accept responsibility for the fraudulent pushing of the help button."

"No, we do need help!" Trotter jumped up from the ground and realized that the man was about six inches shorter than she and was trying to compensate for this with a very tall hat. He didn't look like any practitioner of magic she'd ever seen before. He had an assortment of different sized wands tucked into a special pocket he'd sewn into the front of his shirt, which buttoned up the front and had a high collar. On his face he wore a pair of spectacles that were held together over the nose with wound black thread. "We have to find a way to get to Stoicese, and we have no idea how to get there," she continued, trying to look him in the hat with a straight face.

"Here goes," she heard Prowler grouse to himself.

"Well that should be simple enough," the Engineer answered and removed his hat. He pulled a strange device from inside of it that looked like a tambourine with a sundial and clock gears in the center. The seven metal disks that were attached to the outside rattled slightly as his hands flew across the device, turning this dial here, adjusting that peg there, and spinning the disks after each adjustment. "All I have to do is calculate the current location of Stoicese's kingdom today based on its last known position and adjust for wind speed, fluxes in the incantofield, and the current geological temperament."

"Why don't the maps do that? Don't they work?"

"Of course *they* work. It's Realm that doesn't. It's always off calibration these days. Such a relic of outmoded engineering," he muttered as he returned to his dials.

"Why do you have to do all of that when I can see it right there?" She pointed to a kingdom at the opposite end of Realm that seemed less chaotic and more organized than most.

Barry looked up peevishly and put his device back into his hat. "Oh, I *see*. I wasn't aware that you had spent the last 378 years studying the problems of calibration of eccentric tectonics and apparently don't need *my* help."

"I didn't mean that. I haven't studied any of the problems of, of what you said, and I do need your help. It's just that I don't see why -"

"Precisely! You don't see because you don't have any idea about the vastly complicated processes involved in finding a particular geographic location. Just because you can see it doesn't mean you can find it. Once you've figured out where you're going you'll never know where you are and even if you know where you are you won't know where you're going! Have you learned *nothing* about Bergenheiser's Ambiguously Certain Principle?"

Trotter narrowed her eyes and exhaled slowly. "Listen," she urged, ignoring the twitch in her smiting finger, "if I can just get down off this cliff, I can walk to it. I can see it right there. Now just get me off this cliff!"

Barry laughed disdainfully and ended with a self-satisfied snort. "You silly girl. Just because it's right there doesn't mean it's actually right *there*!"

This time Prowler was expecting her hand to move. Before she'd even fully extended her smiting finger, he'd launched himself into her arms and stretched backward, flailing his paw at the first button he could reach on the sign.

"Gods help us!" He yelled as he and Trotter disappeared from the cliff.

"Well, isn't that just nice," the Engineer huffed. "They didn't even bother to take the customer satisfaction survey!"

*****

For the first time in many months Baron von Proustich took the stairs not only without the help of an aide, but two at a time. He felt *good*. No, on second thought, good didn't cover it. After months of feeling like any breath might be his last, simply being able to walk down the stairs without an attack of intense vertigo and physical pain was incredible.

He felt both the fire and the tension in the sitting room before he even entered. There was a crowd at the bar and Carmony was among them. They all looked vaguely uncomfortable, and no one was even aware of his approach. Except for the one the crowd was focused on, that is. It turned its coal black and orange eyes toward him and opened a mouth full of razor sharp teeth as it broke away from the crowd and ran toward him. The baron was just about to yell for help when –

"Uncle Ludwig, Uncle Ludwig!" It cried out to him. "It's me, your little nephew Arriman, and you've been waiting for me for so long."

And then the baron remembered that this little boy was his nephew and he'd been waiting for his arrival. Somewhere in the back of his mind was a nagging voice reminding him that his siblings had no small children, but that voice was weak next to the certainty that this child was, somehow, his nephew.

"Ah, Arriman, I'm so glad you finally made it," the baron looked confused again. "But how did you get here? You can't see your hand in front of your face in that snow."

"You don't really care about that, Uncle," Arriman said with a smile. And the baron found that he didn't, but momentarily he did wonder why his nephew seemed to have such sharp teeth for a little boy.

From underneath the bar Alice watched the baron's entrance almost protectively. She hadn't moved from the spot since this strange creature entered the inn and was fascinated to see everyone around him pretending that he really was a child. Couldn't they see his tail, his eyes, and those awful teeth? Not to mention the hideous scales. She watched him silently from her perfect hiding place. Therefore, when Arriman took the baron by the hand and led him back to the crowd, she was quite surprised to see the little creature look directly at her and wink.

*****

Trotter screamed as a bouquet of yellow and green zebra-striped flowers appeared in her hand. They weren't particularly frightening flowers, and if she'd stopped to smell them she'd have discovered that they even had very pleasant fragrance. But the appearance of the flowers when she was about to smite that insulting and insane little sprite who called himself an engineer pushed her over the edge.

"Calm down! You'll wake the dead screaming like that, and in Realm that isn't a metaphor. You're ok, just breathe."

She took a breath and looked around herself, ignoring the bouquet she'd thrown on the ground, and realized that they were now off the cliff and somewhere down in the valley. It was a garden in the middle of a wood, and the garden was filled end to end with flowers. There was a hissing sound all around her and as she searched for it she realized that it was coming from the flowers themselves. She took one of the blooms into her hand and stared. It had two almost triangular halves joined at the narrow end with pollen rushing through the pinch from one side to the other as she turned it around and around in her hand.

"Just like little hour glasses," she said to herself.

She found Prowler next to a sign identical to the one that had brought them here. Identical, that is, except for the words "YOU ARE HERE" pointing at a new location in the heart of the map. Her smiting finger throbbed as she turned hotly on Prowler

"Why didn't you warn me about the help button? And why didn't you let me smite him? It wouldn't have even hurt him that much."

"First of all, you pushed the button before you asked. You probably still would have pushed it if it read 'Don't push me!' Secondly, you can't smite here. It's part of the rules. That's why the bouquet of flowers appeared in your hand. It's a sort of divine joke, I think. But if he'd realized that you were even going to *try* to smite him you would have made him really, really angry."

"So what? You just said that there's no smiting in Realm so what could he do about it? Whine at me some more?"

"You wish! The last guy I knew that got on an Engineer's bad side is probably *still* filling out the paperwork. Laugh all you want," he continued when he saw her expression, "but there are some religions that have dedicated circles of hell to the completion of eternal paperwork. He also could have sent us anywhere he wanted, and you never know who they're working for."

"I thought he said he worked for the Guild of Engineers?"

"Loosely. The Guild itself works for whoever pays the highest price. Everything and everyone is political here. Don't trust anyone, ok?"

"We're not so bad as all that, are we?" A voice startled them both. They turned to see a very tall man suddenly perching on a fat tree limb behind them. Her eyes watered slightly as she tried to bring his face into focus; she at first thought he was a very old man with a beard, and the next second was certain that he was a young man not much older than she. She studied him as he continued talking.

"I mean, sure, we have our good days and bad days just like everyone else, but I'd like to think that historically we lean more toward the good. I know at least most of the people around here are pretty unlikely to kill anyone without extreme provocation first these days."

Prowler stepped in front of Trotter protectively. "Not to be rude, but you have to admit that to some of the people around here extreme provocation could be sneezing without covering one's mouth."

Cronus cringed, shaking his head in disgust. "I hate it when people do that. But I'll concede your point. It's always better to be careful when crossing the territories."

Prowler seemed to relax. "Trotter, this is Lord Cronus, the god of history and, last I knew, a friend of your father's." He turned back to Cronus. "Trotter is the daughter of Stoicese and we need to get to him quickly. Can you help us?"

Cronus dropped from his perch and affected a deep and regal bow. Trotter started to respond in kind before catching herself and switching to a curtsy mid-bow and nearly toppled over.

"This is really the mythical daughter of Stoicese?" He paced around her and took her hand, examining it as though he were examining a fruit for ripeness. "Oh yes, I remember now," he stared off thoughtfully and pulled a thick book out of his back pocket. He rustled through the pages until he found what he was looking for. "They've been keeping you among the humans all this time and now that the truth teller has found you and your newly discovered powers they needed to get you here where you could be safe again. At least that's what Miro hoped."

Trotter took a few steps backward. "How do you know all that? I've never met you before!"

He laughed congenially until he saw her expression not softening. "Oh. I thought you were making a joke. Well, I'm the history god," he said by way of explanation.

"And?" She replied, unimpressed.

He sighed with resignation. "The point of being the god of history is knowing everything that's ever happened or will happen."

"How is it even possible to keep that much in one head?"

"It's not difficult at all. The tricky part is pulling one particular moment out of everything. It's like trying to grab a single particular drop of water out of a rushing river. But keeping my memory in the book helps me keep it straight."

"Are you trying to tell me that everything that's ever happened is in that little book?"

"And everything that will happen, although, it has to revise itself constantly as future history changes."

"But if you're the god of history, how can you see the future?"

"Now that's a silly question. Just because it hasn't happened yet here doesn't mean that it's not history already somewhen else."

Sensing one of those arguments that usually set Trotter's smiting instincts into high gear, Prowler pulled urgently at the hem of her dress as her arm started to raise toward Cronus. "Don't even think about it!"

"No, I'm not smiting. That actually kind of made sense in a strange way. But I was just wondering, may I see that book?"

Cronus handed her the book and watched without surprise as she flipped through it with some urgency. Then she handed it back to him crossly. Every page she'd looked at was blank.

"I guess that was just some kind of a trick, then," she said. "I wanted to see what was going to happen to me."

"Everybody does, don't feel bad. But it's *my* memory, see? The book is merely a tool to focus it, so it will only work for me."

"Why didn't you tell me?"

"I used to try telling people that it wouldn't work, but they always still had to see it for themselves before they'd believe me. I guess I don't have a very trustworthy face. I don't know why they don't just ask me what's going to happen instead."

Trotter and Prowler barely exchanged the glance at each other before they both asked, "What's going to happen?"

"Oh, I can't tell you that. It might change future history in some way that it wasn't supposed to be changed."

Exasperated, Trotter pushed. "Then why did you tell us to ask you?"

"Because it saves time. You were going to ask me on your own in a few minutes, anyway."

"You can't tell us anything?" Trotter begged.

"Even just a hint?" Prowler added.

"A hint?" Cronus flipped through his pages and seemed to come to some kind of decision. "Yes, it looks like I actually do end up giving you a hint so I guess that's all right. Ok, what to tell you, what to tell you..." he continued flipping through the pages while his two guests waited less than patiently.

"Here it is!" He cried when he found what he was looking for. "Trotter, for you it will be your mother's gift that will help keep you safe here in Realm and beyond."

"My mother?" She asked quietly. She knew practically nothing about her mother. That a gift she'd given Trotter before she died could somehow save her now made her feel strangely warm.

"Yes, but that's all I can tell you about that. Prowler, you won't always be able to be with Trotter. You will have a choice to make as to how and when to leave her, but you *will* have to eventually leave. If you make the easy choice, her way will be that much harder. But if you make the hard choice, you will possibly save her life." He paused and looked ahead a few pages. "Oh dear. I hope I haven't given away too much."

"No, Lord Cronus," Prowler sighed, "I don't think you have to worry about that."

He brightened considerably at this. "Oh, good! I'm always afraid of that. You'd better hurry now. It says next that you're leaving again via the sign. Don't worry, though, it says that you end up in another safe territory."

They said their goodbyes and Trotter picked Prowler up and headed toward the sign. "Which one should I hit this time?" She asked him.

"It doesn't matter. This time they'll all send you to the same place. It's been arranged."

"Arranged by who?"

"It's by *whom*," he said almost absent-mindedly as he flipped through his book yet again. "Ah, nope. Sorry, I can't tell you that part."

"Fine. Thanks for your help, I think."

She closed her eyes and pushed at random. When she opened them she realized that it was too late to ask him what he meant when he'd said that at least Miro had *hoped* they'd be safe in Realm.

*****

The crowd huddled around Arriman by the warmth of the inn's blazing fire, ignoring the fact that it had a rather more greenish flame than usual, and listened. That they were listening intently was obvious in the way they stared at him as he spoke of childish games and fun, but behind their eyes was a pall that signified something weighing very heavily on their minds. On occasion, one of those thoughts, such as why it seemed like he was floating sometimes rather than walking, might break free in the form of a question to the young speaker, but the question would be turned aside by Arriman and the asker would learn from him that the matter was the farthest thing from their mind. And as he spoke they would find, invariably, that it was true. So they listened, but one of the things that would occasionally stray into the minds already brimming with troubles was that Arriman didn't truly seem to be talking to *them*. They weren't his true audience.

"And what most people don't realize," he was saying, "is that there are so *many* things that a kid can do with their very own horse, so it's obvious that every boy or girl should have one. You can't play a game of Storm the Castle or pretend to slay a dragon without one. Dragons are another thing. It would be so much fun if there were more dragons around like there used to be. We had a lot more fun back then. There's simply nothing left worth having to rescue princesses from anymore without them. Especially since most of the trolls are unionized these days and refuse to work in unsafe conditions."

"But, but," the baron faltered, intent on getting the words out before he forgot them, "how do you remember what it was like when there were dragons around? That was centuries ago!"

Arriman smiled and everyone tried to ignore how sharp his teeth looked for a moment while he brushed the question aside with a dismissive gesture. "Bah, that's not what you meant to ask me," he said. Baron von Proustich looked glassy as the truth of that statement took hold. "What you really meant to ask me was if I liked caramels. Right?"

The baron seemed worried as he responded. "Yes, maybe that was I meant. I don't know where my head is right now. Then do you like them? Caramels, I mean?"

"You betcha! We should have caramels every day for breakfast, lunch, *and* dinner!" He sighed and looked around at the crowd sadly. They wanted to see a little boy in that sad face. They truly did. "But you know what I really want, Uncle Ludwig?"

"What's that, er, nephew?"

"I wish I had someone to play with." Arriman looked meaningfully at Earl and Frieda who'd been huddled by the fire more silently than any of them. Earl jumped nervously as Arriman's eyes fell on him. The terror of falling under his stare was the same terror a mouse feels when it realizes the cat is between it and its hole. And the cat has been waiting for it to walk into its trap.

"What do you think about that, Landlord?" He asked him calmly. "Wouldn't it be nice if there were another child about my age to play with?"

Earl didn't hesitate. "Frieda, get Alice out from under the bar. She should come out 'n play with our new friend." He withered a bit more under Arriman's smile. "She should come play with her new friend," he repeated distantly.

"Really? That sounds like a *wonderful* idea, Landlord! Let's get Alice to come out and play."

He sounds like a boy, the baron thought to himself as Frieda hurried over to the bar. He sounds like one with all the rhythmic highs and lows that children tend to use to emphasize the importance of what they said. He sounds like a boy, he thought, but he also sounds like something trying to sound like a boy. Alice shouldn't be here, he decided.

"Landlord, I don't think -" the baron began before Arriman stopped him.

"No, you don't think," Arriman told him. "You don't want to think at all today. In fact, you just want to sit by the fire and enjoy your breakfast and maybe have some nice hot tea." Arriman's smile remained, but his voice was nearly as sharp as his teeth.

Baron von Proustich stood abruptly, startling those still gathered by the bar. "Breakfast, tea, by fire. Yes, that's all I want. Bring it now." He paced to the fire, sitting rather jerkily as if it took all of his concentration to make his body listen to him.

"Milord," Captain Carmony went to his side at the fire. The baron was staring fixedly at absolutely nothing. He may as well have been looking through the hearth and out into the snow beyond the wall. "Are you alright?"

"He's fine, Captain. You should bring him his breakfast and anything else he wants." Arriman turned toward where Frieda had frozen by the bar when the baron jumped from his seat. "Now, Frieda, weren't you doing something just a moment ago?"

"Yes, yes I was," she simpered. "Alice dear, won't you come out and play with your friend?" She called to the darkness within the bar.

"Do come out Alice," Arriman called to her. "I have some of the most wonderful games to play with you."

After a brief pause were the sounds of shuffling as Alice worked her way cautiously to the door and crawled out into view. Standing with her back to the hearth fire, her hair glowed in a violent halo as the flames gained an even deeper hue of green.

"He's not my friend," she said with her arms crossed against her frail chest.

"That's where you're wrong," he said happily. "I'm the best friend you'll ever have."

CHAPTER 7

The first thing Trotter's eyes registered when she opened them was the most classically horrifying castle she could have ever imagined looming in front of them. As if it were waiting for her to see it, a flash of lightning illuminated the tallest of the curving, intimidating spires.

"I thought he said it was going to be safe!" She yelled over the ensuing crash of thunder.

"Maybe it still is. I'm not quite sure where we are yet." Prowler jumped down from her arms and sniffed at the smoking sign lying in a pathetic heap on the ground. "But wherever it is someone apparently doesn't want us to leave the way we came."

The sign that had greeted them at both of their other stops in Realm had yet another twin here in this kingdom, 'had' being the operative word. What remained of the now familiar sign was a twisted heap of molten metal with the stem of a single sparkler shaking wearily from the top, its flame already burned out. There was a charred circle around it on the ground as if it had only just happened recently. Trotter looked up nervously to the castle spire – and again the lightning struck on cue – and had a pretty good suspicion of what caused the wreckage.

"Stop looking at it!" Prowler cried as he jumped in fright from the resulting crash. "It's rigged to happen every time you look up there for effect."

"Jeez, and some people just go in for flashy hedge sculptures. I can't imagine why they never thought of using lightning before," she rolled her eyes.

"Don't take it so lightly," he admonished. "If they're willing to rig an uncontrollable bolt of lightning just for background ambiance just imagine what kind of brilliant ideas they've got for the main attractions."

She tried taking stock of their surroundings. She left Prowler to investigate the debris to see if he couldn't find the remains of the 'YOU ARE HERE' to give them some idea as to whose territory they were now going to have to cross. Compared with the unreal plants and trees that had surrounded them in the history god's kingdom it seemed to be a fairly normal forest. She climbed up onto a pile of rocks near the black iron gates flanking the path that led toward the castle and mentally corrected her assumption that anything here could be normal.

"Uh, Prowler?"

"Did you find something?" He leapt nimbly up on the rocks beside her.

"I think I have a good idea where we might be." She picked him up and held him high so he could see the valley from her point of view. From here they could see the expanse of the entire kingdom and dotted all around it were giant statues of fearsome, snarling bears standing taller than the trees themselves.

"Oh," Prowler said, sounding relieved. "That's a stroke of luck. We're at Ursula's."

"How is landing somewhere where we can be torn limb from limb by vicious ravening bears a stroke of luck?"

"I don't think a grisly death, pun intended, is likely to happen to us here. You might say she's, well, lost her edge a bit over the millennia. She's lost something, at least. Let's head toward the castle. I'm sure that's what they want us to do."

"How do you know all of this about the gods and about Realm?" She asked him as they headed toward the foreboding shape of the castle.

"Before I was turned into a cat I was a student at the university in Tier Aní studying theology."

"You were going to be a priest?"

"No, no. I was going to be a theologian. Studying religion doesn't make you religious any more than studying psychology makes you crazy."

"Then why did you study it?"

"It was different back then. You've probably never even met a theologian in your life. There used to be a lot of us, but we made people uncomfortable. We were more like the journalists or the accountants of the gods. We kept the original histories, not the fairy tales that are passed now, and we kept up with the movements of the gods. We kept records of their moods, of the atmosphere, and of as much of Realm as we could. Most of us had some magical blood in us somewhere down the line so we could cross the borders into the Wedge and Realm. We could enter any territory under diplomatic immunity."

"I don't see why that made people uncomfortable."

"We tried to educate people about the gods."

"Isn't that what priests do?" Trotter had to wait for his laughter to subside before Prowler could answer her.

"Hardly! You see, the theologians were outcasts as much as any of the citizens of Realm or the Wedge, and were possibly even more hated. We reminded the humans of a time when the gods weren't so aloof and things weren't so easy, but worse, we made them seem *real* again. The priests were a human construct that came along after the gods left the world of man alone to let them rebuild without interference. I think they were a part of the healing process to make the horrors the gods had inflicted on them seem less real."

"You mean the humans used them to put more distance between themselves and Realm?"

"Psychologically, at least. The priests made the gods less real, less tangible. The people still believed in the gods, of course. But there's a big difference between believing that your god is a remote being completely uninterested in your day to day life and *knowing* that your god is only a breath away and could crush you on a whim just to see what color you were on the inside."

"That's horrible!"

"Okay, that was probably an exaggeration, but you get the idea."

"I think I do," she answered, shivering as she spoke. "You know, that's the first time you've ever told me anything about your life as a human."

"You've never asked before."

"Yes I have! Dozens of times."

"Well, you never asked when it was pertinent before."

"Then how did you actually go from Theologian to a cat?"

"That part, my dear girl, is still not pertinent."

"Fine," she groused. So Prowler had been an academic. That certainly explained his habit of sounding like a pompous ass. She'd often toyed with different ideas of what he might have been like, but he was always tight lipped about it. It made her think that there was still much more to the story that he was hiding. Sometimes it frustrated her that he wouldn't talk about it. "You know, I thought we were friends," she said sullenly.

Prowler was shocked. "Of course we are! Why would you say that?"

"Friends confide in each other. They don't keep secrets from each other."

Prowler looked at her face, drawn and clouded. There was something else bothering her. "Trotter, is there something you want to talk about?"

She was quiet for a moment before answering. She stopped walking and sat down on a patch of the soft yellow grass that filled the forest floor and twirled a long stem in her fingers. Prowler sat down beside her but waited for her to be ready to talk. Softly, she answered him without looking up.

"What do you think Cronus meant that a gift from my mother would save me?"

Prowler held his breath. He'd been expecting this question. "I don't think we can take anything Cronus said too literally. What he told us was so cryptic that we could be staring at the event he hinted at in the face and never know it. We can't kill ourselves trying to analyze it because, in the long run, it probably means nothing to us."

"It means something to me. She died just to have me. What could she have given me that would save me now? Did you know her?" There was hope in her eyes, as well as a glistening of tears in the corner.

"Yes, and I can put your mind to rest right now. There isn't anything in the world that your mother wouldn't have done for you. There is nothing that she loved so much as the daughter she knew she wouldn't be able to raise. Your mother is the best person I've ever known and it meant everything to her to know that you would be in good hands and loved."

"Is that why you've always been with me?"

"At first, yes. I owed your mother my life and I promised I'd look after you and keep you safe. But I'm also here because you've rather grown on me over the years, kiddo." He purred and laid his head over in her lap.

Trotter chuckled softly. He only called her 'kiddo' when he was trying to make her smile. Suddenly she felt bad for trying to goad him into telling her more by suggesting that they weren't friends. They were far more than that. Prowler was her family "Thanks," she whispered and smiled. She wiped away the first jewel of a tear that had beaded in her eye and changed the subject. "It seems really quiet and peaceful out here. It's very pretty."

"I agree. Still, we'd better get moving again. We'll be better off at the castle than out here if any of the old avatars are still running around."

"Avatars?"

"Back in the old days Ursula's followers believed that she would come to their battlefields after a battle in the form of a giant bear and carry the fallen away to their reward. What she was really doing was sending her guard dogs down for a meal. Or guard bears, rather."

"Ugh! That sounds really awful."

"Yes, I guess it does. But in a way it's better than leaving the bodies to rot like they'd been doing before. All in all it was a much better way of handling the situation. The bears got fed and people stopped dying of diseases spread by the putrefaction that eventually seeped into the wells. It may seem morbid but it was win-win for everyone."

She shook her head. "I don't think I could ever get the hang of the godding business. There is too much human in me to ever be able to be that cold and that cruel."

"Funny that you say that. I always thought it was the people who had too much human in them that made them cold and cruel."

"Well, we can't all be as loving and loyal as cats." She smiled as she got up from her nest in the grass and started walking away. "Oh, wait. That's for dogs, isn't it?" She turned and winked at him as he got up to follow her.

"Ha! I can just imagine your so-called 'loyal' dog staying by your side through all of this. Anything that eats its own vomit and chases its own tail for fun can't be trusted, plain and simple."

"I'm pretty sure I've seen you chase your own shadow," she teased.

"That was different! That was practically calisthenics. Now can we please get to the castle already?" He turned and walked through the black iron gates marking the path leading to Ursula's castle without waiting for her.

"Aww, I didn't mean to hurt your feelings, Prow." She scooped him back up into her arms and he gave a small yelp of surprise that turned quickly into a purr as she rubbed his ear while she walked into Ursula's kingdom. "You know that I think you're the bravest, most loyal, and smartest cat in the world and I wouldn't trade you for a hundred old flea-bag dogs."

He cleared his throat, a difficult maneuver for a cat, and struggled to be put back down. "You know, it's awfully hard to retain one's dignity when one is being carried around like a –"

"A teddy bear?"

"Exactly! Like a teddy bear."

"No, two of them. Seriously! Are those the avatars? Should we hide?"

"Oh my. Those are definitely *not* the avatars. Let's get closer."

At the bottom of the hill she had just crested was an impossibly long stone bridge that crossed the moat in front of the castle. The moat itself was so wide as to be better described as a lake with the castle sitting at the very center. But the unbelievable scale of what was in front of her now was nowhere near as surprising as the guards that were patrolling back and forth across the front edge of the bridge.

Their faces seemed human enough, except they were protruding from the mouths of humongous bears. They were, fully head to toe, in oversized bear costumes. Not bears like those depicted by the ferocious looking statues all over the valley, but the cute kind of bears such as you would find clutched in a little girl's arms. It didn't take long for the guards to see them as they came down the hill and begin shouting at them to halt where they were. They carried long spears and were shaking them threateningly, but the effect was completely spoiled by the large bows tied around the tips that matched the ones around their necks. One of them even had polka dots.

She couldn't help herself. Trotter started giggling helplessly. Even Prowler had rolled over onto his back and was shaking with laughter.

"Oh, come on," whined one of the guards. "At least *pretend* to be a little intimidated, would ya?"

"I'm sorry," she laughed, "but I can't help it. You're just so *adorable!*"

"Well, at least she didn't say 'precious' like the last one did," said the other guard dismally. "Look, this is really demeaning, but we do have a job to do. Can you try to play along?"

"Sure, we'll play along," said Prowler, gasping as he tried to catch his breath between laughs. "I just couldn't *bear* it if you were mad at us!" He barely managed to finish the sentence before collapsing in another fit of laughter.

"Oh yeah, like we've never heard that one before. No jokes about being stuffed and especially not the one about if he was fuzzy or wasn't. Got it?" The second guard was tapping Prowler under the chin with the tip of his spear. The head on his costume didn't fit very well and kept wobbling up and down as though the giant bear's head was actually talking as he moved. It was actually a bit more menacing than expected from this angle. Especially with pointy bits aimed at his soft bits.

Prowler nodded, though very carefully, in understanding. Suddenly he knew he was going to have some very interesting nightmares when he got back to Sarano.

"We're sorry," Trotter said. "What do we have to do? The sign back there was broken and we have to find some way to get to Stoicese soon."

"Oh, you're *that* kid and cat? Miss Ursula said that a kid and a cat would be coming by about Stoicese."

"You get that many kids travelling with cats around here?" Prowler asked.

"You might be surprised," the guard answered while he used his spear to push the bear's head back into place again. "Cats make excellent travelling companions. They're very loyal, your average cat."

"I *told* you!" Prowler hissed at Trotter.

"Yeah, yeah. So Ursula is expecting us?" She asked the guards.

"*Miss* Ursula is, yeah. She gets upset if you forget the Miss. Follow the bridge to the door and Graham will let you in."

"I thought only grade school teachers insisted on being called 'Miss,'" she answered.

The guard shuddered. "My grade school teacher was bad enough. She had a *ruler*. But I'd still take that over Miss Ursula. You'd better hurry. I'm sure she knows you're here by now."

The second guard clucked his tongue. "Ha! She knew the second they got here, if you ask me. She's got eyes everywhere, she does."

"Just because she knew doesn't mean she remembered it, though," the first one argued.

"But even if she forgot that she knew when she remembers it she'll know that she knew and she'll be mad at us if we didn't hurry up and get the girl there before she remembered that she knew she was here in the first place!"

"Hmm," he pondered as he thought about some of Miss Ursula's previous temper tantrums. He still had burn marks from the last one. "You're right. We'd better get her up there fast."

The guards turned back toward their guests and found them gone. They could still see the pair as they walked quickly farther and farther down the impossibly long bridge, but they were already out of earshot.

"Did we remember to tell them about the last step?" Asked one of the guards.

"Oh, no. Come to think of it, we sure didn't."

"Well, I guess it's not that important. I just hope they aren't walking too fast when they find it."

*****

The snow steamed wherever Arriman placed his feet as he and a reluctant Alice walked out of the Tarbach Inn together. She was angry at being called out from her hiding spot, but even more curious about the strange creature who had fooled everyone so easily. She didn't own a coat, but she'd never truly needed one even in the worst snows. Until now, she was the only person she knew who could be so oblivious to a blizzard.

"You're not even a real boy," she said petulantly.

"I'm afraid you've got me there," he answered with his toothy smile. "I knew you'd figure it out. You're too smart to fall for that kind of a trick. That's why I know we'll be such good friends." He jumped up to perform a complicated turn in the air and landed delicately in the snow by Alice, flourishing with a bow. "I don't look scary, do I?" He asked innocently.

She studied him closely. The creature, with the exception of a shock of white hair on his head, was covered from head to tail in scales so dark a green as to nearly be black. His eyes were huge and a vivid shade of orange, the tiny black pupil in the center almost swallowed up by the brilliance of the iris. His mouth parted into a smile that was altogether too wide for his face and dotted with two rows of tiny needle-like teeth behind which rested a forked tongue that was the purple of a violet. The tail itself pitched at the end into a spade and flicked almost constantly. All of his features when taken individually might have been scary, but altogether the creature was almost comical in his outlandishness. What made it downright droll was the human clothing it wore – a creature from the black depths of imagination wearing a child's sailor suit couldn't possibly be frightening.

"No," she finally said. "You don't scare me at all. You're just strange."

This seemed to please Arriman as he laughed and skipped a little ahead of her toward the river. She followed at a distance, still not trusting what he might want with her. "I was hoping you'd say that," he told her. "I'd rather be strange to you than scary. I think it would be hard for us to be friends if I scared you."

"Why do you want to be friends with me?"

Arriman smiled wickedly at this. "Because you're special, just like me. That's why we'll be such good friends," he answered her.

"I am not like you! You're not even a human!" She stopped in their progress toward the river and stomped her feet. He turned back toward her and looked stricken.

"But neither of us are just humans. We're *better* than humans! I can make humans see what I want them to see, but you're even better than that. You're practically a princess among humans!"

"A princess?" She asked with a tinge of awe in her voice.

"Yes, *exactly* like a princess," he grinned, flashing his purple tongue against his glistening teeth. "I don't know why you'd want to be just a plain old human, anyway," he sneered as if in disgust at the thought.

Alice was thoughtful, but still not convinced. "I'd rather be a princess if I had to be anything, I suppose. Where are we going?" She asked as he picked up his skipping pace toward the river.

"We're going to see Grandfather Tree."

"You know Grandfather Tree?"

"Of course I do. I stopped and spoke to him when I first got here. He told me all about you and how special you are."

"How did he talk to you?"

"The same way he's been talking to you all these years. You just haven't been listening."

*****

The cave was darker than usual. The watcher needed no light to see across the world and his master needed no light as his sense of smell gave shape to everything in the darkness. The watcher did, however, need all of his strength and concentration to focus on the blurry vision he had coming to him from a tiny village that lay beneath the crown of the Stain Mountains. Crouched silently in the corner, the wendigo waited. He had been waiting this way for hours for any word at all from the watcher and could wait for hours more. With a full stomach he had no need to move from the spot and he haunted the shadow like cat stalking prey. Arriman's mission was too important to risk distracting his watcher.

A ripple spread slowly across the surface of the water as the watcher's face broke into a smile. The wendigo heard the tiniest splash as the ripple lapped at the side of the pool and he leaped toward the edge. "What is it? Did he find her?" He asked impatiently.

"More than that, master." the watcher's voice was weak with exhaustion and he gasped for breath as he spoke. "He not only found the girl, but he has won her friendship already. She is in awe of him. He has also found where the door to Laramak was destroyed."

"Was there anything left?" The master was wrought with anticipation.

"Something much more than we might have expected. There wasn't much left at all, but a bit of Laramak's blood remained behind when Stoicese burned the door to his exile. The blood took root under the ashes of the door and found the spirit of the wood it had once been and grew into a massive fir. Part of Laramak has been living all this time in the shadow of where his castle once stood. I believe he has somehow been nurturing the girl through this tree and some of his power must have been conferred to her. It's the only thing that could explain why she's grown so powerful."

"Could it really be? How could we not have detected this before?"

The wendigo waited while the watcher caught his breath. "I don't believe the tree is truly a conscious part of him any more than your hand is a conscious part of you. His desire for vengeance was distilled in his blood and the tree has grown out of that desire. It will act on his will when the opportunity arises, even if it does so mindlessly."

The wendigo was less sanguine upon hearing this. "So it may not be our Lord Laramak behind the girl. The tree could still act even if Lord Laramak were dead."

"The gods cannot die. Lord Laramak is not dead," the watcher reminded his master.

"But they can diminish. We've seen it happen when a god is forgotten. They lose themselves to madness. It's been more than a thousand years since he was tricked by that bastard Stoicese."

"One thousand years is nothing to a god. I tell you he is alive and well. I may not be able to reach him or see him, but I can feel him still. He is too filled with rage for even the walls between this world and the one where he waits to shut the heat of his anger off to me completely. The centuries have only made him more resolute." The watcher's grim smile twitched in excitement.

"When he returns from exile, he will build an army and destroy everything that stands between him and Realm."

*****

The bridge that had seemed impossibly long from the beginning seemed to actually be doing the impossible as Trotter and Prowler walked along it. It seemed to be *growing* as they tried to cross it. With every step they took that should have brought them nearer to the castle they found that they were actually getting farther away. It was shrinking away from them somehow, as though it contained entirely too much length for its size. Even the spires - she was careful not to look up at them again - seemed even farther away than before.

"This is ridiculous!" She said. "How can it be getting farther away?"

"Good," Prowler sighed with relief. "I was beginning to think that I was the only one who noticed that we seem to be walking backward."

"If this is how it's going to be it's going to take forever to - OW!" She was abruptly cut off as her nose came in painfully direct contact with the wall and found herself suddenly against the castle door that had only a moment ago seemed miles away. Prowler had been right behind her, but now... There he was. She had to squint, but she could just make out shape as small as a pinprick far back down the bridge before he disappeared.

"Ow!" Came the sound from her feet as Prowler appeared beside her with his own nose against the door.

"That's what I said. I guess the bridge was all a trick. Not a very nice one, though," she complained while she rubbed the sore end of her nose.

"Agreed. But I don't think I'd complain about that to Ursula if I were you. Let's knock on the door and meet Graham, shall we?"

The doorknocker looked to be an ancient brass that was in the shape of a snarling bear's head, nothing like the cutely costumed guards at the foot of the bridge. This one spoke of the kind of bears from the fairy tales where small children were typically on the menu. She gripped it and banged it against the door, cringing slightly and the tremendous noise it seemed to make as the sound echoed out across the water of the lake-sized moat.

The door opened slowly with a creak that would have been ominous had it been opened by the sort of hunch-backed lisping servant that one would normally associate with dark and odious castles such as this one. Instead, the creak went almost unnoticed because the servant who opened the door was slightly more terrifying than the hunch-back would have been. Unlike the guards at the foot of the bridge, this was no teddy bear costume. It was a man-sized, walking, talking, breathing, teddy bear.

"I assume you to be the Lady Trotter, daughter of Stoicese, and her associate?" The teddy bear asked in the most regal of tones.

Trotter was too horrified to respond. Prowler coughed politely to cover his surprise before answering. "Yes, that's us alright. Are you Graham?"

"At your service," the teddy bear Graham bowed, causing his bow tie to bounce slightly as he rose. In addition to the bow tie, he wore coat tails that gave him the appearance of an extremely formal butler. "Miss Ursula is waiting for you in the parlor. I will take you there directly."

They followed the unlikely butler in through the gigantic doorway and Trotter gasped at the sight that greeted them. Filling the back wall of the entrance hall was an enormous portrait of a fierce looking female warrior astride a vicious, snarling brown bear. Both warrior and mount were standing armored on a pile of bones and weapons, and the warrior herself was wearing a belt of skulls.

"Is that Urs – *Miss* Ursula?" She asked Graham.

The butler sighed wistfully. "Splendid, wasn't she? She has changed quite a bit over the last thousand years or so, but she was always quite the warrior. I'll show you her more recent portraits along the way. It may serve to give you a better understanding when you meet her."

As he escorted them from the hall and into the castle corridors, Trotter began to notice what else was strange about the Ursula's castle. The décor didn't make any sense at all. Here and there would be a bundle of weapons arrayed on the wall, but there would be a large pink bow adorning them in utter disregard of the fact that pink obviously clashed with the dark red bloodstains on the blades. There was a dented suit of armor in one corner that was covered with spikes and blades, but the arm of the suit had been raised and there was a fresh bouquet of flowers extruding from the hand. It was as though someone had taken a dark warlord's castle and tried to add a feminine touch here and there, even if it didn't seem sensible. And then there were the portraits.

All along the hall were the towering portraits of Ursula in different phases. None of them were so dark and frightening as the first, but the early ones all contained elements of the warrior goddess and her bears in battle. As the portraits progressed they began to grow somewhat... tamer.

Trotter stopped in front of one that was starkly different from those previous to it. In this portrait, rather than a young warrior woman sitting astride her bear on some battlefield or another, it showed a woman of a mature age and full figure sitting in a field of lavender with bears surrounding her and bringing her various small animals as offerings.

"Ah, yes," Graham supplied when he noticed that Trotter was studying the painting. "We call this her 'blue period'. This was when her believers decided rather suddenly in a time of peace that she wasn't just a warrior goddess, but a goddess of fertility. They began leaving offerings from each of their hunts for the bears of the forest believing that the bears would take their offerings straight to Miss Ursula."

"Her believers decided? Why did she let them decide what she was going to be?"

"When people think of the gods they tend only to think of what the gods can do for, or to, them. They forget that the influence goes both ways. The gods may have created humankind, but they inextricably linked their destinies to them when they did so."

"But they're so powerful... I guess I just don't understand," she shook her head.

"Maybe the next portrait will help clear things up." He guided them along the hallway to a portrait that was nearly blank.

"What does it mean?" Prowler asked.

"This was created just after the time of peace ended. Her believers were nearly all killed in a war. With barely anyone left to believe in her, she began to diminish. We nearly lost her completely until the survivors began taking tales of Ursula to other villages and towns. Shrines were built by the survivors who credited her with their escape, and their children eventually grew up and built other shrines and taught their children about her. She grew strong again."

As he spoke he led them to the next and final portrait. It held as much in common with the rest of them as a postage stamp. In this one, Ursula was a frail older woman on a lounging chair with a bear cub at her feet and teddy bears all around her on the chair. There was a pink ribbon in her hair to match her pink checkerboard dress. It was hard to believe that this child-like person had ever been a warrior goddess.

"Now do you see the problem?"

"I think I'm beginning to," Trotter answered. There was a thought at the edge of her mind, but it was too awful to voice.

"They kept the memory of Ursula alive, but her purpose as a warrior goddess or even a fertility goddess was no longer needed in a civilized world. Ursula was still worshipped, but only as the bear goddess with no real function to fill. In time, she began to create her own function and cast herself a new image, one that embodied the only kinds of bears that were still loved by the humans." Graham stopped and sighed. "I'm one of the side effects of this, if you haven't guessed."

"Were you one of her avatars?" Trotter asked.

He nodded. "I was *the* avatar. I was her battle steed, her most faithful servant. There was no grizzly or man in the world that wouldn't run in fear of me at one time. I guess in some ways I have it better than Poo-Poo."

"Poo-Poo?" Prowler asked.

"He became the cub you saw in the last picture. You'll understand what I mean when you meet him. We're almost to the parlor now."

He turned toward both of them before he opened the door to announce them. "Just be careful what you say and keep in mind she currently has the mentality of a little girl. She gets her feelings hurt easily but she also forgets things easily, as well. Be careful, but you especially," he said to Prowler.

"Me? Why me?" Alarm tinged his voice.

"No time to explain, she knows we're out here!" He threw open the door to the parlor and with the grace of a royal proclamation he announced

Prowler and Trotter. Ursula sat formally in what might have been a throne had it not been covered in quite so many lace cushions and was dressed meticulously in a long sleeping gown that was covered with images of teddy bears. In her hands she also clutched a teddy bear that seemed to be wiggling trying to get free. This room was nothing like the rest of the castle. It made Trotter feel as though she had walked through a portal into a little girl's bedroom.

"Honored guests," Graham was concluding, "I would like you to have the privilege of meeting her Ladyship Miss Ursula, goddess of bears."

Ursula stood up from her chair and Trotter was surprised to see that the bear goddess was shorter than she was. Her eyes were fixed on Prowler who was currently trying to hide behind Trotter.

"What a precious little kitty!" She exclaimed, dropping the teddy that had been wiggling in her arms. It anxiously scampered away to hide behind a bear cub that Trotter could only assume must be Poo-Poo. It had a large bow around its neck with bells tied on the ends and all of its still long claws were painted in a shimmery pink. It looked up at Trotter miserably before laying its head back down by the fireplace.

Ursula ran around behind Trotter and picked up Prowler and began hugging and petting him. He looked to Graham for help, who gave him a meaningful look that seemed to say 'just go with it.' Prowler gave in.

"Hello, Miss Ursula, it's very nice to meet you. Thank you for – oomph!" He grunted as the wind was knocked out of him when he hit the floor. Ursula was now staring at him in horror.

"Bad kitty! Kitties aren't supposed to talk. You won't talk anymore, okay? Bad kitty!" She said again for emphasis before looking up at Trotter.

"And you? Do you talk, too? You can, can't you?"

"Yes, ma'am, um, Miss Ursula," Trotter answered reluctantly.

134 ■ Alice Will

"Thank you for having us as guests in your lovely castle."

This pleased the strange goddess. She went back to her throne, which Trotter now realized was less a chair than a pile of pillows covered with lace, and flopped down on top of it. "Please, come sit down by me. I'd like to get to know Stoicese's daughter."

"I would like that, Miss Ursula," she began as she tried to find some way to sit down on the couch without sinking in. Prowler ran over and sat by her feet as quietly as possible. "We need to get to my father's kingdom somehow and we're hoping you can help us."

"No. I'm afraid it's impossible. He said you can't go there yet and you have to wait here."

"He said? *He's* the one keeping me here?" She was suddenly angry. She'd come this far to find her father and he didn't even want to see her. "Why won't he see me?" She pushed.

Ursula frowned. Poo-Poo looked up in terror and the small plaid teddy bear she'd been holding when they first entered the room cowered behind him. Graham sensed the change looming in Ursula's mood and tried to jump in.

"Now, Miss Trotter, I'm sure your father will be along as soon as it's more convenient for him –"

"Convenient for *him*?" She cried, ignoring Prowler pulling urgently at her pants leg from the floor. "It wasn't convenient for *me* to have to come here. Do you know what we've gone through to get here?"

"Graham!" Ursula snapped, silencing even Trotter's tirade. "I don't like these guests anymore. They're rude. Take them to the guest room and make sure they're more polite in the morning for breakfast." With that, she disappeared with a disappointing lack of poofing.

Graham heaved a sigh of relief. "You're lucky you're the daughter of the one god she still respects," he said while shaking his head. "If you weren't, you and your cat would probably have been fed to her pets like the last guests she thought were rude."

"I'm sorry." Trotter was downcast. "I didn't mean to be rude. It's just... I've never even *met* my father, and now I find out he still doesn't want to see me after everything that's happened?"

"I think you'll find it's rather more complicated than that. I can't tell you anything more, but he hasn't come to you yet because he's busy making sure you'll be safe while you're here. Not everyone around here loves your father, you know."

"Couldn't he keep me safer by being here with me?"

"It's not what you think. There are rules and rights to passage through the territories. He's been negotiating your safe passage into Realm and out of Realm all this time."

"Out of Realm? I thought I was staying here indefinitely."

"I really don't know any more than that. But I do know that if Ursula comes back and I haven't gotten you to the guest room and out of her sight we might *all* end up being teddy bear food."

"Are you serious?" Prowler asked. "What do teddy bears eat?"

"Anything that can fit into a meat grinder. And I don't mind telling you that she has some pretty big meat grinders."

*****

Alice scrambled behind Arriman through the lowest branches of Grandfather Tree to the hiding place that only she had ever known about before. She was shocked as he began digging under the pine needles in the exact spot where she kept her most prized and private possession hidden.

"That's mine!" She whimpered as he began flipping through the pages. She tried to reach for it but he held her off with a single scaly arm.

"This is what you used to tell your secret wishes to, isn't it?" Alice nodded. "Well, you don't need this anymore. You've got me to tell them to now. We can talk to each other about all of our wishes and dreams. That's what friends do, you know." He tossed the journal casually over his shoulder. Alice barely even noticed as it hit the ground with an unremarkable thud, its pages bared to the soggy snow beneath the branches.

She was intrigued by the word 'friend' that he kept using. She'd had adults who were nice to her, like the baron, and had tried to consider them her friends. But she'd never been able to tell them the things that she would save only for her diary. Maybe Arriman had secrets, too?

"What were those things you were talking to all of the adults about in the inn? About the dragons and the caramels and stuff."

Arriman beamed at her, his sharp teeth sparkling in the faint light under the snow-covered tree. "Oh, you want to hear about *those*. That was just kid stuff. I was telling them about all the things that I wish we kids had. Horses to ride around on, dragons to fight, and caramels to eat all of the time. You know, fun stuff like that. But what kinds of things do *you* want?"

She was thoughtful for a moment. "I like caramels, too."

"But that's easy stuff. Remember, you're practically a princess so you should have anything you want."

Alice bit her lip, almost afraid to say it. "I want a grandfather. I never had one before and I wanted the baron to be my grandfather because he's so nice to me. That's why I wanted to help make him healthy again."

There was the tiniest of stirring in the limbs of Grandfather Tree, but it was enough to please Arriman. "That's more like it! If you want a grandfather then you should have whoever you want it to be. The baron will be your grandfather. You should have a better dress, too, and dolls, and servants of your own to wait on you hand and foot!"

Alice giggled with delight. She was beginning to enjoy this game already. It was much more fun talking to Arriman about the things she wished she could have than just writing it down in a dirty old book. It made it seem somehow *true*.

"Of course I do! All princesses have servants. I also have a beautiful white pony in the stables that will only let me ride it and everyone does as I command!"

"You're really good at this," Arriman goaded her. "Hey, let's go down to the stable and see your pony. Want to?"

Alice looked doubtful. "But we're playing pretend, right?"

"Not anymore, we aren't."

CHAPTER 8

The fire was dying in the inn and the cold was taking this opportunity to dash into every corner of the room with nothing to chase it back out. Earl and Frieda were standing together near the waning embers of the fire feeling lost and confused.

"It's getting cold in here, Frieda," Earl said slowly. "Maybe we should..."

"Should what, Earl?"

"I don't know. I had it a moment ago. If Alice were here she would tell us what to do."

The baron shivered and stood up from where he had just finished his breakfast. "You, Innkeeper!" Earl looked up at him, a plea for help in his eyes. "Put some logs on that fire and get it blazing. I want it warm in here when my granddaughter Alice comes back."

The baron sought out his captain in the kitchens where he was preparing more cider for him. "Carmony, go out there and find Alice. I want to make sure my granddaughter isn't catching a cough out there."

*****

"This is the guest room?" Trotter and Prowler stood by the door of the room to which Graham had escorted them. Despite being led around the castle by a full-sized and quite eloquent teddy bear, they were still completely unprepared for the strangeness of what confronted them. The bed was covered from end to end with small mewling teddy bears, similar to the one that Ursula had been clutching in her parlor, in all different colors and patterns. Some slept curled up in balls while others groomed themselves and chased small toys. They were all over the room, but most of them stopped whatever they were doing to look up at the newcomers curiously. Several of them started to approach them, while a few others shied away and hid. Prowler batted away a plaid one that kept coming close enough to try to sniff him.

Graham looked apologetic. "I'm afraid these are in every bedroom in the castle. You've probably noticed them in the hallways, but when they sleep they look just like ordinary teddy bears. They won't bother you, though. Not really, at least. Once they're used to you being around they'll pretty much just ignore you."

"That's funny. They act just like cats," Trotter said while watching one of the teddy bears stretching and arching his back as he found a better position in the sunlight coming through the window. She ignored the fact that Prowler was giving her a dirty look.

"Actually, since you mention it..." Graham began before Prowler's yowl cut him off.

"No, please don't tell me. These used to be cats, didn't they? She turned them into monsters!"

Trotter picked up the shivering cat to comfort him.

"I wouldn't call them monsters," answered Graham primly. "I don't think there's anything wrong with the way they look."

"No, no, I'm sure he didn't mean it like that. She won't try to turn him into one, will she?" Trotter asked quietly out of the corner of her mouth, trying not to alarm Prowler any more than he already was.

"I don't think so. He fixed that by talking to her. She likes her pets to be cute little fixtures. Not something that can talk back to her."

"But she made you talk, didn't she?"

"I'm not a *pet*," he said, his round button eyes narrowing. She decided she needed a butler, but her idea of butler is probably a little different than most. For the most part, all I do is change litter boxes and act as her filter to keep her from having to deal with people. They tend to scare her a little."

"She's afraid of us? You can't be serious."

"No, she's afraid of seeing herself through your eyes. It's hard to trick a god. They may not be able to read your mind, but they can see the shape of your thoughts. She doesn't want to see herself as diminished as she really is, as you see her. Not when she used to be so powerful. I think it's why she surrounds herself with all of this. It's like she's found her own purpose in her own slightly crazy way."

"Doesn't she see your thoughts, though?"

"She made me," he spread his short bear arms out in explanation. "She sees only what she wants to see through me. Think of me as the part of her brain that still knows what she's become, and what she was once. But she protects herself from it by keeping that part of her mind in me."

Prowler raised his head from where he'd buried it against Trotter's neck. Most of the teddy bears in the room were staring at him now.

"What do they want with me?" He asked.

"They probably just remember being cats before. They're intrigued by you, I imagine. They'll get over it before long. They've learned not to put their noses where Ursula may not want them. The old adage is true around here, you know."

"What adage?" Trotter and Prowler asked almost in unison.

"Curiosity kills the cat. Or teddy bear, as the case may be."

"Understood," Prowler said with wide eyes as a hammering sounded loudly through the halls. It was so powerful that even the echoes hurt Trotter's ears until it died away.

"It would appear we have more guests. My, what a busy day this has been," Graham lamented. "You two make yourselves comfortable. Just shove the bears off the bed if they're in your way. If you should need anything at all, just pull the cord beside your bed and I'll come as quickly as I can." Then he disappeared quickly.

"Well, you heard the bear," Prowler said with a hint of mischief in his voice. "Start shoving!"

*****

Alice squealed and clapped with delight as the pony strutted around the pen for her. It was so pure a white that it even made the fresh snow around it look gray and dirty. The light seemed to glint off of its flanks as it leapt and stretched newfound muscles. Having begun as the mere *idea* of the perfect horse it luxuriated in the feeling of *being* the perfect horse. It snorted in pleasure as it pranced over to her, kneeling down low enough that she could climb onto its back. Having forgotten all about the reason for the blizzard, Alice squinted into the now bright sun. It was a clear blue sky once more with a full sun bathing the country in the heat of a springtime thaw rather than the paltry rays that the Drimmish winter typically permitted across its boundaries.

Distantly, the sounds of the sobs and wailing of the inconsolable wise woman from her cottage were carried to them on a refreshing breeze over the snow. Arriman grimaced, annoyed at the noise, but it didn't pierce the veil of Alice's excitement. She rode easily upon the back of the horse even with no saddle and no bridle as though the horse were made simply for her. Which, of course, it was.

"I'm going to call him Frost," she announced, and the horse knew his name was Frost. "Isn't he beautiful? He was a gift from my grandfather." She smiled confidently, knowing that what she said was as true as she wanted it to be. She wasn't at all surprised when she looked down and realized that instead of the rags she wore when she first followed Arriman out of the inn she was now wearing a beautiful flowing gown that trailed out far behind her as she rode Frost faster and faster in the pen.

"Alice?" Came the voice from inside the stable. Captain Carmony walked out into the pen where Alice was riding. He looked strangely at Arriman for a moment as though his eyes wouldn't quite focus. He shook it off and returned his attention to Alice.

"Alice, I've been looking for you. Your grandfather was worried about you playing out in the snow," he looked confused again, "the blizzard, I mean. Weren't we just having a blizzard? I'm sure it was a tartar snow just a little big ago."

"Oh, we were," said Alice casually, "but I decided to stop it. Is Grandfather still there? I should go and thank him for the pony he gave me!"

"Yes, he's still there. And the pony," he seemed to notice the animal for the first time and brightened. "Oh, of course. The pony he gave you for your birthday. Silly of me to forget."

Alice slid down from Frost and started running toward the inn. She turned back toward Arriman. "Are you coming?" She asked impatiently.

Arriman shrugged as if rather disinterested. "Sure, I guess. We can take a break from playing for a little while. But I have some other games to play when you're finished playing with the humans." He followed her out, his expression dark and contemplative.

He was so deep in thought as he left the stable where Captain Carmony was putting Frost into his stall that he didn't notice Carmony staring after him in shock.

"Did he just call us humans?" Carmony wondered aloud, thinking once again that he was sure he'd seen a tail on the boy just as he'd turned his head.

*****

Trotter was brushing her hair while Prowler was trying to defend the bed from the horde of teddy bears that kept trying to climb up from all sides. She'd given up trying to get him to relax. Eventually he'd figure out that the bears thought he was playing a game and would keep playing just as long as he did.

She looked into the mirror and sighed. The pixie face with the messy brown hair looking back at her didn't look the face of a demi-goddess who'd be trouncing through the kingdoms of the gods and angering former war goddesses. This isn't my life, really, she thought. I'm going to wake up and discover that all of this god business has been a dream and my cat doesn't really talk. And maybe I have better hair in my real life, she added. As she finished that last thought, her hair lengthened and became shinier and thicker, like hair that was more properly thought of as "locks," or "tresses." When it stopped growing, she stared wide-eyed at a beautiful head of hair that, for the first time in her life, was actually attached to her own head.

"Prowler, look! How did I do that?" She was afraid to look away from the mirror in case it disappeared.

"I'm a little busy at the moment!" He complained through a mouthful of teddy bear. One had snuck up behind him for a sniff and he was busy dragging it to the edge of the bed to drop it over.

Exasperated, Trotter stood up from the vanity and yelled at the top of her lungs. "All of you, *off that bed right now!* Do you hear me?" She looked at each and every cowering bear. "No one is allowed back on that bed until we leave!"

She turned back toward an amazed Prowler. "Now, will you take a look at this?"

"Hmm. It's nice. I like it." He barely glanced at her as he kept his eyes on the bears for any sign of disobedience.

"Is that all you can say? I've *never* been able to make my hair work. This time I wasn't even trying to and it just did exactly what I would have wanted!"

"I'm not too surprised. You're in Realm now. This whole place is made of magic and you're picking up more and more of it. I bet you'll find a few other things that you never knew you could do while we're here. Keep at it, it's good practice."

"If I do that, I'll end up more and more like *them*, won't I?"

"You mean the gods?"

"They're all crazy! If my dad is as crazy as they are, then I'm not sure I want to meet him. I don't want to end up being some crazy cat lady who can turn people into whatever I want them to be. They're horrible and evil. But they look so human..." she shuddered.

"That's the trap that people fall into, right there. Humans were made to look like the gods, not the other way around. Yet, somehow the human ego translates that to meaning that the gods must be like humans. The punch line is that most humans don't realize how very like the gods they really are."

"No. I can't believe I'm anything like any of them!"

"First of all, you're *not* anything like most of them. Trotter, most of the gods have never known what it's like to be human."

"What difference does that make?"

"They have no frame of reference for life! They live forever and can't die. Therefore, they have no fear of death. Just because they created something that *can* die doesn't mean they understand the concept of death at all. That's what makes them so dangerous. They don't actually intend to do anything outright evil, even though it seems that way."

"Then why haven't they learned? They've been dealing with humans long enough to learn that *we* value life, haven't they? If they can understand that it's important to us then they *are* being evil by taking it away from us and playing with it so casually."

"You need to remember that it took nearly the extinction of the entire human race and countless animals with it to convince the gods that maybe, *maybe* messing around with human affairs as frivolously as they were wasn't necessarily fair to the humans. For the most part, they didn't value individual humans any more than you value a particular chess piece on the board. Humans were useful to achieving a certain end, and when they are more useful dead or captured than alive, so be it. They don't learn from us and we can't hope to teach them anything."

"Then there's no hope for us. We'll always just be pawns to them."

"No, not quite. They at least learn from their own mistakes, even if it takes a few millennia for it to happen. They eventually became aware of the real damage they caused Aevum, and that the damage was longer lasting that a single life. When they took a life, they usually created a new one, and to them that meant balance was restored. Life was life, and that was it. They didn't understand for a very long time that one life was not the same as another, not to humans. Even when they tried to do something for the right reasons they learned that what was right to them wasn't necessarily right to us. That's why the Accord of Realm marked out a distinct separation between humans and gods. It barred any intervention by the gods into the affairs of humans for good or bad because, frankly, they can't tell the difference."

"And yet the humans still want them around. They still worship at shrines and churches and the priests wage wars with each other over whose god is the better one and it doesn't matter because the gods aren't going to get involved either way anymore. This is just stupid."

"You got me there. I don't think the humans actually want the gods *around* per se, if by that you mean where they can see them. They just seem to like the *idea* of them more than anything. It gives them something to blame when things go wrong. I think if the gods didn't really exist the humans would have invented them for themselves."

"Sometimes I really do think you're crazy, too."

"It wouldn't be the first time I've been told that," Prowler shrugged and glanced at the floor. "Good job with the bears, by the way. Very effective."

Trotter looked around the room and not only were all of the teddy bears staying off of the bed, but they were all trying to hide in any possible space of the room and most of them recoiled when they realized she was looking at them.

"Oh," she said sympathetically. "Now I feel bad for them. They weren't doing anything wrong."

"Not doing anything wrong, my butt! Literally! You try defending your backside from sniffing invaders for half an hour and tell me if you still don't think they were doing anything wrong."

"Alright, take it easy. I'll open the door and let them go out if they want to. That way they won't bother you anymore."

"That would be a relief," agreed Prowler, but his relief quickly dissipated as Trotter opened the door to the hallway. "Oh, no!" He whispered to himself, feeling the hair on his back standing on end.

Graham was standing with another man in the hallway as though he were just about to knock on the door. "Oh! Hello, Miss. I was just bringing a guest to visit you." Even Graham looked a bit nervous. "I know you must be tired, but one doesn't keep Lord Erov waiting, and he said it was very important to speak to you." He bowed a bit hurriedly and backed away. "I'll just leave you two to chat then. Good luck!" He nearly yelled to Trotter as he vanished completely again.

"You're Lord Erov?" Trotter asked the stranger incredulously. He was tall, broad, and handsome but the fact that he was far too tall and far too broad made him seem unreal. His face looked immovable as stone, making the smile on his face seem as though it had been carved by a sculptor who only knew that a smile should show teeth. And there were quite a lot of teeth. He's here to take me, she thought for no real reason at all. With a shock, she knew she was right. This must be some of what Prowler told me. I saw the shape of it in his mind, just as he probably sees in me that I know why he's here.

Sure enough, Erov's smile faded before he spoke. "Yes, I am Erov, god of the seas and all within them. And you, this tiny thing, are the daughter of Stoicese." He nearly spat the name. "May I come in?" His question was merely perfunctory as he was already closing the door behind him when he asked.

"Of course. I have something for you, you know." She dug into the purse on her waist.

He was faintly surprised. "For me? What could you possibly have for me?"

She produced a small shell from her purse that was a brilliant shade of blue and held it out to him. "This is from Miro. She said you would know what it meant."

He laughed bitterly. "She's a smart witch, that Miro. This is a Traveler's Shell. If I accept this shell from you it means I have to allow you safe passage through my lands and through my seas. It would mean I couldn't lay a finger on you."

"Then I guess it's a good thing she gave it to me, isn't it?" Trotter couldn't believe how bravely she was speaking to the titanic god in front of her. I have to be brave, she thought. If I'm weak then I'll never get through this alive. She thrust the shell toward him again. "Here, take it."

"I don't have to accept this shell," he said wickedly. "I could always kill you now and pretend I never saw it."

"No, you can't, Erov," Prowler leaped to Trotter's shoulder to face the god. "You know that by the Accord of Realm you are required to accept this token from her now that she's presented it to you."

"An enchanted cat is your bodyguard? Ha! Now I almost feel sorry for you. It must be terrible to know that your father doesn't care about you at all. He must be hoping something happens to take you off his hands if this is the best defense he gives you."

Prowler's tail swished angrily. "I'm an enchanted *human* thank you very much. And with this shell she doesn't need much of a bodyguard, does she? You can't hurt her and neither can any creature hurt her on your behalf. Just imagine what the Council of Realm would do to you if you broke the Accord. I believe banishment is the going thing these days." Prowler seemed to be relishing the thought of Erov's potential punishment.

Erov snatched the shell angrily from Trotter's hand and started to leave. She stopped him before he opened the door.

"Wait. Why do you hate me so much?" She crossed her arms defiantly, glad to have Prowler on her shoulder to keep her from shaking with fear.

"You?" Erov laughed again. "I couldn't care less about an insignificant brat like you. You're merely the means for me to finally punish your parents for their sins." He slammed the door behind him as he left and Trotter just about collapsed with relief. She took Prowler off her shoulder and hugged him so tightly he could barely breathe.

"Thank you so much, Prow. I don't think I would have survived that without you to remind him that he had to take the shell."

"I think he was testing you. He knew he had to take it. The gods, even the ones like Erov, are tightly bound to the same rules set out in the Accord of Realm. Without it there would be constant war. There is already enough bad feeling and resentment among them so the last thing they need is a new reason to fight. The Accord is something like a code of etiquette in that way."

"He was lying, though. Did you see it? He wasn't planning to kill me. I think he wanted to take me somewhere. And he does hate me, I could see it. I still have one more shell from her to give my father." She looked sadly at her friend and held it out for him to see. "You don't think she's afraid of him trying to kill me, do you?"

"Far from it," he answered her soothingly. "This is a very different shell from what she gave you for Erov. And you heard what he said. He wants to make your father suffer, and if getting at you would make him suffer, then your father must love you very much."

"That's not what he said. He said he wanted to make my *parents* suffer."

*****

The atmosphere at the Tarbach Inn was, for the most part, jovial. The door, which was usually shut as quickly as possible, was now swinging freely to the constant stream of guests coming to visit Alice. Each of them carried arm loads of gifts, flowers, and other trinkets to celebrate Alice's upcoming birthday. There was laughter, and Earl and Frieda were serving beer, wine, and cider to all of Alice's guests and were even discovering lavish foods in the pantry that they didn't remember ever having before. All in all, it was becoming quite a successful party.

The only problem was that the only person who seemed to be truly enjoying themselves was Alice. Underneath all of the laughter was a glimmer of distraction and an undercurrent of hushed conversation.

"I *know* she's a princess," said one guest to another. "All I'm asking is, was she a princess yesterday? That's what I can't really remember."

"If she's a princess, shouldn't we have a king? Who's the king?"

"Why is she living here in the inn? Princesses live in castles, don't they?"

Arriman wandered through the crowd listening to snippets of the hushed conversations and yawning hugely. He was content to not be the focus of attention for now, but he was getting bored very quickly with this child's play. Alice had spent her life to date living in a cupboard under a bar and had no ideas about the vast world beyond the Tarbach Inn. Arriman sniffed in disdain as he thought about it. It wasn't even a particularly *nice* inn by his standards. The indoor plumbing consisted of chairs with holes in the seat over buckets that were discretely replaced and cleaned each morning. You might as well sleep in the stables, he thought. It was no wonder the girl had no real imagination. He was going to have to spur her to think bigger if she was going to be any use to his master. It was time to give her a little inspiration.

"Hey you – you with the funny eye," he called to the guest who'd been asking about the castle. The man was the grubby sort of peasant that seemed to always appear first and leave last anywhere that food or drink might be given away. He was also the type of person that one found anywhere there might be an opinion to be had. The peasant looked around frantically, hoping that Arriman was talking to someone else who just so happened to have a constant twitch in one eye. He, like the rest of the guests, had been doing his best to pretend that the somewhat-kind-of-maybe-boy-creature wasn't there lurking amongst the crowd.

"Yes, Mr. Arriman?" He asked haltingly. This boy, supposing he really were a boy, was supposed to be the nephew of the baron and that made him nobility. This fact alone made him even scarier to the peasants than most of the monsters they could dream existed. Monsters usually stayed in dark places and didn't bother people too much as long as they had a stomach already full of virgins and first-borns. The nobility, however, had a habit of finding ways to get entire villages killed in the so-called defense of the kingdom.

"You were just wondering about Princess Alice's castle, weren't you?"

"Yes, sir. I didn't mean anything bad by it, though. I promise, sir." The peasant looked around for help and discovered that he was completely alone. Then he looked as though he were about to be ill. Most of the guests around him had managed to sidle away from him when they realized that Arriman was only interested in him.

"I'm sure you didn't. I was only going to suggest you ask her about her castle. I'm sure she could regale you with stories all about it."

"Really, sir? You don't think that would be rude?"

"No, don't be silly," Arriman answered him with an expansive gesture. She'd love the opportunity to talk about it. She's just waiting for someone to ask, I'm sure, so go ahead and ask her now while there are plenty of people around to hear all about it. You'll be doing her such a favor."

The peasant puffed his chest proudly. "Yes, sir. I'll be glad to be of service to Princess Alice." He hesitated only briefly in his mission to find the princess when some distant nagging memory surfaced for just a moment. It was a memory of Alice bringing him a mug of beer. Don't be silly, he thought. Why would a princess be serving you a beer?

He found the princess sitting happily on her grandfather's lap enjoying the blazing fire while the citizens of the town took turns complimenting her on her lovely dress and lavishing her with attention and presents. It was exactly as she'd always wished it could be.

"Grandfather, I haven't even gotten to tell you yet how fast Frost is! He might even be the fastest horse in the whole village!"

The baron laughed a bit awkwardly. "My dear, I'm as thrilled as can be that you love your gift so much, but I hate to say that my old memory must be failing because I can't remember for the life of me bringing that horse with us. I know he didn't just appear out of nowhere so I must have brought it, didn't I?" The question was more to Captain Carmony who was staying closer to his baron that usual. He sensed trouble, and also sensed that something was trying to keep him from seeing the trouble. That made him even more wary.

At this, the captain merely shrugged. He'd seen the horse with his own eyes and knew as soon as he'd seen it that it was Alice's birthday gift from Baron von Proustich, but he was beginning to suspect that simply knowing something was true no longer meant that it necessarily *was* true. He cast an askance glare at Arriman as he thought this and was unnerved to see that the boy was already staring through him as though reading his very soul. He looked back toward his baron and the girl who was spilling over with happiness.

"But of course you did, silly!" She teased her grandfather. "As fast as he is I know he didn't fly here so you must have had him with you all this time. You hid him so well to surprise me!"

"I must have done, dear," the baron conceded with a slight air of defeat. "I must have done so well that I surprised even myself."

The peasant on Arriman's mission cleared his throat for attention beside them. Noting that his hands were empty of presents, Alice wasn't terribly interested.

"What do you want?" She asked impatiently.

"Milady, I was hoping that you might tell us stories of your castle. None of us have ever seen it and would love to hear about it." The peasant spoke graciously, if not nervously.

"Castle?" Alice's face twisted in confusion. "I don't know what you're talking about. I live right here in the inn with Grandfather. Don't you know that?"

The peasant visibly deflated with the realization that instead of doing the princess a favor he was about to be prying bootlaces out of his mouth.

"I – I – I only thought th-that since you were a princess you must live in a castle like the baron does, but grander since you're the princess and all," he stuttered.

"Well, where is my castle?" Alice, far from angry, was getting intrigued.

"If she's the princess, wouldn't it be where the king lives, too?" One of the villagers with a suddenly low life expectancy supplied.

"Well, if the baron's her grandfather, wouldn't he be the king?" The first peasant asked with a look of helpful innocence on his face.

Arriman, who he'd thought was still clear across the room, was suddenly breathing loudly right next to his ear.

"There is only one king," Arriman stated darkly. "And it is certainly not this weak mortal." He turned to Alice before anyone could question why he'd specified "mortal." He may have been surprised to know that, due to an innate sense of self-preservation in most people, not one person in that crowd would have been willing to ask that question. Not even Carmony would have, with his now complete distrust of Arriman.

"Alice, come with me. We have a new game to play."

The look on Arriman's face told her that staying was not an option. She asked resentfully, "Where are we going? Why can't we play it here with Grandfather?"

"Because it's time to go get you a castle fit for a princess such as yourself. Don't you want a fantastic castle?"

Alice brightened up and slid excitedly off the baron's lap. "Of course I do! I know *exactly* what I want it to look like, too." She ran out the door following closely behind Arriman, naming all of the different rooms she thought her castle should have as she ran.

Captain Carmony leaned close to whisper to the baron still seated in his chair. He was staring strangely at the door after the two children. With Alice and Arriman now gone, most of the villagers began drifting out, embarrassed as though unsure why they had been there in the first place.

"Milord," he said, "I think we should leave this place immediately. I can have you packed and ready to ride out as soon as you give me the order. There's something wrong here, and I think, honestly, I think we're being tricked by some sort of demon. For starters, I'm sure that Arriman is not your nephew, let alone even a real boy. I also don't believe that little Alice is actually your granddaughter."

Baron von Proustich's face sagged with grief. "I know she's not my granddaughter," he said sadly. "On one hand I feel like she must be my granddaughter, but on the other hand I know for a fact that my son had no children before he died. I know it's a trick, Carmony, but don't you think it's a bit odd that I'm suddenly so healthy and full of life when I've been on the brink of death for the last few weeks?"

Carmony nodded. He had already begun to associate the baron's miraculous return to health with whatever magic was taking place in the village, but he was unwilling to attribute any work of good with Arriman's presence.

"I have a feeling that it's all because of her," the baron continued. "In fact, I'm certain of it." He pulled at the green token from Alice that he was wearing around his neck and showed it to the captain. "I think that I have her to thank for my life. But I'm also certain that if I leave here now I'll die before we get very far."

"We'll take you straight to your doctors, milord. I'm afraid that with the way Arriman has been glaring at you all night you'll die soon if you stay here, as well," he added apprehensively.

The baron shook his head. "That's the other reason that I can't leave, my friend," von Proustich said distantly. "She may not be my granddaughter, but I can't leave her here with that monster. As long as he has her trust she's in danger. She may not know it yet, but she needs me, Carmony, just as much as I need her."

*****

"Why are we back at Grandfather Tree? I thought we were going to find my castle," Alice said impatiently. Since discovering that the world seemed to bend to her will she didn't want to waste time in getting everything she'd ever wanted.

"We don't have to find your castle, silly. It's already there. You just have to tell Grandfather Tree about it and he'll help you make it."

"Really?" Her face brightened. "Where is it? I can't see it."

"Not yet, of course. Just close your eyes and tell Grandfather Tree how much you want a castle. He remembers it. He'll help you make it exactly the way it should be."

"Well, ok," Alice answered dubiously. She closed her eyes and pictured glistening ponds and straight fir lined paths and gardens encircling a gleaming castle of white marble and limestone. She poured her every thought into imagining that her castle was real already and pictured herself sitting with her grandfather upon thrones in the court, entertaining guests from every corner of the village. She envisioned courtyards filled with beautiful flowers and ponies and wished fervently for closets filled with dresses and rooms filled with dolls and friends who would play with her every day. As reality bowed to the pressures of her will, she felt the change prickle across the air and knew that her castle was already there and waiting for her. She opened her eyes.

There, sprawling across the highest peaks of the Stain Mountains was a monstrosity of a castle, far larger than she'd ever imagine a castle could be. It was built from the same black stones of the mountain and it gathered the clouds about it like a shroud. The two tremendous portals that opened in the front of the terrible structure gave it the look of a menacing face looming in the sky over the village. Screams could already be heard from the direction of the inn.

Alice crossed her arms indignantly, trying to hide the fact that she was terribly frightened by the specter she had called into existence. "This is *not* what it was supposed to look like!" She huffed.

Arriman's scaly tail swished and his long tongue flicked at the air with excitement.

"On the contrary," he responded with complete satisfaction. "It's perfect. It's exactly the way it's supposed to be. It's exactly the way it *was*."

CHAPTER 9

Across the boundaries of another reality, Miro stepped into quite a different castle, her first steps into it in centuries. When the immortal Last Wendigo tried to raise an army to take on the gods after Laramak's defeat, the gods bound him within these walls where he could do the least damage. At least, he had been little trouble until now.

There were few of Laramak's demons still in existence since they had been hunted down after his defeat, but the few who still lived were resourceful and good at hiding. They'd been perfecting the art for centuries. Now they provided for the only master they still knew. Miro's first discovery in the castle was one of the things that the demons provided for their predatory master.

She gasped for breath when the putrefaction filled her nose. This must where he kept his livestock. There were no cages to keep the animals contained, and the humans were chained near the feeding trough that they shared with the numerous animals that left waste and fur where the humans were forced to sleep. They looked up at Miro without hope and some of the younger ones even flinched when she opened the door. They had no expectations that she might rescue them, only that she might be there to inflict some new torture upon them. The smallest, a child that couldn't have been more than seven or eight years old, lifted one weak hand toward her briefly before it fell back to his lap under its own weight. The waste, both animal and human was spreading sickness here.

The urge to cry overwhelmed her urge to vomit as she saw how near death so many of them were. She raised her staff and slammed it hard on the cold stone floor. When she did so, the fish upon the top came to life and began disgorging pearl after pearl from its mouth. She placed a pearl onto each lock that held the humans in place, and as soon as it touched the metal the pearl began to sizzle and melt, corroding the metal until the lock disintegrated and the chains fell away from them. Only a couple of them seemed to sense that this meant escape and began to stir away from the trough where they had been chained, but most of the others seemed merely confused.

"Go!" Miro urged. "Take the weakest ones and carry them if you have to. Yes, you are free," she reinforced to those staring at her in disbelief, "but you have to get out of here now. Go and find the healers, no one will stop you."

Miro closed the door behind them as the last of the prisoners left the room supporting each other as best they could. She sealed the animals back in the room to keep them from making a noise that might give her away. She'd risked detection as it was in freeing the prisoners – she couldn't bear to think of them as livestock – but after seeing them she couldn't risk leaving them to become a rotten feast for the horrendous creature if she failed.

She was afraid of what else she might find as she continued down the dark, fetid passageways.

*****

Trotter was beyond exhausted when she finally fell away to sleep with Prowler at her feet keeping a semi-wakeful vigil lest the teddy cats, as he'd taken to calling them, made another hopeful foray at the bed. There were few revelations from this day that were not a source of pain for her, and sleep was a welcome escape.

She'd spent most of her day being frightened in some way or another, and now even her powers were beginning to worry her more than ever. The longer she spent in Realm, the more they tried to escape her control. She'd even had to change clothes before bed when a slight craving resulted in a glass of cold milk materializing over her and hovering briefly before falling and soaking her to the bone. Prowler kept insisting that she needed to use it, to let it out, as though the magic welling up within her was some sort of pet she was keeping chained. It seemed to Trotter that a pet should be trained to obey her before she let it out. Right now she wasn't even sure if it was housebroken.

Sleep was also a welcome break from the overwhelming nature of this chaotic and uncontrolled place. Experiencing Realm was like falling into an entire universe straight from fairy tales crammed within the space of a city block. Realm was far larger than that, of course. It was a sprawling place and didn't feel the need to reconcile potential size with available space or scale. And because it was so much bigger than it actually had the right to be in its given space, it was *dense*. Unimaginably dense. To a creature with a heightened sense of reality such as Trotter, it came with a tremendous sense of ghostly pressure – pressure that wasn't really there but she felt that it ought to be. It was disorienting.

Therefore, when she left the nightmare behind and was truly, deeply asleep, she was very upset to discover that the borders of Realm didn't end at the borders of consciousness.

She stirred. The ground was cold beneath her. She couldn't remember ever dreaming that she felt cold before.

This is a very strange dream, she thought as she sat up and waited for her eyes to adjust to the total darkness.

"You're awake! Hallelujah, she's awake!" A voice said next to her ear.

She recoiled and found only more darkness and more cold beneath her. Then she held her ground, mustering much more courage than she thought she'd have been capable of finding. Catch Trotter on a day when she was feeling especially generous, and she might have confessed that the dark had always been her secret fear. Luckily, actual darkness at night was a luxury that was hard to come by in ever-bustling Sarano.

"I'm not awake. I'm dreaming," she said with a hint of doubt in her voice.

"Only in a manner of speaking. In your warm bed in Ursula's palace, you're dreamin', but you're wakin' up here."

"If I'm awake why can't I see you?"

"Because you persist in the silly notion that you're dreamin', girl! Open your eyes and let an old man have a look at you."

Trotter imagined her eyes opening in bed and discovered she was sitting, not in that warm bed in Ursula's palace, but on a wide and flat stone in the middle of a glade. There was a pond nearby being fed by a waterfall that fell seemingly from a hole in the sky. There were wispy flowers, like the corpses of dandelions, dotting the edges of the glade in a hazy blanket. It was tranquil here and the peace wrapped her soul in a floral-scented blanket. But she wasn't sure she liked the strange man in front of her. He was irrationally tall, although, tall was possibly the wrong word for him. He was long, stretched thin, and built about like a corn stalk with gangly arms. Yet for all his peculiar features, his face was soft and gentle. He wore a tattered black hat pulled low over his eyes and chewed relentlessly on a piece of straw.

"My, my," he whispered to himself as he looked at her face. "The spittin' image of your mother as a young pup, you know. The very image!" He clucked his tongue approvingly.

She sighed. "How does everyone get to know my mother but me?"

He winked at her. "I'm sure if you took a deeper look inside yerself you'll find you know her quite well."

"I suppose that's some cryptic way of telling me I'm just like my mother?" Trotter rolled her eyes dramatically.

He narrowed his own eyes at her and pointed at her with the straw he'd been chewing on. "You've got her tongue, that's for certain. We should have lashed it out of her and replaced it with one from somethin' a little sweeter when she was your age! And don't think that just because you're *his* daughter don't mean we won't do it to you."

She realized what was bothering her about this old man. Everyone she'd met in Realm so far sounded like royalty, but were feeble, inept, and brimming with psychoses of some sort or another. This old man sounded as if he'd already gone crazy, the country attire and accent so absurd in a place of the gods, but his voice and eyes said something completely different than his words. He didn't miss a thing – he seemed to take in every movement Trotter made – and his eyes weren't the dull, glazed look of the used-up gods she'd met so far. He was alert and waiting for something. He was sharp and he was…

"A friend," Trotter said suddenly, causing a smile to spread upon the strange old man's bearded face. "You're a friend somehow, aren't you?"

He replaced the straw in his mouth and nodded warmly. "I'm a friend o' your mother's, and to your father, too, even though he ain't much better than most city boys I known. But most of all," he added, "that makes me a friend to you. The name's Paraben, my dear. And I been waitin' for you for a long, long time."

"*You're* Paraben?" She asked incredulously. "Miro told me I would see you. She told me to ask you for her old staff."

"In due time, child, due time. We got all night, you and me. Don't you wanna see the glade first? You barely even glanced at the water fall," he sounded hurt. "It took me *years* to reroute drops from all the streams in Realm to get it working up here."

"Where is here, exactly?"

He gestured around the glade with his straw. "Here, we're in only my little part of it. But this place, all of it, is where the gods go when they die."

She was taken aback. Die? "But I thought gods didn't die?"

"We don't, not really. But after a while when believers move on, or our purpose is suddenly outdated, we can kinda fade away. There have been soft places between the cracks since long before Realm or Aevum ever existed. This is just another one of those places. Think of it more as a retirement home that I appropriated out of that space. "

These conversations were getting to be like pulling teeth, she realized. Every god she met had a story to tell and wanted to tell it, but they wanted to be practically begged for the story first. Maybe this is it, she wondered. Maybe all they have left are the stories. She felt a pang of regret for them suddenly. Maybe it would be alright to keep playing along.

"Then what are you now, exactly? You were a god, so what happened to you for you to end up here?"

Just then she became aware that his eyes were looking past her. She turned and saw a statue standing by the pond that she hadn't noticed before. The statue was beautiful. The face was carved so exquisitely well that she could almost imagine a tear rolling down the cheek of the marble lady at the pond. Despite the tear, there was a distant look of fondness in the face. Then the eyes blinked, and the statue disappeared.

He sighed and returned his attention to Trotter.

"Me? I took early retirement. I was a god of the fields. It was my job to protect the crops of my believers and make sure the harvest was good and on time. That was before the cities came. They just got so darn *big*. After a while, the cities got so big that the little farmin' villages that I protected became just another part of them, and the little farms were filled with men who measured the soil and brought pipes for the water, and spread herbs to keep away the pests. The fields became a science, and they didn't need me anymore. Oh, they still build them scarecrows in the fields, but they don't remember anymore that they used to build them to invoke my protection."

He stared distractedly at the patch where the living statue had appeared and disappeared before he continued. "I tried to stick it out and pretend that they still needed me, but I ain't as dumb as I look. I knew my days were numbered. Them that stays past their time end up lost like the weeping statue lady over there. Some ends up worse off than that and all you can hear is their whisper. Gods don't die. We just get used up."

"But you didn't," she whispered.

"No," he made a sound that was near to a derisive laugh. "But sometimes I almost wish I had. Sometimes I think them that just float around up here like they're in some kinda dream... sometimes I think they might have been the lucky ones after all."

"Don't say that, it can't be better to be a mindless creature like that. They're practically ghosts! Why is it so bad to be the way you are? And why does every other god I've met except for you seem to be completely crazy?"

"My dear, do you have the foggiest idea of what it might be like to live forever?"

She thought for a minute, then shook her head no.

"Good. If you'd've said yes I'd've sent you back down right now. It's eternity that makes you crazy. We can't die, but we shore weren't made to live forever. It's too much for any creature, human or god or other, to take."

One word in there settled on Trotter's ears as just plain wrong. "What do you mean 'made?' Who made you?"

"Some bastard with a real sick sense o' humor, that's who," he snorted. "Ah, I guess I can't say that. Fact is, we don't know for certain. Our own myths say we were born right from the mind of Chaos, but for all we know we were made by something else that Chaos created first. If we did have a creator they were none too interested in sticking around. That don't mean we didn't try, though. We searched everywhere and everywhen and never could find so much as a 'Dear John' letter." He put his hand on her shoulder.

"See, Trotter, here's the thing. And it's a big thing. We may live forever, but we are every bit as much as alive as you are. We think, we love, we feel, we hate, we eat, and we even crap, though, it may not be quite the way you think of it."

"Eww!" Her face twisted.

"Point is," he hurried on, "point is, that we are alive. Every living thing needs meaning in its life almost as much as it needs air. Gods are no different. We sought meaning for our endless lives for longer than you can even imagine, and when we couldn't find it above us, we started making it below us. We created humans last. There were attempts, *very* creative attempts before the humans. But in the end, we settled on something that was more like us, in our own image, and tried to live through you in some ways. I think we passed some of our own pains through to you, though. I think that might be why that void for meaning burns so deeply in humans as it does in us. If that's the case, then maybe the kindest thing we ever did for humanity was to let their lives end in a relatively short time."

"So without having a reason to exist, some meaning in their lives, the gods wither away?"

He nodded. "Those of us who find meaning some way or another are fortunate. Sometimes they can get it through their believers, but mostly those who try to stay involved in human lives sometimes go another kind of crazy. Like poor old Ursula down there."

"I saw what happened to her," she said with a shudder. Graham's explanation had made sense at the time, but it lacked the Paraben's perspective. She found herself grieving for Ursula and what heartbreak and emptiness and driven her to her current form. "Her butler-bear showed me her portraits from before she went – went, you know."

"You can say it. Crazy. She's gone permanently into some kind of identity crisis just trying to keep up with her human believers. Others are luckier. Your father, for instance, has you."

"Me? I've never even met him!" She swallowed away the unwanted knot in her throat.

"That never meant he didn't love you. He's devoted to you in ways that you may never understand. Having you is the greatest joy in his life, and you should know that. If you haven't noticed, it's not often that gods get to have children."

"Why not?"

He shrugged. "Who knows? It's not really such a big deal since we don't have to worry about heirs and carrying on the family name and all that. On the other hand, a population explosion of gods is kind of a scary thought, so maybe that part is just smart design."

But there's still a part of the story you haven't told me, she thought. She watched him idly switch the piece of straw from one side of his mouth to another while she decided how to frame the question. "But you haven't told me about you, yet. You didn't end up like the others so you must have found meaning of your own."

He sighed so lightly that she had to strain her ears just to hear it. She waited for him to answer and hoped she hadn't pushed too far. What was too far with people like this? She wondered.

Finally, he nodded toward the pond. "That weeping statue had a powerful name once. When used as a curse, your fields would rot and fester and your women would be childless. When used as a blessing, the harvest would be prolific and there would be fat babies everywhere. She was fertility, she was life, and she was death, all in one. And she was beautiful."

She noticed tears in his eyes. Up until this point she had never imagined that a god could cry. "You loved her very much, didn't you?" She asked gently.

Paraben nodded slowly. "That's another thing about living forever. It's awfully hard to find someone that you can imagine spending eternity with, but when you do it's more powerful than any magic that's ever existed. She was one of the primitive gods. We all were at one time, but not all of us were able to adapt. The gods who'd been given sacrifices of blood were the first to be lost as man became more civilized than even we were. That was when I lost her." The tear that had been welling in his eye escaped in a glistening line down his cheek. "Others have drifted here, but I built this place for her," he sniffed and wiped his face with his sleeve.

He pointed at the pond. "That used to be a plain little pond, nothing worth looking at, but for some reason when she did appear, it was always right there. So I made it beautiful for her."

Trotter felt awkward for a moment. She wanted to comfort this kind man – god, she corrected herself – but she didn't know how. He towered over her so there was no question of her being able to reach her arm over his shoulder. She settled for looping her hand around the part of his arm that she could reach when he was standing. "I think that's the kindest thing I've ever heard of anyone doing. I think she knows you're here, and I'm sure she knows what you've done for her," she added, remembering the hint of a sad smile that lurked at the corners of her mouth.

He looked down at her and smiled. "And you're a sweet girl. Just like your mother. Ornery as a mule one minute, sweet as molasses the next."

"Hey, what happened with your accent? It was gone while you were telling me your story, but it's back now. What gives?"

"Eh, I guess you're right. The accent isn't really compulsory anymore. But when you're a god of the field people just expect a certain image, you know?"

"I don't expect anything from you. I just want you to be yourself."

His smile grew wider. "And that, my dear, is why I'm glad you're the one who's going to save us."

"What do you mean by that?" Oh no, she thought. Not me. This isn't the kind of thing I do. I go shopping at the Night Market and play at the pier with Prowler and read my books and I'm only just now learning how to use my powers. What I don't do is run around various ethereal worlds and consort with gods and I especially don't save people. That's the kind of nonsense that generally happens in the books with magical swords and wizards and heroes. The kind that I obviously wouldn't read, she added, somewhat embarrassed in front of her own mind.

"Sometimes a god's gotta do what a god's gotta do. Even if that god is only fourteen years old," he added with a grin. She glared at him until he seemed to shrink a few inches. "Ok," he continued, "that probably wasn't the best time for a joke."

"No, it wasn't. Please just tell me what you meant," she said.

"It's better that I let your father do that, I think. It's time for you to get back down there now, anyway. He's already waiting for you at Ursula's."

"How are you going to send me back down?"

"You're going to send yourself down this time." He produced a short white staff and passed it to her. It reminded her of the shiny bits of coral that occasionally washed up on the shore at home. "This is what Miro's had me saving for you all these years."

"Why didn't she give it to me herself?"

"She didn't want anyone to know she still had it. And," he added sorrowfully, "she didn't want anyone to find out that you have it now. You see, a watcher can't spy on you in your dreams. Whatever you do, use it as little as possible when you wake up or someone might discover it. There's no other staff like this one in the world, and Erov thought this one had been destroyed when Laramak, well, that's another story for another time. Just know that this staff, like most, is a key."

"To Realm?"

"Not just to Realm. To any place and any time in all the universes that exist. Probably outside of some of those, as well."

She held the staff in her hand. It didn't feel like anything special. Something as powerful as he said this was should shoot sparks from the end, or glow, or something, right? This one just sat there feeling as light as a feather. So light, in fact, that it was as if it weren't there at all. As she completed that thought, the staff decided apparently on its own accord that it wasn't going to be there after all.

"Hey!" She cried. "Where did it go? I didn't do anything, I promise!"

He chuckled. "You figured it out pretty fast, didn't you? Imagine it back in your hand where it was just a second ago."

It only took a moment of focus for it to happen. She tested it, and as she pictured there and not there, the staff disappeared and reappeared in her hand over and over again. "Where does it go when it's not here?"

"That staff is tied to every possible world in every possible universe. It only barely exists here in this one, so it only comes when you call it. And only the staff's owner can call it. I could only do it when Miro gave it to me, and now I've given it to you. I think you'll be able to use it better than I could."

"How do I use it?"

"You don't have to use it. Just call it when you need it, and the staff will know what to do. That's the nature of magical things. That's what makes them so dangerous, too. Now you need to use it. This time when you call it back, let it take you back to your bed. You've got a very busy day ahead of you, my dear."

"Thank you, Paraben," she said to him. "If I don't get to see you again after I wake up, I think I'll miss you most of all." She found herself wondering as she spoke why exactly she had said that. It just seemed right to say for some reason as she looked at the living scarecrow.

He bent down and hugged her. "And I'll miss you, my dear little friend. But I'm sure I'll see you again. Now remember everything I told you. It will be more important to you than you realize, Trotter."

The staff came more easily each time she called it. This time, as she held it, she imagined the bed she'd left at Ursula's castle. She pictured herself lying in bed and going back to sleep in her body. She closed her eyes and for one split second experienced something that was to consciousness what weightlessness was to the body. For a moment it was as if she ceased to exist in one world and began to exist in another world. In fact, she *had* ceased to exist due to the fact that even a mind cannot possibly exist in two places at once. Especially not in two places not even on the same plane of existence. And somehow, against all reason, this momentary lack of existence gave her the hiccups when she found herself back in Ursula's guest room.

Where she'd expected to wake up in her sleeping body, she instead was standing next to an empty bed, with the exception of Prowler who'd crawled under the blankets to get away from the pile of teddy cats sleeping all around him. She realized somewhat belatedly that the staff was gone and put down her hand. Then she hiccupped loudly.

"Hrmmpphh?" Said the lump under the blankets that was Prowler. She watched the lump scurry up the bed, dislodging teddy cats as it moved. Prowler's head emerged with a frantic look on his face.

"Oh thank gods! I thought you'd left me! Where have you been?"

"I thought I was right here asleep. I thought I was just dreaming," she said a bit distantly.

"You might have been dreaming, but I was having nightmares," he chastised her. "Most of them involved stuffing and bow ties."

She shook her head. "It doesn't matter now. I have to get ready. I think my father is here waiting for me." She reached over and rang the bell for Graham.

If she was going to meet her father for the first time, she was darn well going to have a cup of tea before she did it.

CHAPTER 10

Stories can be fickle in the telling. As long as the storyteller is careful, and mindful of details, a story can be tamed and kept under control. Alice had been mindful when she began re-writing her story night after night in her journal. Now, as it began spinning out of her control, she was beginning to doubt that she was even still the storyteller. Despite her doubt, she was clinging to her story and desperate to force it back on track. Hers was the story of Princess Alice Will, while the story of Dark Lord Laramak was trying to unfold without her permission.

But this was still her story. She stood with unshakable determination at the door of the castle that she had created. It was nothing like the way she had imagined it, and, try as she might, she wasn't able to make it go away or change anything about the dark and menacing turrets that twisted their way out of the mountain. Still, as she entered the gate, which swung freely open for her by some invisible hand, she was determined to make the best of it. This was still *her* castle, after all.

For anyone who's never been in the presence of a six, almost seven, year old girl, there are few forces of nature greater than the will of a determined child. As she walked into the main hall of the castle, she scowled at the décor. The weapons on the walls were baroque monstrosities and the stone was so dark that it sapped what meager light the green-tinged torch flames were able to provide. She shook her head and stomped from the hall up the stairs of the nearest tower and stopped at the first room she found. It was no more suitable for her in here, and probably worse given the macabre furniture. It consisted of a reclined wooden chair with leather straps from head to foot and a single table with tools arranged carefully. It was only a blessing that her young mind couldn't conceive of the use for which the sharp hooks, knives, and saws were intended.

"This is *not* a room fit for a princess!" She stomped for emphasis. Then she focused. If she couldn't change the castle itself, then perhaps she could change the décor at the very least. Even as the thought crossed her mind a new room began to take shape in front of her. The dark stones were gradually covered with a soft pink and the single narrow slit window expanded into a wide picture window framed in white curtains of puffed lace and silk fringe. The sinister tools on the table became ivory-handled brushes, mirrors, and perfume while the table itself became a vanity fit for a queen. The chair was replaced by a tremendous four-poster bed with a canopy that matched the curtains and the rest of the room was filled with every doll, trinket, or toy that a princess could desire. When she was content with the room, she turned toward the corner and opened an ornately carved wardrobe that practically glittered with gilt-enameled engravings. As the door swung aside she was pleased to see a row of dresses, all nearly identical to the one she wore now.

There was a limit to her creative power. She could only imagine things that she'd seen in pictures. Unfortunately, she'd only ever seen one picture of a princess, and that was in a child's storybook. Her dress, like those in her wardrobe, was the exact replica of the long flowing gown worn by that princess.

Her imagination had other limits as well. She smiled as she looked down on her kingdom from the lace-framed window. Had she ever crossed the high mountain paths or even read about the world beyond she'd have known that, due to the flatness of Aevum, you could almost see to Sarano's far distant shores to sunward from here atop the majestic Stain Mountains. She saw no such thing today. Since she had never been nor seen beyond the mountains, in her mind there simply was nothing beyond them.

Alice looked down the steep mountain slope and saw Klempt, her kingdom, in its entirety. She didn't bother looking down the other side of the mountain. There was nothing there. Her castle was resting not only on top of the world, but on the edge of what was now left of the world.

She closed the door to her room and began playing with her new dolls. It wasn't long before she began to wish she had a playmate.

*****

"Master!" Mouthed the increasingly feeble voice from the pool. The watcher was weakening; the constant focus was draining him. His mind was spread too thinly between activities in Realm, Alice, and Trotter. He was growing weaker almost by the hour, and he seemed more out of touch with his physical location than ever. His mental contact with his body was now tenuous at best, but still he pushed. He had a debt to repay, and his son's murder to avenge. An image of his son's face, twisted in a mask of painful death, kept the watcher tied to a pain-ridden body he otherwise would have long left behind.

She would pay. The sea-witch would pay.

"Master!" He cried again, this time his voice carried weakly across the small pool. The servant, stationed there to alert the wendigo of news from the watcher, was lying in an unconscious heap in the floor at the feet of his attacker. Miro crouched beside the pool and stared at the watcher in a mixture of disgust and pity.

"You call that miserable, evil creature Master?" She asked sadly. "You once served the gods themselves, and now you work for Laramak's rabid guard dog. You were a good man once, Baden. I'm going to offer you the chance to be one again."

The watcher was silent for a moment that was long enough for Miro to doubt whether the creature had even heard her. Then a slow toothless smile crept across his face. It was a horrible smile that bore no semblance to an expression of happiness. It was a smile that spoke of torments yet unimagined; it was the calm before a storm.

"Baden," he repeated, laughing darkly at a memory. "I think I'd forgotten the sound of my old name. There wouldn't be many other than you who would remember it. How kind of you to remember those of us you wronged."

"You knew, old man. You knew that Pardo was working against the Accord for the wendigo. Your own son was betraying the very Accord you helped draft!"

"He would have come back to us if you'd given me time!" The watcher snarled, half rising out of the water before slipping back with exhaustion.

"There was no time," she responded. Regret tinged her voice. "You knew that, as well. You were there when the council voted and you allowed it to happen. There wasn't a choice, Baden. Pardo would have destroyed the fragile peace we'd worked so hard to achieve if he'd managed to free the wendigo. And now you're working for the same beast of Laramak's that turned him in the first place."

"The wendigo didn't kill my son!" The watcher's leathery face twisted in agony as he pushed himself further into the pool away from Miro. "You did, you witch. You did," he whispered, his breath coming in shallow gasps.

She paused for a moment and studied the wretch. It was so hard to believe that this was somehow the same Baden that spoke so movingly for peace during the first negotiations after the Reconstruction. Then she corrected herself; this *wasn't* the same Baden. That man died with his son. She remembered his face on the day of the vote, and the image still pained her. The discussion regarding Pardo's punishment had been short, but heated. The Accord was clear when it came to the penalty for violating the tenants of the Accord: death for mortals and interminable banishment for the immortal gods. Laramak was the first to be banished for his refusal to end his warring among the humans. The wendigo was second for his attempts to save his evil lord, though his prison was far less horrible than his master's. Pardo was, among his various other sins of greed and malice, mortal, and his sentence for trying to help the wendigo escape was inexorable. Still, the decision had been nearly split between those who wavered in favor of imprisonment for the son of the great Baden out of a sense of friendship, and those who knew the danger of setting precedent by not resolutely abiding by the strict letter of the law. Especially so soon after the Accord had been signed, when the peace was still so fragile.

And during all of it, Baden had sat silently, neither arguing for his son's salvation nor casting a vote when it was time. His vote for his son's life would have divided the vote evenly, and his words would have easily swayed the hearts of those for whom a vote of death was hardest. He'd known this then, and because of this he kept his silence and he let his son die for what he believed then to be the right reason.

Grief, however, knows no reason. It twists itself in burning ribbons inside of a mind until the horrible truth begins to look like something different altogether. In Baden's case, the truth became utter betrayal, not by his son, but by the council he'd fought for.

"Your guilt did this to you, you poor man," she shook her head sadly. "You couldn't live with letting Pardo die. How you must have suffered for your grief to have warped you like this. The enemy is still here, Baden. Does any part of you still see this? The man who corrupted and bent your son to his will is in this castle. *He's* the one who took Pardo away from you. I may be the one who was sent to carry out the sentence, but I wasn't the enemy. You knew that once, my old friend. You can help me stop him now so he can never take another son again."

His sightless eyes opened – he'd been blind since before the time of the Accord – and the clouded gray irises rotated until they rested on the place from where Miro's voice issued. His breaths came more slowly as he opened his mouth to speak once more.

"Pardo," he answered feebly. "I want to avenge Pardo. I can't. I can't, without your help," he spoke falteringly and lifted his emaciated hand toward her from the water.

With no hesitation at all she slipped into the pool and reached for the man she had once respected and loved as a friend.

She never even reached his hand.

*****

There was darkness here, but even in saying that it must be understood that it is as gross an understatement as has ever been made. It was dark, yes, but in this place no light had ever, would ever, or could ever exist here in any form. There was simply nothing but the perfect, uninterruptible dark.

This is the mind of Chaos itself. And Chaos didn't sleep, but it dreamed magnificently. In the dreams of Chaos, the potential for everything is created and destroyed; potential universes spiral from birth to collapse, and dreams of anything and everything that might exist wait on coiled springs for an existence that may or may not come to pass. In this mind that contained absolutely nothing, the potential was everything.

In the darkness of one of these dreams, the potential that was the former Lord Laramak ignored the spiraling majesties around him and watched a door that was not really there. Stoicese had burned that door a day ago, or an eternity ago, time was not measurable here. What mattered was that if Chaos still dreamed of the door then some part of it somehow existed in some form, and Lord Laramak would continue to pour his own potential into it until the day it would finally open for him again.

*****

Miro gasped in pain. She tried to fight her way out of the water, but it was too late. The water around her took on a pale glow as it seeped into her body, the murky blue tracing along her veins in dark lines and invading every corner of her body. It burned terribly as it raced across her flesh and then, just as suddenly as the burning had overcome her, she was left completely numb. She sank down in the water limply next to the watcher. Hurt filled her sea-blue eyes.

"Baden, I thought you wanted my help!" She was unable to move her limbs and unable even to transform into a stronger form. It wasn't so much a paralysis, but more as a though a terrible weight were attached to every cell of her body, keeping her from being able to move anything but her eyes and mouth. Worse, she knew that in time it would drain her completely until she was no more than one of the ghostly whisperers in Paraben's garden.

She was glad she couldn't see the watcher's face when she heard the grim laughter that cracked dryly from his lips.

"I did, sea-witch. And you helped me. I wanted revenge, yes. You call what you did to my only son carrying out a sentence?" He spat the word. "You *murdered* him. My son! I have dreamed of this, sea-witch. I'm too weak to pull you in, and I doubt even the master could have forced you in. But now you're mine! He promised me you would suffer beautifully for every year you denied Pardo his life. Master!" He called weakly. His voice hadn't needed to carry far; the wendigo had been waiting behind the opposite door, listening with something nearing delight.

The wendigo let his eyes wander over the deep-blue lines that dictated the uselessness of Miro's struggle and smiled expansively. "Why Miro, former goddess of the surf, tender of the lost, and finally the treacherous queen of Erov. How many still remember you as that, do you think? How many still think of you as a queen in your tattered robes instead of the homeless traitor Erov cast out of Realm?" His smile became a leer as he spoke.

"And yourself? How many people do you think really believe that you are lord and master in this castle prison and don't see you for the slavering dog of Laramak's that you are and have always been?"

The wendigo laughed. "I'm sorry. I'm sure you meant that as an insult, but I consider the comparison flattering. You see, people tend to underestimate dogs. They think of them as brainless, affectionate, panting little loyal pets. Loyalty they have, and that counts for something. But what people forget is that, left to their own devices and uncoddled by humans, a dog is a single-minded hunter, undeterrable from its quarry. I am a hunter, witch. I smelled you as soon as you entered my castle. But, unlike a dog, I laid a trap for you."

"Erov's water. This pool is from Erov's realm," she said simply, almost with disinterest.

"You don't sound surprised."

"It takes a lot to surprise me. The only thing that can bind me is the water in Erov's sea where I was cursed, but the only person who knew that was Erov himself. So go ahead and brag as much as you want, but this trap wasn't yours. You may like to think you're the real hunter, but you're only just someone else's dog now. Tell me, why serve this new master?"

He bared his teeth at her. "To finish a war that never should have been stopped! This time there won't even be time even to choose sides. Those who value survival will serve Laramak, and those who don't will be punished in the manner of his choosing. They will *beg* for mere banishment."

It was Miro's turn to laugh, though the gesture sapped her strength even further. "Is that your plan? You think so small. And where does Erov fit into this? He's not the type to sit back and hand over power."

"Perhaps you gave him all the motivation he needed," answered the watcher. "He loved you very much once, you know."

She scowled. "He was always an evil, selfish, bastard. He never loved anyone more than himself."

"But you were still his queen. It's amazing how love betrayed can turn into the blackest of hate. His desire to see you suffer was stronger than even his own ego." The watcher's voice trembled with anger. "It was Erov who helped me see clearly. He helped me see that we had a common goal in destroying you."

182 ■ Alice Will

The wendigo chuckled airily. "My, my, witch. You're just making friends everywhere, aren't you?"

She ignored him. "Where is your master now, dog? Bring him to me."

"He isn't here."

"He will be," Miro said confidently.

The watcher's sightless eyes narrowed. Her confidence in the face of her capture made him curious and he sought out Erov in Realm. His shock was apparent when he found him. "He is coming!"

Miro smiled with satisfaction from her confinement.

*****

Trotter spent rather longer than was necessary grooming herself for a being that could command her hair to do itself. An observer would have called it stalling, but she needed time to gather her thoughts. Prowler waited helplessly and quietly on the bed for her to speak, but she was silent until she left, asking him to wait in the room for her to return. One last stern look at the teddy cats assured that they wouldn't bother him even after she left.

It's really happening, she thought as she followed Graham from the bedroom to the parlor where her father waited for her. The whole purpose behind her coming to Realm had been finding her father, but until now it had all felt so surreal. Just the knowledge that he was in the same castle with her, let alone the same plane of existence for the first time in her life left her feeling frightened. *I don't even know if I'm going to be happy to see him.*

"I think you'll know when you see him," Graham answered her soothingly. She hadn't realized that she'd been talking to herself until that moment.

"What's he like?" She'd seen him in her dreams, but dreams always seemed to blur at the edges. How could she trust a memory from a dream?

"He's a good man, and he's strong. Stronger than any of us. Except perhaps for you," he added thoughtfully.

Graham left her at the entrance of the parlor door where she stood, marshaling the courage to simply turn the handle. Instinctively, she was aware that her father knew she was there, but he was letting her proceed in her own time. For this, at least, she was grateful.

Remember why you're here, she admonished herself and reached for the door.

At the table, waiting for her with an untouched cup of tea, was a man who was more familiar to her than she'd expected. He was starkly handsome, but had a serious air to him that would have made him seem cold and distant if not for the warmth in his eyes and slightly nervous smile when he stood to welcome her.

Graham had been right; she knew the moment she saw him.

"Dad?" The word welled up in her throat behind the tears struggling to the surface. She'd never, even in her most private thoughts, used the word in conjunction with him. It felt alien and wonderful all at the same time coming out of her mouth.

He stood from the table and came half of the distance to the table to meet her. There was no hiding the sheer excitement and happiness in his face as he opened his arms to her. He did want her, and that knowledge was all it took to propel her the rest of the way across the parlor to his embrace. This time she didn't even notice the childish décor and the sad bear cub Poo-Poo grumbling at the teddy cat that kept trying to climb up his back. She didn't notice anything until her father turned her tear-stained face up toward his own.

"My girl," he said as he brushed his fingers urgently through her

184 ■ Alice Will

brown hair. "I wish I had more time just to look at you, but I need you to come with me now. There's so much to do. Are you ready?" She nodded and he kissed her gently on top of her head. "You're as good a liar as your mother," he said with a loving smile.

"Wait! We have to get Prowler," she remembered, turning toward the door that had been there only a moment ago.

"Not a problem," he answered. She was still facing the direction that would have led to the guest room, had the guest room been there. Instead, a mere few feet away crouched a very discontented Prowler with one of his back legs hoisted in the air.

"Ok," he was saying to himself. "Nothing strange about this. Nothing at all. Perfectly good explanation is on its way, I'm sure," he finished with a theatrical yawn, pretending that his compromising posture had been merely an elaborate stretch.

Trotter looked around her and fought the urge to drop to her knees and hug the ground, if there was one. Whatever was under her feet felt solid, but she couldn't see where it ended and walls began, if there were any, or where the walls ended and the ceiling began, if there was one. It was an endless wash of white, for lack of a better description. There was no color, but there appeared to be light, despite the shocking lack of shadows or depth. She looked helplessly at Prowler who was now the very picture of dignity, and back toward her father.

"I know what you're experiencing, Trotter," Stoicese looked back at her, a wistful expression in his eyes. "It's still amazing to me and I've seen it for thousands of years. There weren't any words I could have said that could have possibly prepared you for this, and believe me that I tried desperately to find some. I finally decided it was best just to bring you here."

"Where are we?"

"We're at the bedrock of everything. Think of the worlds you know as a castle with layers. You might think of the world where you live as the main floor, the Wedge as the second, and Realm as the towers."

"Does that make this the dungeon?"

Stoicese grimaced. "On second thought, this might be a poorer analogy than I thought. No, not the dungeon. Where we are would be the foundation, possibly even the rock below it."

Prowler's ears twitched nervously. "Are you saying that this is the Canvas? Here?"

"That's what I prefer to call it, but while it's descriptive it's misleading as to what this place truly is." He laid his hand on Trotter's shoulder. "My girl, calling it a canvas is an understatement. A canvas can be painted with a masterpiece, but if you paint over it with another it would be as though the original masterpiece never existed. And real masterpieces have been painted here. The world you grew up in, the Wedge, and many, many others you've never known all began here."

"Then how is it so different from a canvas?"

"This canvas remembers each and every masterpiece. It holds the memory of all that has existed, and is tied to the realities spun from it for eternity. Unlike an ordinary painting, if the masterpieces created from the Canvas are destroyed, they can be remembered here and rebuilt. Exactly as they were, even."

There was a hesitation in his voice and she suddenly had the feeling that he was working up to telling her something terrible. "Sarano has been destroyed, hasn't? That's what you're trying to tell me."

"And nearly all of the world with it," he conceded. "All because a lonely little girl couldn't imagine that the rest of the world existed. Here, you should sit down. I know this must be hard to hear." He gestured behind her to a chair that hadn't been there only a moment ago. It was broad and piled deep with comfortable cushions. All in all, it was completely incongruous with the rest of the strange blankness around her.

Still, the appearance of a comfy chair was by far the least frightening thing that she could imagine at the moment and she sank into it without argument. As he moved to sit across from her a stool appeared beneath him just as though it had always been there.

"I've asked this so many times in the past couple of days and I still haven't gotten an actual answer. Please be the first to tell me; *what is happening?*" She asked. Once she began, however, she found she couldn't stop the flood of questions that had battering at the walls of her heart. "How am I involved and what is the truth about Laramak? And while you're at it, will you please tell me why you've never brought me here before, and *why did you let my mother die?*"

The pain on his face was clear, even through the haze that her tears had flooded over her vision. Then she remembered Paraben and the beautiful lost woman he would spend an eternity trying to love. She wasn't the only one who'd suffered in the loss of the mother she'd never known. "I'm so sorry" she said, embarrassment damping the anger she'd carried for so long. "That was completely unfair of me."

"No, no it wasn't," he said softly. "It was unfair of me to keep you in the dark all of these years, but I can promise you, Trotter, that if I could have done any differently I would have. I can also promise you that things will be so much clearer when this is over. But first, there is so much I have to show you. Are you still with me? Can you trust me?"

She wiped her eyes and nodded. Prowler leapt up beside her in the chair and purred softly, soothingly.

"Then listen closely. You know the story of Laramak's defeat, right?"

"Yes. At least, I know the story they tell, about the blacksmith and the key. But that's just a fairy tale."

"I'm glad you recognize the difference. That saves us some time. The reality is nothing like the story, but it seldom ever is. You can't imagine how bad the fighting was during the Reconstruction, and I have no desire to draw the picture for you, but as bad as it was, it was nothing compared to the horrors that Laramak was unleashing. It was his abominations that drove scores of gods to finally understand the need for cooperation, and they aligned against him. There were hold-outs, of course, but eventually every last one of them signed the Accord of Realm. The very first provision of the Accord was the banishment of Laramak. The final battle was terrible, but we captured him finally."

"How do you capture a god?"

"By posing as a lowly blacksmith in his kingdom who claimed to forge an armor that would make him untouchable."

"You were the blacksmith, weren't you?" She asked in pure shock. "You lured him into the forge?"

"Yes. The story tells of one key, but there were actually two. One that locked us in together, and the other in my hand locked the other door as I slipped out when his attention was on the first door. The locks were magical, but not strong enough to hold him forever. So I banished Laramak while he was bound and then burned the forge so no one would be able to open the door to him again."

"Where did you send him?"

"To what is the next best thing to death for a god; the sleeping mind of Chaos where very few could ever reach him again. And when I say very few, I mean only me, at least, only me until recently," he said, giving her a meaningful look.

Trotter shook her head in frustration. "So that's why they've been watching me. And why everyone is so afraid of me, isn't it?"

"It's also why I've kept you away from Realm and away from as many of the bad influences as I could. I mentioned that there were those who were less enthusiastic about signing the Accord, and there are some who would rather return to the dark and bloody days of Laramak than live peacefully and quietly. They dream of conquest, of being kings again. They've forgotten that Laramak has spent nearly a thousand years, an eternity in the mind of Chaos, dreaming of his revenge. There would be no other king but him when he was finished."

"Can't you explain that to them?"

"It's hard to explain anything to someone who fights you in the dark. As soon as the first tremors began and the Wedgequakes began, they started vicious rumors to divide Realm again. It all should have been completely unbelievable to anyone with half a brain, but I'm starting to think there just aren't enough halves to go around up there." He shook his head with disgust. "Since the ability to change reality has been only in my line since the Accord was signed, it was inevitable, I suppose, that they said I was plotting to break the Accord and make a move toward dominion again. The rumors started in the Wedge as well, saying that I was using you to build an army in the world."

"That's ridiculous!"

"Yes, it is. But they couldn't see what was really happening. All they knew was that Wedgequakes meant reality somewhere was being changed and there were only two in existence who could make that happen."

"Then where are the changes coming from?"

"There is a girl in Drimbt, in the same village where I captured Laramak. I don't know fully how it happened, but something has been making her stronger and stronger, and I'm afraid that it has something to do with him. I sent Falcon, my servant, and he tells me that, whatever she is, something seems to be adding strength to her powers. She believes in her illusions fervently, and in that belief, plus this added power, they are becoming real. He also tells me that she doesn't seem to be completely in control of her power anymore, and that she's just recreated a castle for herself on the top of the Stain Mountains. The castle is more than just identical to Laramak's. He says it *is* the castle of Laramak. The villagers pulled it down stone by stone when he was banished, but there it sits, just as new as the day it was built."

"Then we have to go and stop her!"

"Almost, my dear girl. And this is the part that hurts me," his eyes showed his pain, "but you are the one who has to stop her. Everything I've told you is why I have to stay here. War is coming and when it does, it will be fought here in Realm. For a god to leave Realm is against the Accord. If I were to leave even to help stop Laramak it would unleash all of Realm to pour back into Aevum. I almost wonder if they aren't trying to lure me into breaking it to justify their attack. But the war is inevitable, and I have to prepare."

She stared at him. It wasn't with shock, or concern, but confusion. "Why do I feel like I already knew that? Everything you're telling me, it's like you're telling me something that I knew and have just forgotten. It's like déjà vu."

"It's part of your powers, Trotter. You've been trying to use them more since you got here, haven't you?" She conceded that she had. "The more you use them, the stronger you'll be. But *especially* while you're here. Realm is magic distilled, and that's flowing through you right now."

"I don't even really know how to use them yet, though. How am I supposed to stop this girl if I don't even know how to use my powers?"

"Ingenuity, my girl. I didn't use my powers to capture Laramak. I tricked him into doing it for me. Use what's at hand. Do you understand me? *Use what's at hand,*" he repeated urgently. "But the girl isn't truly the problem. According to Falcon, she's being used and she's already beginning to suspect it. She's powerful, but what makes her most dangerous is that she has no idea of the consequences that come with power."

"But she's destroyed most of the world! How can she not realize that?"

"Because she never really knew it existed. She's never been outside of that tiny village, Trotter. When she began to remake the world, she remade only the part that she knew. None of this is her fault, and you have to keep that in mind, no matter how frightening the implications of her actions are. Her name is Alice, and she isn't even seven years old yet. Laramak and his servants are using her in terrible ways, but she is still just a child. One who needs rescuing as much as the rest of the world."

She sighed, waiting for frustration, fear, or anger to come. When none did, she asked him, "Why here? Why did you bring me here to tell me all of this?"

"Because no one else can reach us here, and this is the only place I can teach you how to use reality as a weapon."

CHAPTER 11

The villagers of Klempt gathered quietly behind the baron and Carmony at the edge of town. When Arriman left, much of his illusion faded and the senses that had been screaming for recognition during his visit began permeating the mists of memory that he had twisted in their minds. The distant thought that he was not a boy was no longer so distant, and they were afraid. And the only difference between a large crowd of frightened people and that angry single-minded organism known as a mob is having someone say the wrong thing at the wrong time.

This anger was held in check, however, by the fact that the most terrifyingly dark and ominous castle had suddenly loomed over them and blotted out the sun by reaching higher than the Stain Mountains had ever dared. It was a nightmarish silhouette penned in black and gray against a sky that was spreading red fingers across the horizon and racing toward them. There were frequent mutters along the lines of 'someone ought to do something about that...' but never a volunteer.

And so they waited while the baron and his captain discussed the problem quietly and tried to exude a confidence that they were far from actually feeling.

"Sire, the garrison isn't far," Carmony was saying. "I could ride there and be back with troops in just a few hours, and have the rest following us within the day."

"You're so certain that we'll need them?"

"And you're not?" The captain asked incredulously, abandoning etiquette in his surprise.

"It's not that I don't believe we'll need help, son," he looked sadly at Carmony. The eagerness, the strength, the fortitude, all of these things he saw in Carmony, he wished he could feel right now. But all of that was beyond him. He'd learned to recognize futility in his nearness to death these past months. "I know we need help. But I don't think all the baronies in Drimbt could stand up to this."

"But sire, it's just one castle!"

"Doesn't anything seem familiar to you about this castle? Sitting atop the Stain Mountains? That demon that tricked us all so easily?"

Carmony blushed slightly and shook his head. He was very intelligent, quick-witted, and had a natural instinct for leadership, but he was not an educated man. This fact alone was a prime reason that the baron had been unable to promote him above the political machine of the nobility. He might be lord and master of his barony, but he was powerless against the inertia of tradition.

"Did you never hear stories of Laramak, god of war, in your village?" Baron von Proustich continued at Carmony's continued silence. "The fables talk about the dark days long ago when the gods were here in Aevum and ruled over us, using us as slaves."

"But those are fairy tales, milord." There was a hint of uncertainty to

Carmony's voice.

"Fairy tales are usually based on something, Captain. Whether the grain of truth behind it is a pebble or a boulder, who can tell? But in those fairy tales, Laramak was the worst of any of them. And his castle sat higher than any other in the world. It was said he created the mountain range precisely for this purpose. There was an etching in a book that I read once..." his voice drifted thoughtfully as he stared at the hulking castle.

"Sire, if you suspect something like this, we should take these people away now and meet the garrison."

The baron shook his head sadly and turned to face him. "You take them, Captain. And take this." At that he slipped a signet ring from his finger and pressed it into Carmony's hand.

For centuries, the barony had passed from father to son in the form of that ring. It was every bit as much the barony as the baron himself. It was the ring that he would have given his own son, had he not outlived him.

"Milord –"

"Put it on. As my last order as your baron, put the ring on and take care of the people."

Carmony was horrified. "What are you doing? I can't take this, sire!" He tried to give it back to his baron but von Proustich steadfastly refused.

"I'm finished, Carmony. I know Alice is the only reason I'm still alive right now. I also know that she's somehow involved in this and she has no idea what's happening. If anything happens to her I'm lost anyway, so I owe it to both of us to try to help her. The best thing I can do for my people now is to go in there and try to stop this before it's too late. But the first thing I will do is make sure they're still in good hands when I'm gone. Carmony," his voice softened, "you are the only son I have left, and I should have treated you more like one all along. Wear that ring and be my heir, and for gods' sake, protect the people!"

"How can I possibly?"

"You have always been an inspiration to me, whether you knew it or not. Now go and be the symbol and the strength they need," he answered. Then he leaned in closely and whispered one last thing to him and then abruptly turned back toward the castle, cupping his hands to his mouth before the shocked captain, now baron, could argue.

"Alice!" he roared. The echo bounded heavily from wall to wall in the village and flew up the mountain side to the distant castle. Before the final echo returned, the former baron was gone.

*****

As he had for centuries, Erov sat alone in his castle far beneath the shimmering and perilous Erovian Sea, the only large body of water in all of Realm. The gardens of Realm had a peculiar ecology that didn't rely on streams, ponds, or any other source of water to thrive. The gods willed that the grounds were lush, and so they were. It was a horticulturalist's dream.

The Erovian Sea, of course, had no gardens to speak of. Its forests were of coral mountains and peaks more than a mile under the sea, and such flowers as it had were beautiful and deadly creatures forever attached immobile to the coral structures that lured small fish into the venomous grasp of their fleshy petals. Even more frightening were the lionfish that hunted among them. They were more lion than anything and more amphibian than fish, since they stalked the edges of the beach for prey of any size almost as nimbly as they stalked cat-like among the coral structures deep under the sea.

Everything about this sea was a trap. It was warm, calm, and inviting from the surface, but every fish was a carnivorous predator or scavenger, the jelly fish were cow-sized with a mouthful of rotating teeth like razors, and the mermaids weren't mermaids at all. These were Erov's own private joke. True to the name, their bottom half was piscine, like the powerful tail of the great white shark. But there was nothing feminine or gentle about the upper torso, though vaguely human in form. Their powerful arms were half-webbed to their bodies to give them the speed to fly through the water faster than anything else in the sea and their stomachs were elongated and rippled with muscles. These muscles enabled them to coil and spring out of the sea high enough to pluck sailors from boats, if there were any brave enough to sail Erov's waters. But most gruesome of all were the heads. They were hairless, and had very small brains so the skull was almost flat in the back. This left more room for the mouths. Though they didn't have a pronounced nose, their teeth filled three-quarters of their face in jagged rows, and their throats were wide, flaring into their shoulders. The jaw could unhinge like a snake's in order to help it swallow larger prey whole.

They were terrifying. In their limited capacity for thought were two prime commands: Kill everything, and eat when necessary. They were death to anything near enough to see them, plucking even the mighty lionfish from their lairs in the coral for an easy snack. And they were Erov's favorite sport. This is the most important thing anyone needs to know when dealing with Erov. He fashioned a creature as terrible, vicious, and deadly as he could imagine and stocked his sea with them in order to hunt them and capture them for his own amusement. They were to him what a rhino was to a big game hunter, except that even a seasoned big game hunter would have crapped his pants on sight of one of Erov's mermaids.

Erov enjoyed a challenge.

His current challenge, however, wasn't nearly as much of a challenge as he'd expected. In fact, it was almost boring him with how astoundingly easy it had been to turn so many of the gods of Realm against Stoicese. And the matter of the girl...

He sat pensively in the uppermost tower of his castle where he spent most of his time these days. Despite the terrors of his sea, Erov's castle was a gossamer work of art. It rose from the coral on the sea floor majestically, blending at the base until it was impossible to tell where seabed ended and castle began. As it reached higher and higher the coral was replaced with mother of pearl, not just reflecting the light beautifully but seemingly creating its own pulsing glow. It was a dry oasis on the seafloor, the air forming a protective globe around it where the water lapped calmly at the edges. This was the castle he'd created for his queen, but he no longer dwelt on that fact. Now, if he thought of it at all, it was simply where he kept his throne.

Still, his mind lingered on the girl. He frowned as he thought of the traveler's shell in his pocket that Miro had provided her with to keep her safe from him. Miro and her trinkets! As if he would have actually harmed the girl. She was too important to Laramak. It served his plan well for Miro to think that his intentions toward the girl were violent, but the convenience of it bothered him at the same time. As much as he hated giving her credit for the fact, Miro was smarter than that.

He thought of the centuries he'd spent waiting for an opportunity like this one, how carefully he'd poisoned the mind of the last watcher until the man could barely distinguish between Erov's words and his own thoughts. Then he'd given the watcher a touch of immortality and left him with the wendigo and his demons to serve his purpose. Centuries had passed; frustrating, agonizing, taunting, and seemingly endless. Then the wendigo had called for him. The watcher had discovered a secret that

Stoicese could have kept from anyone else, from everyone else, but not the watcher. He'd concealed his daughter along with the secret among the mortals to keep her hidden from Realm. An adolescent, a Changer as powerful as her father and even farther-reaching, and one who still thought of herself as a human rather than a god.

Very well. Let her be human. Her love of humanity would be a powerful weapon for Arriman to use against her.

A bat-like creature with a long and transparent abdomen hung by its feet from the ceiling near the window. It had hooks at its feet and arms, and had a pinched waist in the center of its clear stomach where a sand-like substance was trickling slowly through to the bottom. As the last grain of sand dropped through the pinched waist, the creature yawned noisily with chime-like pipes, stretched, and rolled itself lazily over to hang from its hands and allow the sand to begin flowing downward again. A nearly identical creature would be doing the same in every castle in Realm; the chiropticks, as they were called, were the only form of timekeeping the gods used.

Erov took note of the chiroptick's rotation with a mixture of pleasure and apprehension. It was time. All across Realm the gods he'd allied with would be gathering their strength and preparing for war. A challenge had been issued to Stoicese during an emergency meeting of the Council of Realm that Erov had carefully timed and crafted to leave no other option than war. Most of the council avidly supported Erov and believed that the truth god was responsible for the destruction of Aevum, a mere third remaining loyal to Stoicese and his word. The gift of changing reality was exclusive to Stoicese and his line; it was impossible for the council to think that he wasn't involved with the utter chaos happening among the humans. Stoicese tried to convince them that the real danger was still coming, that Laramak was using a small child in some way to try to bring him back, but he received nothing more than uncomfortable laughter even from among his supporters. There was only one thing the council agreed upon, whether it was out of conviction or fear, and that was that Laramak was gone.

Erov, in turn, capitalized on this. He argued that Stoicese was using the name of Laramak to frighten the council and misdirect their fear at a legend long gone from their world so they wouldn't discover his own plan to break the Accord and establish a kingdom of his own on Aevum using his daughter as his agent. When the meeting adjourned, Stoicese was left with the ultimatum to deliver his daughter to the council for interrogation by morning or have her taken by force. It was all an elaborate farce filled with legalistic and flowery debate in which every member of the council knew the unspoken intent. There will be war, and here is our reason.

A thousand years of fragile peace were more harrowing than many of the gods could take. It meant a thousand years of comparative idleness, each longing for the days of conquest and glory and worship, but none willing to risk banishment for breaking the Accord. It could only be all or nothing, and now they had their chance. They had lined up so easily against Stoicese once they realized this, and Erov had given them the final provocation for war.

When he'd demanded that Stoicese turn over his daughter everyone had known it was an impossibility. True to character, Stoicese immediately took Trotter to the canvas where no god could reach her, and Realm prepared for war.

*****

"A weapon? For real?" Trotter was embarrassed at the over-eagerness in her voice. She almost expected a scolding for it, but if he noticed it he was too kind to say it.

"Yes, a weapon. But it's one that you can only use when your life depends on it. Everything in reality is completely connected. It's easy to think of it as so many individuals or things, or places, but it's *all the same thing*. Do you understand?"

"No," she answered a bit hopelessly. "I don't at all. I mean, I can see how everything might be connected, but all the same thing?"

"You're still thinking of it in individual terms. You're thinking that you can't possibly be the same as your house, or that the pastry you ate the other day is the same as the seagulls on the shore or that the torches in the street are the same as the water in the sea. But no matter what they look like, or what they do, or if they're alive or if they're just the rocks on the ground, it's all made from the same fabric."

"What is the fabric?"

"You're standing on it. The canvas is where the gods created your world back before the Accord made me the only god who could create and change reality. It's really just another part of the mind of Chaos."

She gasped fearfully, as did Prowler at her side. "But you said Laramak was here!"

"In a manner of speaking, yes. But you have to understand that the mind of Chaos spans across entire universes, most of those not reachable even by us. Laramak is in one that was only reachable by me, and then only with the help of a staff," he looked sideways at her, "but we destroyed that staff when he was banished."

She suddenly remembered Paraben's words, "...*in all the universes that exist.*" Her father was trying to tell her something important, but why not come out and say it? "Are we really alone here?"

He looked pleased. Apparently she'd asked the question he was hoping for. "In a matter of speaking, we are, and in another manner..."

He paused, prompting her to think of the answer for herself.

"And in another manner, we're among everyone who has ever lived. Is that right? Because we're all a part of the fabric and that fabric that connects everyone and everything is all around us right now."

He smiled and nearly jumped from his stool. "How did I get such a brilliant daughter?" He laughed. "I'm sure anyone listening right now would say the same thing." Again, he gave her that meaningful look.

That's the problem, then, she thought. Not even this place is safe from the watcher. He wants me to use the staff, but no one can know I have it, Paraben said. But if it's the only thing that can free Laramak, why do they want it with me when I'm not even sure I can protect it?

Why not just leave it safely hidden with Paraben? She wished fervently that she could ask that question.

"Ok," she continued, her mind racing in directions that frightened her, "so back to the question about reality as a weapon. You said that everything is not only just connected, but it's of the very same fabric. That means that any change I make could affect the whole fabric, right? That's why I have to be careful when I use it."

"Precisely. And that's why Alice has caused so much trouble."

"I still don't understand. Why couldn't one of the gods just go down and see for themselves? Then they could stop her and no one could be blamed for breaking the Accord. All of this could have been avoided. Sarano could still be there!" The frustration she was expecting earlier found a hole in her temper and spilled all at once.

"It's all a part of the Accord, I'm afraid. No god can set foot inside of your world, or even the Wedge. The agreement was for the good of our own creations, you see. We had to step back and let them live their lives as they saw fit, no more meddling. That meant for good reasons or for bad reasons. Mankind has to control its own destiny if their lives are to have any true meaning."

Meaning is so important to the gods, she remembered from her dream-talk with Paraben. But at the cost of what? "Can you all really stand back and watch as the world you created falls apart?" She was astounded. "*Someone* isn't content to just sit back and watch. You said yourself that something or someone was making her stronger. That means someone *is* meddling!"

He nodded, his face looking resigned. "And that's all the more reason that the rest of us have no choice but to stand by the Accord. You can't understand how fragile the peace has been all these centuries, Trotter. It's more important than ever. If someone is breaking the Accord then they must be punished, but we can't break the Accord in order to stop them. Do you understand that?"

"No, I don't. This is stupid! You're really going to tell me that even though someone else is already breaking the rules and about to cause the end of humanity and destroy the world in the process, none of you will do *anything* to save us because it would also be *breaking the rules*? What's the point of having rules if only the good guys are going to follow them while the bad ones run around trying to take over the world?" She dislodged Prowler and left the chair, storming away. Prowler jumped down to follow her and as he did so he heard the tiniest 'pop' as the chair went back into a state of non-existence.

"Trotter," Prowler called to her, "he's absolutely right. I know it seems defeatist, and probably cruel to you, but you don't know how much worse things were when the gods *did* get involved. Divine intervention goes both ways, you know, especially when they don't realize that they're doing anything wrong. It has to be this way. Please listen to him," he called to her.

She stopped walking and sobbed quietly. "But it's all gone," she said softly, sniffing back her tears. "Everything I knew, everything I loved, and they sit there and do nothing about it."

"No, my girl," Stoicese said behind her. He hadn't moved from his seat as she walked away but he may as well have been standing beside her for as soft and loving as his voice was in her ear. "Everything you knew is all still here in the long memory of the canvas. And I'm not doing nothing. I'm sending you. I can't go into your world and stop her myself, but I'm also going to fight a war in Realm to keep anyone else from doing it. It has to be you, Trotter. It's always been you, though I tried hiding you for years hoping it wouldn't really happen."

She turned back to face him, her arms hugged tightly across her body. "Then it looks like I need to learn how to use reality as a weapon, doesn't it?" She hoped that it had sounded more like determination than the resignation and fear that she felt. She closed her eyes tightly, blinking the last of her tears away. When she opened them Stoicese stood beside her, wrapping his arm around her shoulder. He kissed her again on top of the head.

"Please don't hate me for this," he said. "If there was any other way…"

"I know, Dad." She realized she hated seeing how much this hurt him. I barely even know this man, she thought. But I want to know him better, she added. She forced herself to smile and tried to sound more confident than she felt by a mile. "Just don't think you'll ever be able to ground me for anything after I save the world."

*****

The hermit crab was slowly waking up from its hibernation. It had been crafted with a single purpose and, for the first time in its existence, it was needed. The world in which it awoke was dark and confined, but it wasn't bothered by this. The crab crawled out carefully and unnoticed, leaving the shell behind forever, and worked its way quietly through the folds of clothing. Finally, it sensed the warm skin of its target, and plunged its claws deep.

*****

Erov howled in surprise at the sharp pain and clawed at his robes until he found its source in his side. He pulled aside the last layer too late to stop the hermit crab from wriggling the rest of the way into his body from the hole it had opened in the soft flesh above his hip. He pounded uselessly at the wound, knowing he couldn't stop his body from absorbing the crab now. His limbs turned leaden and pulled him to the ground as the castle faded in front of his eyes and another familiar scene began to take its place. Still, he grinned. He'd dealt his cards carefully enough to know that the war would begin with or without him leading the charge. But for the first time in centuries, he was about to face *her*.

*****

There are some people for whom the sense of duty is strong enough to pervade every cell of their body, their physical reactions being guided just as much by this instinctive sense as by coherent thought alone. Carmony was one of these people, and his sense of duty was now ignoring the state of shock trying so hard to overpower him. While his mind was still staring at the empty footprints left behind in the snow where his lord had been standing solidly just a moment before, his body had shaken off the disbelief and led him to the knot of townspeople who were not as able to avoid the paralysis of shock.

The baron... He tightened his jaw and cleared his head; he didn't have time for grief to overcome him. The baron was with Alice presumably, but who knew what else was within the black stones of that horrible place? There were barely subdued sobs from the villagers, and the sound reminded him that they shared his fear. No one could look at that the nightmare looming above them without feeling that the baron was already dead. No one could go there without going to their death. The thought seemed to emanate from the castle, as though instilling terror and dread in anyone approaching were a part of its natural defenses.

It was working.

He clenched the ring the baron had given him tightly in his hand at his side as he reached the cluster of frightened people. The baron had, in front of these witnesses, made him his heir. Carmony had no delusions that the inheritance would hold up against the ranks of greedy, power-hungry nobles once they honed their teeth on the vitriolic self-righteous indignation that was bound to follow the announcement. No, if anything was to come of this title it would have to be now, while the villagers were still caught off-guard enough to not question his authority and follow his orders long enough for him to protect them. This would be the only time he would have the power to follow the baron's wishes, and he would have to make it count.

He stopped just short of the huddle and let his gaze drift over them. There were fifty of them, maybe less, but they were all looking to him, some more anxiously than others, as the leader for at least the moment. Their eyes told him that it wasn't out of a deep sense of respect for either Carmony or the baron's bequest, but out of the sheer fact that someone was going to have to do *something* and none of them wanted to be the one to do it.

People are fantastic creatures in that regard; a new baron that every last one of them would have complained about to anyone who would listen during a time of peace and plenty was welcomed eagerly as long as it meant that none of them would have to be the ones to make the hard decisions. Let him play at being Baron for now, their eyes seemed to say, but when things are better someone will give the whipper snapper the boot. Let someone with more *experience* be the baron.

The unbearable part was that the average citizen, far removed from the political melee that passed for administration, mistook simply being born into the right family as experience. Those who had been groomed for the job were sent off to schools at a young age in Tier Aní and returned to a country that was unfamiliar to them when it was time for them to take command of their family's soldiers. Soldiers they'd never known, never cared for, and wouldn't notice if they were absent from the banquet the night after a particularly bloody battle. While they were attending elegant university dinners and teas hundreds of miles away, Carmony was fighting beside Baron von Proustich, beloved of his people, and learning daily by his intrepid example. This was the education a future baron truly needed.

But it was not the education that a baron would have, he reminded himself. Not in this day, not yet. Truthfully, he didn't want the barony. He loved the barony, of course, but in his mind, the barony was the people. He didn't have the gauze over his vision that nobles were born with that enabled them to see the barony only as a stone upon which to hang their coats of arms. Even if he managed the retain the title and do for the people what the baron wished, he would be fought at every turn by resentful nobles who thought that his policies gave too much strength and prosperity to the peasants rather than lining their own already gilt-lined pockets.

"Everyone, listen to me!" He called to them, and, for a while, they would because he was the man who would make the hard choices, who would take the risk now that their own nerves failed them. To seal the deal, he theatrically slid the signet ring over his finger, waiting for the last murmurs to die away. The villagers watched him expectantly. It was time for him to do the only good for his baron that he would have the power to do. He cast one last glance at the castle and resisted a shudder. All he had left now was the hope that this one thing would be enough.

"I need your fastest rider on your fastest horse."

*****

Trotter watched her father perform miracle after miracle on the canvas in a state of awe. She'd been wrong in thinking that the canvas had a memory. It *was* memory. And those memories danced in front of her violently under her father's control. It was like watching him conduct a symphony where the instruments were forces of nature. She felt herself being transported by the feeling of power as he showed her how to create, then turn the canvas over and create something else, then simply change it. She might have created a frog, but when she turned it into a bird it had somehow *always been* a bird. That was the danger of changing reality. One small change altered the very fabric of the world around it.

It was exhilarating how easy it was to pull a creature, a place, a stone, anything from the memory of the canvas and change it to suit her will. She'd pulled a building at random into existence and destroyed it simply by turning the stones to dust. She laughed as it crumbled and moved onto her next miracle. Stoicese frowned at her enthusiasm and called on her to stop, but she was having too much fun.

She should have listened.

Trotter felt the reins metaphorically yanked from her fingers and suddenly found herself standing in the middle of a field under a sky that was too evenly crimson for a sunset. There was a sickeningly sweet smell to the air that nearly made her gag.

"Where are we?" She'd asked him fearfully, trying to cover her mouth and nose with her hands. What she'd at first thought was the sound of fire was the buzzing of flies covering piles of something unidentifiable on the field.

"We're in a memory now. It's one I think you need to see. This is what happens when Reality is taken for granted." He gestured for her to follow him to a nearby hill. As they got closer she could just begin to hear the sounds of battle beyond it, but when she drew beside him on the peak she nearly fainted at the scene below them. She hadn't even realized she was screaming until her father sent the memory away and they were once again standing on the blankness of the canvas.

She dropped to the ground hugging her knees against her chest and sobbed. Crying seemed the only way to cleanse her eyes of the horrors she'd just witnessed. Prowler hadn't been with them in the memory, but it was apparent to him where Stoicese had taken her.

"You showed her the Reconstruction didn't you?" He let Stoicese's aggrieved silence answer him. "She's not strong enough for that. She's only fourteen years old! She can't even handle smiting without feeling guilty, and even then the people she smites are barely even burned. What did you do to her?" Prowler tried to comfort Trotter. She'd stopped sobbing, but she was trembling now.

"They were people. Just ordinary people on the field. All over it, in pieces. Those things did that to them, and then the ground just swallowed them all. The monsters, the villagers, everything. It really happened, Dad, it really happened!"

She screamed the last words nearly in hysteria. Stoicese dropped to

208 ■ Alice Will

his knees beside her and pulled her to him while the sobs wracked her body once again. "You had to know, Trotter. What you saw is the kind of power we have. I had to show you our power at its worst so you could know how to use our power for the best only. And that means not using it at all when it can be avoided. If you have to beat Laramak by changing the world, then we haven't really won at all. Do you understand?"

"I do," her breath came in shudders, "but I don't want this. Dad, I've never been this afraid of anything. I don't think I can do this alone."

"You aren't going alone. You have Prowler, and I'm also sending Falcon with you. He'll be my eyes and help guide you for me. But you have to go now, my girl." Stoicese bit back his own emotion. He'd waited so many years to hold his daughter, and now he had to let her go fight a battle he'd have given anything to be able to fight for her. "It's time, Trotter. Are you ready?"

"I don't think I'll ever be ready. So I guess that's all the more reason to go now. How do I get there?"

"I'll send you both there. Falcon is waiting for you already."

"Wait!" She cried urgently and leapt to her feet. She began digging in her pockets.

"What's wrong?"

"Nothing," she answered with relief as she found what she was looking for. "Miro wanted me to give this to you. She'd said you'd know what it was."

Stoicese took a black shell from her hand. It looked as though it had been carved delicately from stone. He smiled and clasped his hand gratefully around it. "I know *exactly* what to do with this."

She picked Prowler up into her arms. "Are you ready?" She asked him.

"No rest for the wicked, I suppose. I'm ready when you are, but for the record, I wouldn't mind if wherever we end up had a seafood buffet."

"I'll see what I can do," Stoicese answered. "Trotter? One last thing," he said as he squeezed her shoulder. "I have always been proud of you, but never more so than I am right now."

And then they were gone, but not before Trotter was able to see the glint of tears forming in his eyes. For the first time in her life, she had a real family.

It was something worth fighting for.

CHAPTER 12

Miro was still smiling when Erov appeared in the pool beside her, almost as helpless as she was.

He didn't bother looking around himself; he knew the water of his own sea as he knew the fingers on his hand. Erov tried to stand, knowing he was being watched, but found his legs could barely lift him to turn and face the one he knew would have to be there. Before he gained the strength to find Miro, the sound of her low laughter rippled toward him, filling him with enough anger to fuel a lunge to wrap his hands around her throat. Her face was filled with surprise as gasping replaced the laughter. He stared down into her face with absolute hatred and tightened his weak grip, determined to force her under and squeeze as much of the life out of her as he could before his strength gave out.

Those eyes… the same sea-blue eyes that had tricked him once before into loving her were red with the lack of air and fear as she pulled feebly at his hands to free herself. Erov willed all of his strength into his hands as her thrashing became weaker and weaker, and suddenly he felt a crushing pressure like a vise around his own neck. He looked deeper into her eyes. Fear? No. He'd been mistaken. It wasn't fear that lit her eyes. It was anticipation. He saw the unmistakable glint of grim amusement as his own pain became unbearable.

He dropped her and fell back into the water, tearing at his throat to remove invisible fingers that felt like iron bands. The wendigo plunged into the water beside him and pulled him, panting for breath, to the edge of the pool where the watcher chattered excitedly.

"Master, we have the witch!" The watcher shrieked. "We have the witch!"

"Idiot! We don't have the witch, the witch has *me!*" He turned hate-filled eyes toward Miro's smug, though still gasping, face. "*She* broke the Accord. She planted a Hostage Crab inside a Traveler's Shell that I was required to take."

It was one of the oldest tricks in the god business. The Hostage Crab lives in a dormant state until a threat awakens it. The owner of a Hostage Crab would secretly transfer it to whomever the owner felt was a threat. When the owner was in danger, the crab immediately awoke and burrowed into the possessor, essentially holding them hostage to ensure the safety of the host. It was an old trick, but also a trick not seen since the signing of the Accord. One that he wouldn't have had the chance to fall for had he not given in to the desire to see the girl in person. But he'd wanted to scare her, to make sure Stoicese was frightened into making the wrong choices. Now he knew he should have stayed away and trusted in his own plan.

"Oh, so now *I* broke the Accord. That's funny," Miro said her voice hoarse and cracked. "If you hadn't been interfering with her in a manner that would require you to accept the token, then you'd be safe at home, tucked happily into your little sea of horrors right now."

"Why did you even think I'd see the girl in Realm?"

"It was my little insurance policy, Erov. Who else could I think would possibly be behind this?" Her eyes burned with contempt. "For a plan this lacking in imagination I knew it had to be you. You waited for a thousand years, and it takes a little girl to do your work for you? Tsk, tsk," she chided. "Some all-powerful god you are."

"My poor imagination captured you, didn't it?"

"Well now," she said theatrically, "I guess you've got a point there, big guy. What are you going to do with me now that you have me?"

"Burn her!" The watcher cried. "Burn her as she burned Pardo!"

"Don't touch her!" Erov spat. "She bound me to her, wretch! I'm *infested* with the witch," he gestured angrily at the spreading maze of blue pulsing in his own veins and sapping his strength. It wasn't as pronounced as the network of poison coursing through Miro, however; these were *his* waters after all. What bound her still returned some strength measure to him. "You won't do a thing to her as long as I'm her hostage. What she feels, I feel three-fold."

"And what do you feel like now, Erov?" Miro taunted.

"Like seeing the wendigo tear your flesh from your body," he snarled. The wendigo's eyes brightened with the thought.

"I thought as much," she responded lightly. "Hence the insurance policy. You've never been much for pain, have you? I, on the other hand, am willing to take quite a bit of it if it means seeing you squirm again like you did a moment ago. It looks like we're in this one together, big guy."

Erov clenched his teeth. That was the name she'd always used when she wanted to mock him. It was time to show her how big he could be.

"It seems your insurance policy is only good for you, witch."

"It only had to be. I knew you wouldn't dare lay a finger on Trotter."

"Not if she's as useful as I think she will be," he agreed. "But she's not the only one you want to protect, is she?" Miro's cold silence caused a smile to spread thinly across his bearded face. He couldn't lay a finger on her, but he could still make her wish for something as simple and selfless as torture. He turned his taunts down a different path. "It only takes one member of the council to release the wendigo. Did you know that, witch?"

"You wouldn't! It would break the Accord. The council wouldn't stand for it!"

"Haven't you heard? The Accord is already broken. Realm is at war, princess," he pierced her with the nickname she had always hated.

"War?" She half-whispered. Her eyes were wide with shock

He was pleased with her reaction. "War," he confirmed with a self-satisfied smile. "All Stoicese had to do to stop it was turn over his daughter to the council so they could be sure she wasn't involved with the destruction in Aevum. Not one stone in Realm will be left standing when they are finished with Stoicese. And when Realm is nothing but a memory, the war will spread to the Wedge and then to Aevum."

Miro was silent while she absorbed the impact of Erov's words. "Where is Trotter?" She said finally, her voice quavering. "Where is my daughter?"

"*Your* daughter?" Erov said in mock surprise. "Did you think we didn't know the two of you were hiding her for a reason? Just think... A full blooded goddess, walking around in Aevum completely unaware that she could control the entire world with a snap of her fingers. It's only a shame I couldn't banish you to Chaos for infidelity. Banishing you from Realm alone wasn't enough. Did it hurt all these years, pretending she was another woman's child? I hope it tore your heart out," he said vengefully.

"Just tell me where she is."

"Already gone from Realm," the watcher trilled happily. "Stoicese has sent her right to Arriman. Arriman will make her bring back Lord Laramak!"

Realization spread across Miro's face, twisting her beautiful features in fear. "You *wanted* her to go there all this time, didn't you? Even the Leshy in Sarano was a ruse to get her to Realm where she would incriminate Stoicese just by being there. You knew he would have to send her on her own once the war started."

"Still think I'm unimaginative?" He taunted.

"No. I think you're a loathsome son of a bitch who was never fit to lick wendigo crap from Laramak's shoes. What will you do when he starts hunting down everyone who punished him? As you pointed out, you *are* a member of that same council, Erov."

"I guess that's a challenge I'll have to deal with if it comes. I may have been a part of the council, but I'm also the one responsible for freeing him."

"You think that will save you?" She asked derisively. "He wasn't one to show mercy, if you recall. If he returns, no one will be able to stop him. Not even you."

"Master –" the watcher began to interject.

"Be silent, old man!"

"But master, she's lying –"

Miro was the one to interrupt him this time. "You wouldn't even be able to hide from him, Erov," she continued quickly. "Not with a watcher still alive. Laramak would use him like a tool to hunt you down."

"Don't listen to the witch, master! She lies to protect herself!" Baden begged.

"Is the daughter truly on her way to Arriman?"

"She is there already!"

"And she will be able to open the door that Stoicese burned?"

"She is the only one, yes. She will bring Laramak through. Arriman will see to it."

"Then it looks like your job is finished, old man." Erov reached across Miro and laid his hand on the watcher's head. When he removed it he drew away with it the last breath of the twisted creature, surprise etched into his face. Then the body of Baden, the last watcher, sank beneath the waters.

Miro shook with grief. She had executed the son for his crimes against Realm, and now she was responsible for the death of the father. It was unavoidable, but it didn't make it hurt any less. Baden had seen through her and was trying to warn Erov. "What did you do to him?" She asked.

Erov shrugged. "I took back what I gave him. Did you think he lived this long on his own? I'd call it a mercy releasing him from that twisted body. And at least this way no one can ever use him against me. Not you, not even Laramak," he added with satisfaction.

"Master," the wendigo interjected. He'd been practically panting since Erov mentioned his freedom. "What you said about releasing me…"

"Chomping at the bit are you?" Erov asked sardonically. "Very well. As a member of the Council of Realm I release you from your bonds and into any world of your choosing. But first, go to Stoicese." His lips curled into a sneer. "When you find him, rip him to shreds, and when he heals, shred him again!"

*****

Her guest having departed, Ursula sat chewing her lip in her parlor, shrouded in self doubt. There was fear in her eyes as she squeezed the teddy cat in her hands nervously.

"No," she shook her head as though coming to a decision. "He asks too much this time. Too much."

Graham was ever-attendant and ever-patient with his mistress, but he wished he could convey to her a sense of the true urgency of the situation. An avatar is never completely free from its master, nor by their very nature do they wish for that freedom. They are one and the same with the master. Graham was created by Ursula at the peak of her power from a part of her own mind. Perhaps the only part of her original warrior mind that survived was that with which Graham was thinking now, and that warrior mind smelled a return to glory.

"My queen, Stoicese doesn't ask any more from you than that you defend your own borders. He will protect you from his side, but he can't be everywhere."

"He wants me to fight?" Ursula squealed like a schoolgirl, a sound that was in complete conflict with her shriveled old body. Her hand covered her mouth in an equally dainty and fragile feminine gesture.

"Yes! To fight, or let Erov and his horde of monsters destroy Realm and everything that it stands for."

"No, it just won't do," she responded, struggling to maintain a grip on her delicate composure. "Fighting is barbaric. We no longer do that."

"*Barbaric*? Fighting is what you are!" He fought utter exasperation. "Please, come with me." He held his soft fabric hand out to her and urged her to take it. He led her from the parlor and to the hall of portraits.

"This," he indicated her frail body, "is not Ursula, the Bear Goddess. You've let yourself be taken and twisted from shape to shape by the humans and your wish to be adored by them." He stopped in front of each portrait to let her absorb the changes.

"But they can't make you change. You were complicit in your own

218 ■ Alice Will

defeat; you let them *bully* you into giving up all of your strength, all of your glory, just so they would continue to honor you in smaller and smaller ways. They used to lay down their lives defending your name. Then it was just an occasional slaughtered calf. When that became too much for them they would burn the first of the harvest in offering. Now what is left in their minds of the great Ursula?" He felt her hand tighten on his and he dared not stop, but he also didn't dare turn around to face her. He nearly ran with her to reach the first portrait. "Keep looking! Here, this is who you are. *This* is the goddess you were meant to be. The Accord of Realm is broken and the armies are already assembling in the territories. Some are already moving on Stoicese. This is war, my queen. This is why you exist!"

She dropped his hand and gasped. I pushed it too far, he thought sadly. He stared up at the portrait completely without hope. "This is why *I* exist," he added in a heart-broken whisper.

"Graham," a voice in a rich contralto addressed him. It was a voice he hadn't heard in hundreds of years. "You poor, wretched thing. What have I done to you?"

He turned slowly and faced Ursula, the Bear Goddess. Right down to the scarred and shapely armor, she was the very beauty from the portrait.

"My queen?" He asked, unbelieving as she reached up to his fabric-furred muzzle.

"Damn straight. Now let's see about getting your teeth back."

*****

Something terrible churned in the depths of the Erovian Sea and was slowly approaching the shoreline. As it advanced, the foam of its wake was stained with the red gore of fish, squid, and any other life that waited in its path. Here and there a dorsal fin broke the surface before disappearing beneath the sea once again, giving rise to a sense of dread in the few lionfish that hunted the small animals along the edge of the shore. They each fought for speed to be away from the coming tide of death. As the wave reached the shallows nearer to the shore, hundreds of heads could be seen in addition to the dorsal fins. Heads with small skulls and tremendous mouths of razor-sharp teeth.

The mermaids, a species that hunted and lived alone, had massed into an army by command of Erov, and the time had come for them to rise. They would fight the way they hunted; without pattern, without remorse, and without fatigue. As they reached the shore and emerged from the sea many of them stumbled briefly, adjusting to legs which were entirely new to them. A gift from their master.

The monsters of Erov's sea poured by the hundreds out into Realm. They were hungry.

*****

Stoicese absently ran his fingers along the ridges of the shell from Miro. He could see the armies advancing already from the top of the tower, and the soldiers he had were too few to spread along each of his borders. He had no idea if he could count on Ursula to defend her own borders, and he dreaded the thought of an additional attack from that side if they came straight through her land.

From the top of the castle keep he could see all sides of his kingdom and protect it as best he could, but there were limits to what he was willing to risk with his own powers. His strongest servants lined the parapet walk with bows and arrows, and those not able to fight huddled together under the shade trees of the bailey in the safety between the castle walls. This war might have been only a distraction from what was happening in Aevum, but so many of the gods were starving for the excitement, passion, and release found only in battle and willfully blind to the ruse. They simply didn't want to see it. Because of this, he had to depend almost completely on Trotter, and the thought left him with a fresh hurt. He wished fervently that he could see her still. Her visit had been so brief, but it had reminded him of how very much he stood to lose. A millennium separated him from Miro, the goddess he would love for eternity, but their daughter had been in his arms only an hour ago. For Miro, for Trotter, he thought as he held her gift in his hand. For all of us to be together again.

He walked to the very center of the keep and circled and wide area in the floor. Where there had been nothing but stone before now appeared a small fountain with a low lip and a wide pool. Water spouted from a statue of a leaping fish in the top of it, a fish very like the one on the top of Miro's staff. He bent over the lip of the fountain and dropped the shell from Miro into it. As soon as it hit the water the shell expanded and became a long black eel that nestled immediately out of sight at the ornate base of the statue. It became almost invisible in the shadows.

Stoicese returned his attention to the coming battle. He could hear the archers taking aim and turned his eyes to follow their commands. Already the first army was in range.

The first, only. There would be many more. Nearly all of Realm, in fact. All but a very important few.

*****

Trotter held her breath as the featureless white of the canvas became the muddy swirls of melting snow. She wasn't surprised to see the castle above her, dominating the mountain tops utterly with its sprawling ramparts. It was the same castle from the bloody vision of the battle her father showed her. She shivered violently, more from the memory than the icy wind that suddenly kissed her neck. What did surprise her was the sunset glow that imbued everything around her with the pink reflection of the setting sun on the snow.

"It's almost night already," she muttered aloud while Prowler was dancing frantically trying to find anywhere that he could stand to keep his paws out of the wetness. "How long were we in the canvas?"

"Not night," a harsh voice cawed from the tree branches behind her. Sitting low in the limbs of a young fir was a brilliantly red and fierce looking bird of prey. Prowler huddled in closer to Trotter.

"Please tell me that didn't just come from the bird," he whined.

"I think so. Don't tell me a talking cat has a problem with a talking bird?"

"No. I have a problem with a talking bird with talons the size of my head!"

"I don't think you have to worry about this one." She looked up at the bird. He was vaguely hawk-like, if hawks were three feet long and the color of flame. His feathers sparkled in the red light like the embers of a dying fire. "I think he's on our side. You're Falcon, aren't you?"

The bird dipped his head in acknowledgement. "Not night," he repeated. "Laramak's sky."

"Is Laramak here already?" She asked rather more quietly.

"Not yet. Come," he flew from the low branch to a place further ahead of them on the mountain path. The trees were thinner here at the very edge of the forest, where the rocky peaks of the mountain emerged from the forest that climbed the lower slopes and in which Klempt was nestled. Trotter picked Prowler up from the snowmelt and followed Falcon's direction to a broad and ancient tree near the edge of the path. "Look," he commanded.

Carefully, she peered around the side of the tree. Where the path emerged from the forest, the mud and snow gradually gave way to dark stone shaped into a massive staircase, wide enough for an army to march down side by side. It followed a slow curve up the side of the mountain and ended at the mouth of the castle, which gaped open as though defying anyone to enter.

"Guarded," Falcon added.

This drew her eyes back to the base of the stair where, almost masked by the sheer enormity of the stairs behind them, prowled two gigantic creatures that were as related to dogs as Falcon was to a hawk.

"This is bad," Prowler said. "If Laramak isn't back, then *something* is already rounding up his rogue creations. Those beasts were the wendigo's pets, and they're practically indestructible." The hair on his back stiffened as he watched them pace, their muscular bodies tense with anticipation. "If we can see them then they can probably already smell us."

"Upwind," Falcon shook his head briskly.

"Then we're safe only until the wind shifts." Prowler sighed heavily. "Cronus was right. I do have a choice to make," he said almost to himself, jumping down from Trotter's arms onto the cold ground.

"What are you talking about?" Trotter asked.

"Look there, at the base of the tower closest to us," he nodded his head in the direction of the castle. There was a fluttering at the wide window that looked light and lacy even at this distance. There was a warm glow coming from that room despite the darkness of the rest of the castle. "If I were you and I were looking for a little girl, I'd start there."

"What do you mean, if you were me? I'm not going without you. It's not safe out here for you alone, not with those awful dogs!"

Prowler edged away from her. "That's the point. It's not safe for *you,* either. I only have about thirty seconds to do something noble for once in my life before I change my mind and hate myself forever, so don't interrupt me. Wait here and don't follow me. When they're gone, take off and run up the stairs as fast as you can and don't look back no matter what you hear." He looked at Falcon meaningfully as only a cat can, "Bird, you make sure they both follow me and not her."

The tears were already stinging Trotter's cheeks before Prowler leapt away despite her gurgling attempts to plead with him. "No, no, he can't!" She finally managed to croak before Falcon's broad wing extended in front of her protectively.

"He must," he answered brusquely, turning his attention back to the wendigo's hounds.

Prowler was out of sight, following along the inside of the trees that skirted the mountain path. When he had circled to the side of the staircase opposite from where Trotter and Falcon waited, he began to yowl loudly as though he were an injured animal. The hounds sniffed the air, growling and pawing at the ground in excitement as they looked to each other, both making motions as though starting after the sound. Finally, it seemed a decision had been made between the two of them and the one nearer to the forest sprang toward Prowler's hiding place. A flurry of motion gave away the exact spot where Prowler had been hiding and his words as he launched into a run pierced the forest canopy. "This is going to hurt!"

The one remaining behind howled with something that was either encouragement or jealousy as he held his position guarding the stairs.

Falcon grunted and dove from the branch, his powerful wings snapping as they caught air just above Trotter's head. "Not you, too!" She called after him, but it was too late.

Falcon swooped from the sky tauntingly over the snapping jaws of the hound and screamed at her as the hound snarled and hurled itself into the chase leading away from the stairs. "Run now! Run now!"

Swallowing the bitterness of panic and grief, Trotter was surprised to find that she was able to run blindly through the tears and hit the stone stairs hard, nearly jumping up them two at a time. Don't look back, don't look back, don't look back, she reminded herself. Don't look back, or he sacrificed himself for nothing.

"Prowler..." she half-whispered, half-sobbed a mournful farewell as she ran even harder, determined to outrun the sounds of snarling and snapping coming from the forest. The sounds of chase had been replaced by triumphant and satisfied howls.

Her legs and lungs burned as she climbed faster and faster, but it was completely overtaken by the pain of the loss she felt right now. Even Sarano's destruction hadn't left her feeling so empty as this. She was almost relieved when the anger somehow boiled to the surface over her grief.

They will pay, she thought, letting the anger propel her faster up the stairs. No place in any of the universes would be safe for those who got in her way now.

*****

There was a trick to the godding business, and most of all in remaining a god. The trick wasn't in the unimaginable power, and it wasn't in appearing seven stories high and causing worshippers a shortage of clean underpants. It wasn't even in the agelessness. That came naturally to a creature that could only measure its life span in terms of galactic revolutions and supernovae. The trick, the secret, was that no matter the sacrifices, the worship, the belief showered on you by your creations, you couldn't let yourself be duped into *believing* in *yourself*. Belief in yourself, in your supposed omnipotent powers and your fundamental place at the head of the world of humans... Now *that* was the ultimate trap for a god, though it was an irresistible one while the belief was strong and the soil ran red with sacrifice. But when that belief ran its course and the humans turned away to another source for strength and inspiration as they unfailingly did, to whom could a god turn?

In the old days, long before the Reconstruction and the Accord of Realm, if the gods were faced with blasphemy they would have destroyed humans one by one until not only did the entire kingdom believe, they *knew*. They *knew* that their god was all-powerful, unforgiving, and that they were completely at their mercy.

But longer still before that, before they were gods, they were just beings searching for a reason to live forever. It had been an act of longing and love that inspired the creation of humans, to give them the gift of a chance at a meaningful life, and to care for them as parents would a child. But then the love became worship, and worship became a drug. It became *belief.*

Belief itself was both the divine and the disease for a god. This was a lesson Stoicese recalled bitterly. We were all just creatures together once, so long ago, he thought. We didn't become *gods* until we created humans and ultimately demanded their worship as the price for their creation. We never knew that there would also be a price for their belief, or that belief would be the poison that drove us mad.

Here, standing on top of the world as it were and watching Realm devour itself in war, it was a lesson that he couldn't fail to remember and regret. The regret was not over creating humanity and Aevum, but of letting their position over humanity turn them into power-mad monsters. From the highest point in his tower he watched the advance of more of the monsters from Erov's sea to the east, while Avis' army had nearly reached him from the south. Ursula and her legion of ravenous bears were handling the borders to the west with ease. That had been a surprise; he was sure when he left her palace that he still hadn't reached her, the real Ursula, under the shell of a discarded goddess that she'd worn for so many centuries. He didn't know what had happened, but he was grateful. With her capable tactics he was able to focus his energy solely on the south and the east. Behind him to the north was simply nothing. His kingdom was at the very edge of Realm and rested against the borders of Chaos.

Stoicese pulled all of his mortal servants back to the castle keep to be with their families. He'd already lost too many lives to the poisonous jart birds that were the arrows of Avis, arrows that needed no bow to propel them and would fly for miles until they found a target to inject their venom and drain the blood of the wretched paralyzed victim. The flocks were always preceded by a shrill and angry whine as of the wind through the thinnest reed, but never soon enough to run. It's hard to escape an arrow that steers itself in the search for meat.

He wasn't willing to lose another life in this farce. Not any of the lives under *his* protection, anyway.

He turned back toward the relentless swarm of mermaids and raised his hand into the same field of vision, holding his fingers together beneath the swarm in a line. Slowly, he separated his fingers, grimacing with effort as though his flesh were made of unyielding lead. As the space between his fingers grew wider, a chasm opened in the ground in front of the mindless beasts and those at the front of the group were propelled down into the infinite depths of the pit. They scrabbled and clawed as they fell and pulled many of those down behind them as they sought some purchase on the crumbling ground.

Stoicese scowled as he looked at the scar he'd just created on his border. Realm would not heal as easily as the Wedge or even Aevum.

This place existed in the minds of the gods themselves instead of Chaos, so this was the only place in all the universes that wasn't recorded in the canvas. Rebuilding would be long and take a concentrated effort, and it was his intention that Realm would be returned stone for stone, tree for tree, to what it was before this war. And what it also was, and perhaps more important than anything, was a symbol. He would not destroy a symbol, not for his sake, not for anyone's sake.

One more trick to godding is not confusing omnipotence with omniscience. The gods were far from omnipotent, except when compared with the relatively powerless humans, but they were no more omniscient than your average cat. They had merely honed keen instincts over the eons, but sometimes even those still failed them. He remembered this lesson too late as he was suddenly aware of the scratching of claws on the stone behind him and the searing pain as something cannoned into him from behind, sinking its teeth deep into his shoulder between the bones.

Stoicese hit the ground hard with his attacker on his back tearing deeper and deeper into him. With his one free arm he shoved at the ground at the same time willing the castle stones below him to arch upward, allowing him to roll free over the top of the terrible teeth, wrenching himself loose at the cost of his own flesh. He suppressed a howl of pain as he rolled quickly away and turned to see his assailant before the creature could get to his feet. The mermaid snarled as it tried to free itself of the stones entangling its feet. Stoicese was raising his arm to finish the creature when he felt another set of claws sink into his remaining arm and twist the muscles under the flesh.

"You like my pet?" The hot voice whispered wetly into his ear, particles of blood and flesh from a recent meal spraying onto Stoicese's face as it spoke. "I just picked him up down in the valley. I only thought he'd make a nice distraction, but I got the added benefit of watching him nearly tearing your arm off. Not bad for a creature with the intelligence of a gadfly."

Stoicese struggled to free the arm his captor now held while his other hung limply and uselessly at his side. The gods may be immortal, but this would still take hours to heal and his weakness lay in the fact that he needed to guide his powers with his hands. If his other arm were damaged badly enough he would be helpless to defend himself or his kingdom until he healed. His attacker was unfortunately aware of this. He twisted his head and saw a tremendously clawed foot attached to a long double-jointed knee. This was a creature that could spring at will in any direction, and it shouldn't have been out of its prison in the Wedge.

He let his hand drop as though weakened, and concentrated on the ground under the feet of the wendigo. There was a howl of rage behind him and his arm was suddenly free as the stones turned to razor blades and spikes everywhere the wendigo tried to step. Stoicese threw his hand in the direction of the mermaid and rolled the rest of the ground around it, sending it swirling like a whirlpool of rock and stone until even the toothsome head was buried from sight. When the ground settled the mermaid was gone.

Stoicese turned his attention back to the wendigo who was struggling to balance on the parapet while attending the mangled and bleeding foot he'd hoisted high into the air, making him look more dog-like than ever. It was no wonder the humans had recast the wendigos in legend and myths as werewolves, with their long ears and deep blue-black fur. But what really cemented their resemblance to wolves was the muzzle, too long for a human and with canine teeth meant for tearing flesh from bone. The wendigo curled his lip over those teeth now and a low growl began building in the beast's throat. Stoicese knew its feet were already healing – Laramak had given these, these filthy carrion eaters of all things, the gift of almost instant healing, though he'd granted immortality to this one alone. It had made their capture and execution a bloody fight for the gods. As an immortal, the last wendigo had not been banished with Laramak only because he had exchanged imprisonment for the whereabouts of the others.

"When I banish you, do you think your old brothers and sisters will be happy to see you?" Stoicese taunted.

"You banish me? That takes two arms, I do believe. One to hold me and one to open a doorway. You've barely got one left. When I'm finished with you, you won't even have that much." The wendigo snapped at the air, flexing its powerful jaws. "Where do think you're going?" It asked as his quarry inched closer to the fountain.

Stoicese moved more quickly now to the back of the fountain, trying to place it between himself and the crouching wendigo. He paused behind it, waiting.

The wendigo laughed, a short barking sound, and stood firmly on its now undamaged feet. "Are you trying to hide from me? Behind a little fountain?" The double-jointed knees flexed in reverse as the creature leaned forward and it leapt across the plaza clear to the fountain's edge while the stones rippled with spikes underneath him, trying impotently to impale him.

Stoicese resisted the urge to flinch as its claws gripped firmly on the edge of the small ornamental fountain so close to him. "Everyone knows dogs don't like baths, wendigo," he goaded.

The comment struck as bitterly Stoicese hoped, and the wendigo's face twisted in anger. He jumped from the side into the fountain and crossed it too quickly for Stoicese to evade and grabbed the god's robe.

"Let's see if you can still make jokes while you're bl–"

The voice, in fact, the entire wendigo, halted and Stoicese pried his robe from the stone hard claws. He looked into the base of the fountain and saw the medusa eel detach from the wendigo's leg and slither back to its hiding place in the shadows, satisfied with its meal. The wendigo, through sheer unnatural strength, fought the toxins surging through his body just enough to open his mouth in the rise of a howl, but ultimately failed as his blue-black fur was replaced with dark gray granite.

Only now did Stoicese allow himself to give into the searing pain and he grabbed at his useless arm, shoving the bones back into place where he could to speed the healing process. He tore away a strip of his robe, and as he tore it the cloth wound around his arm on its own until he had a workable sling to immobilize it. The wound in his other arm was excruciating, but at least he could still use it.

He rushed back to the parapet to see the consequences of his distraction. A few of the brighter mermaids, those that had more than two brain cells to spare for anything other than eating and killing, were trying to find long trees to lay across the chasm, but the longest of those were still far short and spiraled hopelessly into the pit. Those trying to find a way around the chasm to the south were engaging Avis' army and causing such confusion that the soldiers of the army were killing almost as many of their comrades as the darting mermaids were.

"Interesting," he said to himself.

CHAPTER 13

"Alice," von Proustich pleaded again as she tried to hand him another cup of tea, "please listen to me. We can't stay here any longer. It's not safe for anyone or anything. Do you understand what I'm trying to tell you?"

Alice put down her cup and stared at the former baron with childish impatience. "Not safe? Of course it is, silly! I made this place, so nothing here can hurt you because *I* would never hurt you." She nodded her head firmly, ending the discussion. "Now, when you finish your tea," she continued blithely, "we'll play dress-up!"

As she spoke, a full suit of ornamental armor appeared next to another piece of kingly regalia that was purple puffed velvet with more gold brocade than adorned the officer ranks of most of the armies of the world combined.

Von Proustich sighed inwardly. This had been happening since she brought him up into the tower. Every time he tried to reason with her she would conjure some new toy, or gift, or sweet, all as though she were trying to keep him happy as she would a pet.

"Alice, my dear girl," he said, trying another approach.

"Yes, grandfather?"

"You may have created this fortress, but outside of this room, is it anything that you wanted it to be? When you dreamt up a castle of your own, didn't it have beautiful spires, and gardens, and wasn't it supposed to be perfect for a princess?" Alice was glumly silent. "This place is not the castle you wanted, my dear, is it?"

"No," came the mumbled reply.

Progress, he thought with relief. That was the first acknowledgement she'd made that she wasn't totally in control. "This castle is the same as the one that belonged to a very bad man a very long time ago. Who do you think it was that made it this way? Was it Arriman?" He prompted.

"It wasn't Arriman," she said almost contemptuously. "He's just a stupid boy. He's not even a *real* boy, but he's still stupid."

"So you can see him for what he is, then," he said almost to himself.

"Stupid? Of course."

"No, I mean, you can see that he's not a human. That he's a demon of some sort," he said gently, not sure if the word would scare her. Many of the villagers were uncommonly superstitious. Living on the constant brink of either freezing to death or starving to death tended to have that effect on a population.

"Oh," she said thoughtfully. "So that's what a demon is. I've read about them, but I got the impression that they were bigger. And not so stupid."

"I can be whatever size or shape I want, and I'm *not* stupid, thank you very much Miss Smarty Pants," came the acerbic reply from the doorway. Arriman stood there looking more serious than before, having exchanged the comical sailor suit for a leather shirt of sorts. It covered him fully, though what there was under the scales to cover von Proustich didn't want to know.

"And I heard what you said about my master, human." Arriman left the doorway to approach von Proustich and poked him in the chest hard with something that was half finger and half talon. "It's only too bad you won't live long enough to say it to his face."

"He's coming here?" he backed away from Arriman and stood protectively in front of Alice.

"Who's coming?" She asked with the slightest hint of nervousness creeping into her voice. Her grandfather was worried and she considered him the bravest man in the world. If he was worried, then something must really be wrong.

"Only the most powerful god who ever ruled in Aevum. Your so-called grandfather was right, you know. This is *his* castle, not yours. You only helped him restore it. Now that you've done that, I finally don't have to put up with your whining anymore, you little brat!"

Arriman moved closer with his slit eyes focused on Alice and von Proustich lunged at him, picking him up in the process and pressing him against the sword attached suit of armor, business end first.

"You bastard!" Arriman screeched as he pressed his dangling feet against the suit of armor and slithered his way off the sword. The noise as the blade slid from his back made Alice cry out more from disgust than fear, but the wound itself – even the leather shirt - closed tightly the moment the sword was gone. Except for the puddle of blood on the floor, it was as if it had never been there.

Both von Proustich and Alice shrank away as Arriman ran at them again, this time snarling with teeth bared, but the generations of ancestors sitting on the baron's throne had bred gallantry and nerve into the man as obviously as his inherited blue eyes and heart problem. Once again, he stood between Arriman and Alice, the child who wished so much to be his granddaughter.

"Stay away from her." He spoke levelly and softly, trying not to panic Alice any more than she already was. "I don't know if a creature like you can even be killed, but I *do* know I can make you feel pain over and over and over again. Pain like you've never imagined before."

"That's adorable coming from you. You're only standing upright at the moment because of a child keeping you alive. You know, I *was* going to kill you, but now I think I'll leave you in the dungeon for Lord Laramak's experiments. You'll probably make a sorry berserker, but I'll still enjoy watching him twist you and send you out to kill your own soldiers." Arriman flattened his hand in the air and as it arced back downward, von Proustich began to grunt with physical struggle. Arriman pressed his hand down harder and smiled as the man groaned aloud and pushed at the sky above him as though a weight were trying to crush him.

"Stop it!" Alice shrieked and threw herself at Arriman, her tiny hands slapping and clawing at him. "What are you doing to him? *Stop it!*" He ignored her completely.

The floor under von Proustich buckled before collapsing, and Alice just barely missed his outstretched hand as he disappeared from sight. She leaned over the hole left in the floor and saw that all of the floors underneath him had crumbled away just the same.

"Grandfather!" She yelled into the depths of the hole.

Aside from the complaints of bending and broken boards, she heard only silence.

And then the silence was broken by Arriman's angry scream, followed by the sharp smell of smoke in the air.

*****

The gods had been born to immortality, if they had indeed been born at all. Prowler, however, having been born a terminally mortal human, had come about immortality the long way around. He could still die as a cat, of course, but he had gained a series of Get Out Of Jail Free cards in the convention of instantaneous serial reincarnation. Given that the world drifted somewhat on its foundation in the billowy mind of Chaos, he never returned to the exact place that he had been when he died. On the whole, he viewed this as a very good thing because generally whatever or whoever had killed him was still hanging around when he reincarnated. Usually he would end up far enough away to be able to leg it for his latest life, but he was never so far away as to lose his bearings.

This time was different. This time was... *wet*.

Prowler shook his coat irritably and opened his eyes, expecting that he'd arrived in a puddle or something in the forest. What he never expected was to find himself standing in the spray of a waterfall that rushed from a slice in the air above a small pond. There was a statue of a woman at the edge of the water and he hid behind that to get temporarily out of the spray while he got his bearings, but the water still dripping from his whiskers made it impossible to think about anything else. He set to drying himself and rubbed the side of his face briskly against the stone folds of the statue's robes.

"I'd appreciate it if you didn't do that," said a gentle but firm voice.

Prowler jumped and looked up at the statue warily. "I'm sorry, madam, I didn't mean any harm. Let me just take care of that for you." He pawed gently but urgently at the streaks of moisture drying on the stone to remove the offense.

Paraben sighed. "No, Cat. I'm over here."

Prowler turned and saw a man he could only describe as 'long' lighting a corncob pipe on a stone bench nearby. He shook the final remnants of water away as he trotted over to the bench. This is fine, he thought. Nothing wrong here. I've already seen far stranger things today.

"Where am I?"

"You're in what I like to think of as the Rest Home. Thanks to you, our friend Trotter made it to the castle just fine. That was a mighty fine thing you did for her, Cat." He pointed his pipe at him and nodded approvingly.

"My name is Prowler," he said reprovingly.

"All cats are Cat on a farm," Paraben answered with a glint in his eye.

Prowler narrowed his eyes. "I wouldn't know. I've never consorted with a farm cat. Now can you tell me how to get back to her? She might need me again."

"I'm afraid you can't get there from here. But you don't need to worry about our young lady friend. She's got a number of people on her side that she doesn't even know about yet."

"If I can't get there from here, how on Aevum did I get *here* from *there*?"

"Oh, that. I'm afraid I intervened."

"Why would you have done that?"

"I have a little task for you in Realm. No rest for the wicked, I'm afraid."

"First, who *are* you?"

Paraben laughed heartily. "Have I really changed so much in the last seventy years? You really don't recognize old Paraben?"

Prowler's mouth dropped open as he studied the man's face. There was the sharp line of the nose, yes, and the sandy colored hair. The mouth was the same if he imagined it not so... so *stretched.* "Is it really? What happened to you? I don't remember you being so long, and tall, or so hayseed for that matter."

"They say the pull of Chaos is lighter up here, but I'm not sure if I believe that. I know it's been a devil of a time trying to keep the petunias from growing up like sunflowers and the corn from growing up like redwoods, though. As for the hayseed part, well, I just picked that up for fun." Paraben winked and took a theatric puff from his corncob pipe. "But back to business," he continued. "I need you to take a message and a gift to Stoicese."

"Can't you get back into Realm if you tried?"

"I could, I could. But Realm is a place of madness right now and I'm afraid I may not be able to make it back here again. Or if I do make it back, I won't be myself any longer. War can do terrible things to who we are. At least, who we think we are. And if I know anything at all, it's that she needs me still." He nodded his head toward the pond where the statue stood. Prowler looked back and was surprised to see that it was gone.

"Was that really, I mean, is it really *her* in there?" He asked carefully.

Paraben only nodded sadly and repeated, "And she still needs me."

He tucked the pipe away into the fold of his plaid jacket and pulled a small bundle of ribbon out of another pocket. He let it dangle in front of Prowler. There was a large pearl knotted at the end of it. It was dull and lifeless, as though every bit of sheen had been squeezed out of it.

"I need you to wear this and protect it until you can get it to Stoicese. And no matter what, you have to keep it dry until he can get it to Miro, do you understand?"

"Of course, but do I really have to wear it?" He protested as Paraben reached down to tie the ribbon and pearl around his neck.

"Oh, how silly of me. Would you rather keep it in your pocket?" Paraben asked ironically.

"Never mind," Prowler groused. "Just please don't tie it in a bow, if you don't mind."

"Same old Prowler I see. It's time to go. Are you ready?"

"As long as you promise me that there's a seafood buffet somewhere at the end of all of this, I'll be ready for anything."

"You know," Paraben grinned, "I think that might be even closer than you know."

*****

Every fall the farming towns outside the peninsula of Sarano had tremendous festivals to celebrate the last of the harvest. Trotter had visited these festivals out of sheer curiosity at first, then found herself looking more forward to them every year. Sarano had its own festivals, of course. There was Beer and Pretzel Day every year when the city practically shut down to go watch the toughest members of the Iron Workers Guild and the Ship Builders Guild play a game of splatball. This was a game played in a valley between two tall hills, where the object, apparently to Trotter, anyway, was to run into other players as often and as hard as you could while trying to carry an oddly shaped ball across the other team's goal at the tops of the hills. The 'splat' came in if the player carrying the ball wasn't fast enough to dodge the full beer kegs that the other team rolled down the hill to defend their goal.

There was also May Day, although it was a bit of a conundrum to most of the citizens because no one was really sure what a 'May' was, or what they were supposed to do with one if they had one. They continued celebrating it, however, because the city spiritual leaders swore that it was an ancient holiday mired in tradition and not to be forgotten. Again, most of the city shut down and everyone celebrated by giving each other, in addition to confused looks, chocolate covered hard-boiled eggs, which nobody ate, and had city wide duck hunts. Not that they shot the ducks, of course. They simply hid them in various cupboards, alleys, and trees while the children tried to find them. Getting them to not quack was the trick.

But these festivals, as enjoyable as they were, paled in comparison with the week-long Cornucopian in the fertile valley between Sarano and the tropic region of Ostano. The people of all of the farming communities converged on this spot after they pulled the final fruits of their labor from the soil and built a small city practically overnight for the occasion. Almost as soon as the first carts arrived in the morning, tents and ramshackle buildings and stalls were hammered up and by nightfall the smells of roast pig, lamb, chicken, and candied everything from squash to apples to crickets filled the air. On the final day of the festival, the villagers celebrated the relatives who were no longer with them in a peculiar way. Everyone worked all week on the decorations and on fabulously adorned masks that all shared one theme: despite the added feathers, beads or paint, the masks were all the faces of skeletons. On the last evening, the tents and stalls hastily hung their decorations in an attempt to outdo everyone else, and the small city of lights and festivities quickly became a city for the dead. There was a parade through the cobwebbed, ghost-laden avenue that passed by every tent and shack, and it always ended at The Haunt. The Haunt changed every year depending on who built the biggest shack, but it was also always the same. All throughout the shack were skulls, hideous visages, stuffed weasels, bats, and other creatures in vicious attack positions. When you passed through The Haunt, you were supposed to feel that you had passed through the bowels of hell and emerged on the other side stronger and wiser.

Laramak's castle reminded Trotter very much of The Haunt. At least, the part about the bowels of hell.

Since hunting was back in fashion among the elite of Sarano, Trotter was no stranger to seeing stuffed animal heads hanging as decoration in homes. The bulging glass eyes made her uncomfortable and she thought it was probably some clinging primitive instinct that urged an otherwise perfectly civilized individual to take a trophy head, but she accepted it nonetheless.

There were many such heads on these walls, and some were creatures she'd never seen anything like before. Some of them even had two heads sprouting from the same neck. There were hunters in Sarano who would simply *die* for a trophy like that. Judging from the teeth on the heads, possibly quite literally. But the heads that bothered her the most were all hanging in places of seeming honor next to the weapons that removed them from their former bodies.

And they were human.

Every story of Laramak, every dark fable and fairy tale she'd ever heard about the atrocities he committed, none of them could match the evil that she found when she realized that the heads were lined up oldest to youngest, and the youngest were so young that they couldn't have possibly understood what was happening to them when death came. She clenched her fists and headed faster down the hall, fairly certain she was heading in the direction of the tower Prowler had spotted from the ground.

Her instincts proved right when she heard the first hint of voices coming from deeper within the dark chambers. She ignored the echoes and tried to focus on the direction where it seemed that the sound had originated. She ran as quietly as she could when she heard the first words clearly and saw light spill from a doorway as she rounded a corner. What she heard made her run faster.

"You'll probably make a sorry berserker, but I'll still enjoy watching him twist you and send you out to kill your own soldiers."

The sound of a little girl's scream followed this, and as Trotter peered around the corner into the room she saw a man disappear beneath the floorboards and a little girl, she presumed it was Alice, try to reach for his hand as it followed him into the darkness. Trotter's hand jerked upward of its own accord and her smiting finger took aim at the horrible little lizard-like creature standing over the girl.

At first, she thought nothing had happened, but then she noticed a trail of smoke beginning to curl up from his toga, and the scales on his back began to smolder as well. The lizard creature didn't seem to notice this until he actually began to burst into flames.

The creature shrieked, but whether it was in pain or anger Trotter couldn't tell. And she didn't wait to find out. She reached her arm out to the girl who was cowering away from the creature flailing to put his flames out.

"Alice, come with me! We've got to get out of here." Trotter beckoned to her. "Please, I'm a friend, I promise," she continued when she sensed the girl's reluctance.

"Did you kill Arriman? Who are you?" Alice asked as she took Trotter's hand and ran into the hall.

That thing had a name? Trotter wondered to herself. "I'm Trotter, but I'm also someone like you. I can make things happen, too." She noted that the screaming behind them had stopped and tried to pull the girl along faster. "I don't know if he's dead, but I hope I at least slowed him down."

"Where are we going?"

Good question, Trotter thought. "Away from here, and as quickly as we can!"

"I won't leave Grandfather!" Alice stopped running and dug her feet into the ground, effectively becoming an anchor to Trotter's steamboat.

"We have to go get Grandfather!" Alice stamped her foot.

"Ok," Trotter gave herself a second to breathe. "Where is he?"

"In the dungeon. It's this way, I can feel him," Alice said distantly and began pulling Trotter down the nearest stair.

The dungeon, great. Creepy castle, now a creepy dungeon. I'm sure it will be just lovely, she thought, and there will be all sorts of fun toys to play with. *Or things that want to play with us,* the part of her brain that wanted to survive the trip reminded her.

"Alice, wait," she pulled the girl by the shoulders to an unwilling halt. "We don't know what's down there. We need to be careful. I want you to go behind me, ok?"

A pout of pure stubbornness puckered Alice's otherwise cherubic face. "But *you* don't know where he is. *I* do."

"Then tell me which way to turn, but I want you safely behind me where I can protect you."

"I don't need protecting!" Alice said angrily. She grabbed Trotter's hand and...

.... And suddenly they were standing in the dungeon staring at a man tied to a chair with a gag in his mouth. So much for caution, she thought. He was bloodied in places, and large bruises were already blossoming in black and purple across on his face. Most of his shirt and coat had been nearly ripped off of him as he plummeted through the floors into this bondage. For some reason, more than the blood or his fearful eyes, Trotter noticed the small green stone hanging incongruously around his neck from a piece of twine.

The man looked woefully at Trotter as Alice wrapped her arms around his neck after Trotter untied the gag. "You shouldn't have come," he said weakly. "You should have gotten her as far from here as you could."

"That was the plan, but she wouldn't go without you. Can you walk?"

She asked while she worked on the restraints binding his arms and legs to the chair.

"How predictable. Pathetic, but predictable," Arriman tutted at them while shaking his head. Trotter spun around to face him with shock on her face.

"Let me guess," he answered her questioning look. "You're wondering how I got here so quickly, right? You forgot about the shortcut." He jerked his head toward the hole in the ceiling and floors above that led straight to the tower room where she had left him burning. He was still smoldering slightly at the edges, but the scales she'd seen shriveling in the heat looked new and shiny. Still, there was the definite stench of cooked snake in the room.

Arriman waved toward the baron and all the bindings leaped back into place on von Proustich. A second wave produced another chair beside the first one and Alice was shoved into it, held in place by unseen hands as the bonds magically snaked into place to secure her as well. One final wave slammed her head against the back of the chair with a sickening crack, and she fell forward with her eyes closed.

Use what's at hand, Trotter remembered her father saying. She'd had a pretty good idea that he was alluding to something else at the time, but right now it still seemed like pretty good advice.

Arriman had already turned toward Trotter. "Now we can finally talk sensibly. You're going to do something for me, and you *want* to do it for me," he said, his voice somehow speaking directly to the back of her brain.

She found that a part of her really *did* want to do whatever he asked, but it was being beaten to death by the rest of her parts that remembered that this vile little thing needed to die. She twitched her fingers furiously and tried not to look at the cinder block she was mentally working loose from the wall.

"And why would I want to do something for you?" She asked, stalling for time. Another piece of mortar pulled loose and the block began to slide silently from its niche in the wall.

"Because I asked you so very nicely, and you don't want to hurt my feelings, do you? I'm just a nice little boy, after all."

Somehow there was still a part of her brain that wanted to see a sweet little boy. It was a good thing that part was so small, because if it had been much larger she would have felt just awful when she flung her arm around and cast the cinderblock into the demon's head. It made a wholly satisfying crunch when it connected. He fell hard, smashing a table underneath him. She tried to bring it down on his head again, but he reached a scaly finger out as it swung nearer and the block exploded into dust.

"Did you think you were the only one who could smite around here?" He goaded as he pulled himself up onto his feet. His broken features rearranged themselves and snapped back into place like elastic.

"You can't trick me like you do the other humans, you know," she cast her eyes around the room looking for something that would cause more damage.

"And you can't really hurt me, if you haven't figured that out. But if you help me, maybe I can say we'll go easy on the girl and her pet human."

"I could just will you out of existence, you know," she said, fighting the temptation to do just that as she spoke.

"Oh, I'm sure you could, child of Stoicese," he said. "But I'm sure you know that if you do that, then it will be as though I never existed. But that wouldn't actually solve your problem, now would it? If I weren't here now, then my master would have sent someone else and someone else might have already killed the little girl and her pet. Did you think of that? Could you live with yourself if she died because of you?"

He was right, and it burned in her to admit it.

"Maybe. But I've still proven that I can at least slow you down." She closed her eyes and focused everything she had and *pushed,* trying to imagine Arriman far, far away from them.

When she opened them, he was gone. At least, he wasn't standing in front of her anymore. She rushed to start untying Alice when his voice whispered right into her ear.

"Silly girl. You still haven't seen all of my tricks."

She spun frantically around looking for him and saw nothing but a shimmer floating in the air. She picked up the fragments of a table leg and swung it in circles through the air.

"Where are you, you little snake?" She yelled at the untouchable swirls as they began to converge on her.

"I'm everywhere," came the whisper. "And now you're about to see my best trick yet."

Trotter swung wildly at the air, missing von Proustich narrowly enough to rustle his hair. She could hear the demon's laugh ripple through the air around her. "That tickled," he teased. "Does it make you feel better to try to fight me with sticks?"

She froze. Then she cursed herself. The first trick she'd tried didn't work, so she'd reverted to a fit of panic and flailed around like a scared little girl instead of thinking of something else. Some hero she was turning out to be. *So I need something that can affect the air*, she thought.

She dropped the table leg and concentrated. Almost immediately a lacy frost pattern began weaving its way up the walls as the temperature in the room dropped farther and farther. By the time the room was colder than the deepest Drimmish winter could have dreamed of reaching, the air was clouded with frozen droplets. The droplets vibrated, radiating heat in the intensity of the anger pouring off of them, until she pushed the temperature in the room even colder and they fell with a crash to the hard floor. It wasn't until she heard the small whimper from von Proustich that she realized the effect it would also have on him and Alice. The baron was covered with a thick layer of frost and was visibly trembling, but Alice appeared flush and warm, steam rising from her tiny body. Given what she'd already seen from of the girl's power, Trotter wasn't surprised.

She nearly slipped on the ice as she ran to the chairs to help. *Small changes*, she thought. *The smallest change I can possibly make.* She focused on the rope restraints envisioned a past in which they had been damaged in just the right places, and one by one they fell away from both Alice and von Proustich with the barest of tugs. As weak as the man was, he still grabbed for Alice and cradled her in his arms, the blood dripping slightly from a cut on the back of her scalp.

"Please help me get her out of here," whispered von Proustich. "It's not her fault, she's just a girl!"

Trotter slipped her arm around him, struggling to keep him on his feet with Alice in his arms, and guided him toward the door. He was wracked with wet coughs and spat blood on the floor as they walked.

"What is your name, young lady?"

"Trotter, sir." Despite his apparent weakness, the man spoke with a confidence that seemed to expect to be answered and she found herself applying the honorific almost automatically to this man she didn't know. That wasn't something that came easily to her. All gods suffer from a disposition toward egotism, and despite growing up in the overly-genteel seaport of Sarano, 'sir' and 'ma'am' tended to grate on her inherited ego.

"Trotter? You mean you were named for a pig's foot?" He asked with a small smile.

"Yes, sir. And in knowing that you know almost all there is to know about me," she said it with the bored tone of someone who had offered that explanation more than once in her life.

"That's hard to believe coming from a young lady who is currently risking her life to save a total stranger. Not to mention when she is doing so by magic." He coughed again, this time longer and harder. She had to take Alice from his arms while he knelt on the floor until the spasm subsided, leaving him out of breath.

"It's not far now. I think I can carry her the rest of the way if you can still walk. We can get you help at the village," she offered.

"You're an optimist, too, I see," he said hoarsely, his strength melted away. "Trotter, I'm bleeding somewhere deep inside, I can feel it. Even if I make it out of the castle you know I won't make it down the mountain."

The frankness of his words surprised her, but he deserved an answer every bit as frank. "Yes, sir. You're right. For some reason I can't move Alice with magic. I've been trying, but it's like she's rooted here, somehow in these stones. But I still can't leave you here."

"That's where you're wrong. Do you know whose castle you're standing in?" She nodded. "Then you know you have more important things to do than be hindered by a dying old man. The entire world may be depending on you and little Alice Will."

"What's left of it, you mean," she said before she caught herself.

"It's gone further than here already?" He asked fearfully.

"Right now, this valley is all of the world that's left. That's why you and everything in it just became so much more important."

"Is it really gone? Forever?"

"I might be able to fix it, but only if I can stop Laramak from coming back. If I fail…" she faltered. "Let's just say that even if I'm still around to rebuild the world I wouldn't do it if it meant handing it over to *him*."

He stood still, looking grief-stricken. "Then you just defined the very reason why I'm not important at all right now. Go, *go,*" he repeated firmly when she opened her mouth as to protest. "Go and take her out of here and find Carmony. He's the baron now that I'm gone. Tell him not to fear and always remember that fear paralyzes and anger mobilizes."

Alice stirred in Trotter's arms, softly at first but then sat bolt upright and struggled free of Trotter's grasp. "He's here. Arriman's here!" She exclaimed, looking around frantically and lunged for the safety of her grandfather.

"Take her and go!" Von Proustich was frantically peeling Alice's frightened arms off of him and trying to shove her toward Trotter.

This time, however, Trotter couldn't obey. She tottered to and fro, her limbs flailing wildly. "I c-c-can't!" She stuttered, having difficulty making even her own lips follow her mental commands. It felt as though every muscle of her body had suddenly declared independence and was trying to go its own separate way. Then she watched in horror as her own finger rose and shook angrily in her face.

"You're a naughty, sneaky little girl, aren't you?" She heard the words come from her own lips and nearly choked in surprise. Alice and von Proustich looked as terrified as she felt.

"Get out of her!" Alice yelled, and Trotter found she was completely unable to respond.

"Now, now," Trotter felt her mouth forming the words despite the urgent messages she was sending to her lips to be still, "I told you I was about to show you my best trick."

"And now we've seen it," von Proust answered. "But why would you want the body of a little girl when you could have the body of a baron? Let her go and you can take me!"

"Don't be silly!" Arriman trilled happily off of Trotter's lips. Her body bent and shook as though laughing, but no sound came out. It was like watching a marionette show. "You're less than useless to me. You're basically dead already, but you're still standing for some reason." To her horror, Trotter found her finger lifting again and jabbing hard into the baron's stomach, causing him to choke violently and vomit blood onto the floor.

"Besides," he continued, his words turning Trotter's voice low and malevolent, "This isn't even the final trick. This is barely even the appetizer. You see," he danced Trotter's arms about as though illustrating the point, "bodies are *easy*. Just wait until I have her mind, too!"

Swirling beneath the surface of her own traitor flesh, a wave of fear washed over Trotter as she felt her own thoughts being suffocated deeper into non-existence. "That's right!" Arriman answered her thought. "That means I'll be able to do anything you can do. And anything you can do I can do *better*!"

Then, as suddenly as it began, the marionette show was over. All that moved for a moment was the surging, bitter aroma of the dungeon as the expression on Trotter's face locked into place. This expression wasn't the fear that had surged fleetingly to the surface under Arriman's control before. It was pure pleasure. At least, it was pleasure until she looked down at her body.

"Ew," said the voice. It was still Trotter's voice for the most part, but now there was another layer just above it and that layer was unmistakably Arriman's shrill cadence. "How disgustingly *fleshy*," it said in a tone of disgust.

"Trotter? Are you in there? Fight him!" The baron commanded.

"Oh, do stop that. You just sound ridiculous. She can't hear you anyway, so you might as well save the few breaths you have left."

Arriman dismissed him and turned thoughtful. "I know the switch is in here somewhere," he said almost to himself before lighting up again with delight and clapping Trotter's hands excitedly. "Here it is! I found it! Just watch *this*."

Before their eyes, Trotter's light skin began turning black and shiny as the scales formed on the surface. Horns began curling outward from her head and a tail swished back and forth behind her. When her eyes fell on them again they were the yellow slits of a snake.

Alice squealed, part in surprise, part in anger, and rushed toward him.

"Let her go, lizard-breath!" She cried as she pushed into what was once Trotter's very human chest, fighting the urge to draw back in revulsion as her hands met hard scale instead of yielding flesh. She pounded against the hardened chest with her fists.

"Bor-ring," Arriman announced as he brushed her hands away as casually as a speck of dust he'd found on his shirt, sending her tumbling to the ground beside von Proust in the process.

"That's better. *Now* I'm ready to meet Lord Laramak. And won't he have fun with the two of you when he returns. Maybe," Arriman gloated over the former baron, "just maybe, you'll live long enough to see the new world, old man." He then turned away from them, bolting for the exit toward Grandfather Tree and the last remnants of the doorway to Laramak's prison in Chaos.

"Then it's all over. I failed." Von Proust slumped against the wall, his breath coming in wet, strangled gasps.

"No, Grandfather." Alice patted him on the hand after pulling herself unsteadily to her feet. "He's just a stupid boy. And I'm stupid for letting him scare me so much. I'm going to go stop him for you."

"What can you do?"

"I don't know. But I think I can do just about anything I want."

CHAPTER 14

"Is this really all of them?" Carmony asked, unable to hide his shock.

"Yes, sir, every unmarried and childless man in the village who's of age," replied old Henstrich, a retired sergeant. Not many career soldiers in any of the baronies lasted until retirement, and the many battles he'd fought had left their marks, some more jagged than others. He was near seventy, but the crisscrossing pattern of deep scars on his face made him look past a century. When Henstrich retired he'd left a legend behind him, one carefully augmented by himself at any opportunity, so the former sergeant was treated with a great deal of respect by the soldiers Carmony had requested by messenger. These soldiers were capable and he could rely on their skills, but mostly he had chosen them because they were younger than he was and less likely to balk at his role as baron. If he was going to have to command an army, at least he could start with one he could manage.

"But there are only three of them!" He appraised the three men.

Granted, the winters were horrible, long, and dangerous, so the first thing the Drimmish wanted to do when they entered adulthood was find a husband or a wife to set up a warm household and share the many hardships that came with life in the Ice Bowl. For that reason, proximity and thick skin were among the most important factors in finding a spouse. Beyond that, the Drimmish simply weren't picky.

But these three… The best of them looked like a plucked and starved chicken.

"Sir, some of the married men asked to volunteer."

"I don't want to take anyone with wives or children dependent on them," Carmony answered without hesitation.

"Come to that, sir," Henstrich answered cautiously, "we take care of our own here for the most part. None of our widows or orphans have ever gone to auction, and the men take comfort in that. They won't feel right if they can't do their part to protect their families, sir."

A baron for barely half a day and I'm already screwing up, Carmony berated himself silently and wiped the beads of sweat from his brow. The late afternoon glare of the sun had cast a pall over the land. Its heat was becoming oppressive rather than rejuvenating and the snow that had begun as a blizzard that morning had melted into the ground, slowing their progress as carts and horses alike floundered in the mud. He rallied as best he could.

"You are absolutely right, Sergeant," he recovered. "But I think three will actually be enough for what we're trying to do. These three only have to be guides for my soldiers since they know the mountain and we don't. Please tell the married men who have volunteered that I am touched by their honor and their courage, but if we fail, they'll protect their families best by being right here with them."

"Yes, sir."

Carmony sighed and shook his head. "I hope to every last infernal god that it doesn't come to that, but there's so much we don't know! Those two hounds that we killed in the forest, how many more of them could there be? Who knows what else might come out of that castle."

"Yes, sir," came the ever-obedient reply, despite the obvious discomfort that was etched onto Henstrich's face.

Carmony knew that unloading his fears on the man was unfair. The baron is supposed to be the one man who is sure of what he is doing, who is sure of victory. It was Carmony's job now to give strength and courage to his people, but who would give it to him now that *his* baron was gone?

He changed the subject. "Were you able to get everything I asked for, Sergeant?"

"It's all loaded on the carts as you asked, sire." A question dangled in the air trying to free itself from the tired former sergeant's lips. He seemed to add the honorific as if asking forgiveness for having doubt.

Carmony had instructed that everyone call him nothing more formal than 'sir,' but apparently when the world became a fearsome place they wanted a baron more than an amiable young man. That was another good lesson today already.

"But?" Carmony offered as amiably as he could.

"But do you really think it will work, sire?"

There it was. The question was also in the faces of the three men who were all trying to hide behind Henstrich at the same time. They had all seen the monstrous bodies of the hounds they'd pulled from the woods, and they'd also seen the bodies of the men carried out beside them that had been ambushed by the second when subduing the first. There was reason to fear, but that in itself, contrary to all belief, wasn't reason enough to fight. Fear paralyzes, anger mobilizes. That was a favorite phrase of *his* baron. Now Carmony thought he finally understood it.

He gestured for Henstrich and the three young 'men' to follow him. He stopped at the cart that had carried the bodies from the woods and pulled the sheepskin away from their faces. Only one of them had much face left to show.

"Did you know these men, Sergeant?" Carmony asked softly. He knew that the sergeant was no stranger to gore, but he could tell from the gagging noises behind him that it was having the desired effect on the other men, as well as those eavesdroppers who'd been lingering near.

"Yes, sire," Henstrich said tightly. "These were Hane and Hedi, the Meghin twins. Young Burlen," he pointed to the youngest corpse, "was to marry my great granddaughter in spring."

"Listen to me, then, Sergeant." He put his hand firmly on the old soldier's shoulder. "This could only be the beginning of what might be waiting in that castle and already lurking in the woods. For the sake of these men and their families, it *has* to work."

He let his voice drop sonorously as he turned to the others who had gathered nearby. "For the sake of Hane, Hedi, and Burlen, we will make them pay!"

Murmurs of assent began spreading through the crowd and some of the men were already repeating "For Hane, Hedi, and Burlen!"

For The Fallen, insert name here. Carmony reflected bitterly as he walked away from the chanting crowd. It might not be the most original battle cry, but it was the only one that never seemed to go out of style. These people needed a symbol, and damn the creatures who had given them one.

*****

War is the one thing created by humans that comes closest to being immortal. It might begin as a disagreement over territory, resources, or whose god is more divine, but once the atmosphere becomes bloated with pain, fear, hatred, rage, and the thrill of killing, the creature called War is born and the reasons for fighting cease to matter. It stalks the land on the legs of armies and brings death, perpetuating deeper and deeper hatred in every heart it touches.

Worst of all, some of the scars left by War are permanent. The scorched earth beneath a battleground might, in time, be lush and fertile again, but the memory of the village that once stood there filled with families will scorch souls for generations. The battles might end and a fragile peace may be attained, but War still rages in the hearts and minds of the people, searching for a more closure than a treaty can bring and contained only through the strongest efforts of diplomacy.

Of course, therein lies a great distinction between humans and gods. Humans didn't create the original notion of war; they inherited that from the gods themselves. However, humans were the first to recognize the weakness that drove them to fight, and thereby they were the first to conceive of diplomacy.

There were no diplomats in Realm. Perhaps if there were, then it wouldn't be tearing itself apart quite literally right now.

As it has been mentioned before, Realm stood apart from those worlds spun from the fabric of Chaos because Realm itself had been spun from the fabric of the minds of the very gods who inhabited it. In essence, it was a collection of completely different kingdoms held together by no more than common consent. And since the lands and everything on them drew their existence from the minds of the gods, the lands were highly reflective of their masters' temperaments. As it stood now, the eccentric and lush beauty that had been the blanket of Realm was withering and dead, the waterfalls that stood ten miles high were dry and their cliffs crumbling, and the jeweled sky was simply no longer there, only the vastness of Chaos stretching beyond the borders of the kingdoms. Even the kingdoms themselves were becoming unfettered and Stoicese, with so much of his concentration on forcing back the inexhaustible mermaids of Erov, wasn't strong enough to hold them together.

His own kingdom as well as Ursula's had become crowded. The mermaids seemed to be pouring from the sea infinitely as though Erov had planned to choke all of Realm with his monsters. The part that had taken them all by surprise, however, was not the sheer number of his bloodthirsty mermaids, but that they had been set against all of Realm, not just Stoicese. It became apparent when Sylvia joined Avis with her archers mounted on stags. She had been shocked to find Avis engaged in battle with Erov's army, and had only been more shocked when more mermaids approached and attacked her flanks. Now both Sylvia and Avis along with a few others had moved their armies into Stoicese's land and were effectively protecting his borders in defense of themselves, allowing Stoicese to focus on the mermaids beyond his land and those that had breached Ursula's borders.

Deep in the valley in Ursula's forest, dead pine needles crunched under her iron-sheathed feet. A moment later she heard another crunch that she knew was neither hers nor Graham's and swung her tremendous battle axe in a violent arc that cleanly severed the head from the body of the mermaid that had been sneaking up behind her. She smiled as she shook the blood from the blade.

"It's been far too long since I've properly vanquished an enemy, you know," she said.

Graham padded up silently behind her and inspected her kill approvingly. "Yet it wouldn't appear that you're out of practice, Mistress," he answered her.

The sounds of fierce and guttural animal fights filtered through the dying woods to their ears and the shape of a bear flitted through the edge of eyesight chasing after an already mauled mermaid. In the face of creatures as relentless and violent as themselves, the mermaids were finally learning fear. Having captured its prey, the bear trotted back into the clearing near Ursula and Graham and dropped it neatly at their feet. The only item out of sync with this act of homage was when the bear stretched its back languidly and began using its own paw to groom its mouth and ears. Graham grimaced.

"I know, I know," Ursula interjected before Graham could comment. "In any form there's just something about the cat that won't go away. But you can't fault them in function. They're as merciless a hunter as you please."

"Yes," he grumbled, "despite the fact that they have a tendency to bat at shadows and purr at me, they're at least getting the job done." And anything is an improvement on the teddy form, he added silently.

She laughed, a deep and hearty sound, and slapped him on the rump. "I do believe all those years of cuteness have left you grouchy," she teased. "But that's my fault, I suppose. Come on then, let's get the taste of blood back in your mouth to replace some of that old stuffing."

Graham obligingly knelt down on the ground while Ursula grasped the horn on his saddle and swung her leg over. When he stood back up on his four legs with her astride him they were together, warrior and mount, an image of both perfect majesty and perfect ferocity. His armored faceplate was tipped with a rhinoceros horn and ended at his muzzle, allowing his teeth to be free to rip and slash. The weight of the armored harness, glinting with jewels and ruby splashes of blood alike, didn't even stop him from galloping with the speed of a horse. And gallop he did, with his warrior mistress guiding him, until he found a quarry of mermaids feeding off of a bear-cat they had ambushed.

Finally, he thought happily to himself as his mistress slashed about them with her axe and he tore muscle and bone alike with his teeth. Free!

*****

Arriman let the feeling of power grow within him as he skimmed through the woods heading for Grandfather Tree. The power this girl had and didn't even know! Every time he plunged deeper into her mind he found new and wondrous abilities, some of which he put to use on the occasional hunter or forest creature he found. The first villager he simply smote, leaving a blackened patch of char where he'd stood and found it very unsatisfying. For the second one he reached deeper, and turned a nearby squirrel into a rapacious creature ten times its normal size and left it to devour the villager. He watched, drooling with excitement, until the screams stopped and the fun turned boring again.

He paused again on his way only long enough to leave a few more such creations to guard the path from the castle and finally reached Grandfather Tree with anticipation tingling from his horns to his tail. The very branches seemed to tremble with eagerness as though they acted for the mind that rested so far beyond, connected only tenuously to the world through their leaves.

The time had finally come.

He stood watching the tree and swishing his tail anxiously as he sought inside of this mind he'd captured for what he needed. Deeper and deeper into Trotter's mind he plunged, ignoring the occasional resistance he encountered as she tried feebly to fight him back.

"It's too late, sweetheart," he said. "I've already got the trick. Now watch this!" He crawled under the branches to the spot where Alice had taken him before and pressed his hand against the tree and told it to *remember*. Where it shuddered with anticipation before, the tree now shook violently with effort, as though it was trying to lift its roots from the very ground.

"Remember!" He shouted at the tree, urging it forward. He clenched his fist and pounded it through the bark, opening a wound into the tree that ran thick with red sap. From the bare wood beneath the wound a hint of metal began glinting darkly as the tree pushed it to the fore from inside. Splinters and branches fell away around it as it came to the surface and saw light for the first time in a thousand years. In the broad trunk of the tree, now shorn of branches and exposed, the outline of a tremendous door suddenly appeared as though carved into the wood of the tree. The edges were crusted with char and moss grew into the corners quickly. It seemed suddenly that the ancient door had been there all along, weathering and waiting through the ages.

Arriman touched the lock and giggled anxiously. Even the metal vibrated under his touch.

"Now then, how do I open the door... let's see." He peered within Trotter's mind again, ignoring the brief surges of fear and anger as he turned over the memories like pages he came to a place where the whole of her consciousness seemed to be focused intensely, as though trying to build a wall around the memory. He was instantly intrigued "What do we have here?" He asked.

He pushed through the shroud of anger as she tried to keep him back and found something... interesting. He opened his hand and let the staff fill it, the weight dropping into place with deadly intent.

"You were going to use *this* little thing to destroy Lord Laramak?" He pulled the unwilling response from her memories. There had been a plan, though a feeble one. She was going to use this staff to transport Laramak to a place that he'd never escape. In her mind he saw the list of possibilities including the heart of a mountain or volcano, or take him through both time and Chaos so that he couldn't be found by anyone ever again.

"And then what, demi-god? Were you going to sacrifice yourself along with him? Wherever you took him I could make you bring him back again just like I'm about to do now."

I'd hurl us both into the volcano first, came the angry reply.

"Well then!" He giggled fiercely, and it sounded vaguely like a woodpecker on a chalkboard. "I guess I'll just have to make sure that can't happen, now won't I?" He dropped the staff on the ground and grinned at Trotter's mental anguish as the flame leapt from his hand and he reduced the staff to charcoal, then scattered the ashes to the wind.

"Now then, where were we? Ah, yes…"

He held his hand open and looked into the past. There was a key he needed, and since that key had once existed he could make it exist again thanks to Trotter's powers. He had only to feel its weight, to know it was there, to *believe* it was there…

And then it was. The phantom weight he'd envisioned became solid and a small key, so innocent in appearance that it could have belonged to a child's toy box, appeared in his hand.

He put the key in the lock.

"Stop it! Bad demon, you stop that right now!" Alice yelled as she grabbed his tail and pulled with all of her might until she managed to drag him away from the lock, clawing desperately at the ground all the way.

"Don't you *ever* stop? Gods, what a pain you are!" He shook his tail free of her grasp and turned on her. This time she didn't flinch when he came toward her.

"I want Trotter back. She's a lot nicer than you and I don't like you at all. So get out of her before I make you!"

"Go ahead and try it. I'll enjoy feeding you to one of my new pets!" He jerked his tail at her intending to knock her over with it but was stunned when she simply snatched it from the air and stood immovable.

"I said I'd make you, and now I will." She began to twist and pull at the tail, wedging one of her feet against his leg. Try as he might, he couldn't dislodge her foot or her hands and where she touched him he was beginning to burn.

"I said get out of her!" She cried at him.

Arriman screamed and tittered and his voice, the one that had sounded as two closely joined in harmony, began to crack and another voice could be heard again under Arriman's shrill cursing.

"Alice, keep pulling!" Trotter finally managed to make her lips form her own words. "Pull!"

The black scales that Arriman had covered Trotter's flesh with began to ripple and pull away almost like taffy, exposing pale flesh beneath. Suddenly Trotter's arms were free of her possessor and she pushed away from her with everything she had until she'd finally freed her body and legs as well.

"That's it Alice, hold him!" She raised her hand, her own hand finally of her own will, and as she brought it down a blue flame arced and came down with it, engulfing the creature completely. Arriman twisted and screamed again. At least some good had come of his possession of her; Arriman had unwittingly shown her how to access her own powers on a level she'd never been brave enough to try before.

His last words were nearly lost as the rest of his body burned away. "I still won, you know," came the bitter whisper. Then Arriman was gone.

"Are you really you again?" Alice asked, her small hands raised defensively.

Trotter looked down at her own arms and rubbed frantically at her skin as if rubbing away the memory of the scales, then felt her head for the horns that were no longer there. Finally satisfied that she was back to herself she sighed heavily and nodded. "It's all me again, thanks to you." Then concern etched across her face. "Let me see your hands, are you ok? You were burning."

"I'm fine," she answered, showing Trotter her untouched ivory hands. "I was burning him, but it wasn't hurting me."

Alice jumped forward to hug her and Trotter happily reciprocated. "You saved me, Alice. And not just me. You saved everyone."

"I'm not so sure. What did he mean when he said he won?"

A chill ran over Trotter's newly released flesh and she looked to the door standing quietly in the tree. "I don't know. But I think we should destroy that key right now."

As soon as Trotter's hand touched the key Alice gasped behind her.

"Oh, no," she said. "I think I know what he meant now. Can't you feel him coming? Laramak's almost here!"

Trotter pulled at the key again and again but it wouldn't budge from the lock for which it had been forged. She could feel it beginning to turn itself counter-clockwise in her hand and she pressed back as hard as she could to keep it from moving.

"Alice, get out of here!"

"I want to help you!"

"And the baron wanted me to save you! Do it for him, Alice, just go!"

"Grandfather," she whispered sadly.

The key finished its turn and disappeared inside of the lock, burning Trotter's hand as it went. The lock began to glow and the tree around it began to smolder until the lock melted away, leaving a hole behind that spread wider, burning at the edges. And now something was coming out of the hole...

"Go *now*!" Trotter yelled at Alice and tried to run away, but something that was more claw than hand reached out and held her arm. Alice backed away with wide eyes and, to Trotter's mixed relief and dread, disappeared. Please stay gone, she thought.

She turned back to face the creature that was using her arm as an anchor to pull itself out of the now gaping hole in the tree, and all of her remaining courage poured out of her in one long scream.

It had no face. There was a mask, a piece of armor, but there was no face within it and nothing but sharp metal teeth where there should have been a mouth. But nothing was as terrible as its eyes. Instead of emptiness behind the mask there was a deeper darkness and it seemed as though she might fall into them if she looked too closely. They were direct windows into Chaos, and from within the eyes of the mask inches from her face she felt as if infinity waited to swallow her whole.

Lord Laramak stood up straight and looked out over the world as though waking up from a dream. He didn't seem to be aware of the quaking girl in his grip at all. In fact, he didn't even seem to notice the pounding hoof beats thundering up the path toward them until a club slammed into his mask with all the force the rider could muster. Granted, the blow didn't seem to damage Laramak, but it did at least have the effect of making him drop Trotter's hand and raise both arms bemusedly to its face.

"Come on!" The rider called to Trotter while the creature was momentarily confused. Trotter took his proffered hand and climbed up behind him just as Laramak was gaining awareness of the situation, and as they thundered down the path they heard him roar.

"That one wasn't like the others. What *was* that thing?" The rider asked her urgently as they galloped furiously. Spittle foamed at the corners of the horse's mouth and its eyes rolled wildly as the rider tried to keep it from panicking.

"That thing was Lord Laramak." She answered slowly when the shock finally released her frozen tongue. *And I lost the staff. I lost the staff. I lost the staff,* she repeated to herself in silent dread.

"Gods help us, he was right," was the rider's strange reply.

CHAPTER 15

Spinning slowly in a timeless dance, the dreams of Chaos swirled past one another, spanning from birth to death and birth again in form after form as the potential blossomed here and there in bright, fleeting bursts. Within this vastness rested thousands of worlds, including Aevum and the Wedge, that had begun as ideas and then been concentrated into being. Dreams floated past them on occasion, jealous in their own feeble shrouds of potential, but they had no power to influence what had become reality. But now one of those dreams has opened a hole into one of the tiny worlds held in the mind of Chaos...

For the first time in eons, Chaos stirred from his Dreaming.

*****

Lord Laramak shook his head, trying to clear his mind. Was this another dream? His purgatory in Chaos was laced with dreams, but they were never real enough to touch, neither had he possessed solid hands that could touch them if they were. But in this dream something did just reach out and touch him. Hard. He roared, furious, daring something to approach him again.

Shaking off the disorientation of the dream, he flexed his arms and looked at them in amazement. He *did* have arms again. At the end of those arms were not the hands he remembered, though. The metal gauntlets that he wore in battle looked very much like these, but he was certain that there were no gloves on his hand. He opened and closed his fist several times and turned his hand over, and then examined his chest and face likewise. There was no flesh, no weakness, anywhere on his. At least there would be no need for armor. He *was* armor.

This time he was aware when the sound of hooves filled the path above him. Two horses with their riders came into view around the corner. One of them was dragging an enormous creature behind it that looked like it might have been a herculean relative of a raccoon.

Arrows jutted out of the creature's body from every direction. It had apparently taken many to bring it down.

Laramak stepped onto the path and the horses skittered to a nervous halt, ignoring their riders' anxious commands as they fought to turn the other way and run. But the sounds of Arriman's other distorted creatures closed in on them from behind, leaving the horses with no direction in which to bolt.

The first rider grabbed for his bow and reached into his quiver to find it empty. "Galt, this one's yours. I'm all out," the rider called with as much bravado as he could muster.

The one called Galt was already loading his own bow and loosed two quickly at the figure in the path. Both arrows not only missed their mark, but shredded into pieces as soon as they left the bow. All that reached Laramak was sawdust. The world no longer felt like a dream to him now.

This was something he knew. This was *battle*. He raised the clawed hand he'd finally accepted as his own and pointed at the first rider.

"Make War," Laramak whispered with a voice as dry as the sawdust at his feet.

"Vander, let's just go," Galt slung his bow over his shoulder. "We'll come back with more –" He broke off as he heard the snarling, expecting to see one of the other creatures behind them.

Instead, for a very brief moment before he died, he saw the first berserkers to exist on Aevum for a millennium.

Laramak was impressed by the viciousness of the horse in particular. It took far less effort to turn humans into berserkers; by the duality of their nature they were always battling their primal sides so unleashing it was a simple matter. Domesticated beasts seldom showed this level of initiative when turned.

Laramak smiled. Perhaps his powers had been distilled during his purgatory.

When it finished devouring the second rider's horse he sent them both down the path toward the village. One of the creatures that Arriman had twisted into a monster blundered out of the woods and stared at Laramak, unsure suddenly where to attack or run.

"Amateurish at best," Laramak said, his voice already stronger. It had been an owl, now far too heavy to fly, but still able to pounce on its prey and shred it in a single bite with a beak like a scimitar. But it lacked Laramak's touch of rage. "Make bloody War," he commanded it. Suddenly it howled as no owl should have ever been capable and plowed down the village path in tremendous leaps, buoyed by wings that were now tipped with razor sharp bone.

Overhead the sky deepened from the sunset glow to the crimson of blood and it burned hotter than ever. Where the snow and ice had melted away, the puddles were now boiling away in clouds of steam that hugged low to the ground.

Pleased with his new world, Laramak turned up the path toward home and the castle doors opened for him in welcome.

*****

Stoicese winced when the damaged muscles in his arm flexed as he brought his arm up hard, lifting a wave of trees, rocks, and dirt against a surging tide of mermaids that were bearing down on what remained of Avis' army from the east. Avis was currently too busy defending himself from the horde to his south to have even been aware of the danger. When the ground swelled and he saw the mermaids churning under the rocks and his army safe from the attack, Avis reached into his pouch and pulled a token from his arsenal of creatures with deadly beaks and talons; it was one that he had never expected to use. He sent it flying through the trees toward the tower where it landed near Stoicese and cooed softly, fluffing its luminous white feathers as it did so.

Never let it be said that even the smallest flutter of wings is meaningless. Avis' dove signaled an alliance and changed the nature of the war in Realm. It startled and flew away, however, when a sleek cat with blue-black fur wearing a pearl necklace suddenly appeared just a few feet away from it on the parapet.

"Oh gods!" Prowler cried as he teetered uneasily on the wall. "An entire tower and he sets me right at the edge of it. Gods should *not* be allowed to have a sense of humor," he complained.

Stoicese picked him up with his one good arm and set him down gently on firmer ground. "I'm guessing Paraben sent you here, but what about Trotter? Tell me everything that's happened so far."

"There isn't much for me to tell. As soon as we got to the castle we found the Wendigo's hounds and…" Prowler's voice drifted off as he noticed the snarling statue in the fountain. "My gods, is that him?" He asked incredulously.

"Yes, at least, it *was* him. You don't have to worry about him anymore. What about his hounds?" He pressed impatiently.

"Falcon and I had to distract them so Trotter could get into the castle. They ate me, obviously, and I can only assume they did Falcon, too."

"Falcon?" Stoicese's brow creased with thought, then relaxed. "Possibly, but I feel almost bad for the creature that ate him. It will be the worst case of heartburn he's ever had when Falcon heals and claws his way to freedom. And Trotter? Is she ok?"

"According to Paraben, yes. And he also wanted me to give you a message." Prowler looked down at his feet and frowned, which, for a cat, deserves some measure of acknowledgement. "But listen, I swear that I'm repeating this word for word no matter how looney it sounds, ok?"

"I believe you. What is the message?"

"He said, oh gods. He said 'The eagle has landed.' And then he giggled. See? I told you it sounded ridiculous!"

Stoicese rolled his eyes. The borders of Chaos were a little thinner where Paraben was. They said that because of that sometimes bits and pieces float in from other universes somehow, and that sounded very much like one of the odd bits that Paraben was likely to pick up just because he liked the way it sounded.

"It's ok. I think I know what he was trying to say. It means I've got to call the Council." He looked back down at a wretched feeling Prowler. "By the way, why are you wearing a bow?"

"It's not a bow! This is for you, too. Paraben said to keep it dry until you got to Miro." He tried to shove the ribbon off of his neck with his back paw and fell over on his side in the process. "A little help would be nice."

"Actually, hold onto it for me for bit longer. I'll be right back."

"Where are you –"

*****

Prowler's voice was lost as Stoicese stepped out of the illusion of time the gods had created for the diverse life that populated Realm. He left the cold stones of the rooftop behind and stepped into another place that had been created long ago to serve only one purpose. Here, bathed in simplicity, was the court where the Council of Realm met when decisions were needed that must be made jointly and on neutral ground.

There was little by way of decoration in the predominantly gray room aside from the austere chairs that ringed it. He strode to the foremost of these now. The Bell of Rostrum tolled deeply when Stoicese struck it with a hammer. The sonorous tones would reach every god in Realm and they would know that a council meeting had been called. By the rules of the Accord, the call was not to be ignored no matter the circumstances.

Almost immediately the gods began appearing in various states of disarray and damage. Ursula was the first to arrive and was covered in blood. Stoicese was pleased to see that none of it appeared to be hers.

"It's about time somebody rang that damn bell. Has this farce finally gone on long enough?" She spoke heartily and winked surreptitiously at Stoicese.

"Wait, we're not all here yet. Where's Erov?" Kaito asked suspiciously. Several of the more abused gods turned toward him irritably. Kaito with his turbulent winds was one of Erov's most loyal supporters, and also the type of person who would be voted most likely to be related to a weasel.

"You're surprised by this?" Sylvia snorted at him. "Why would he show his bastard face? He was the one who encouraged us to attack Stoicese and then turned his army against all of us!"

"Did you see how many there are?" Asked Cronus. He flipped though his book and added, "I'd forgotten there were going to be so many of them."

Stoicese was relieved to see that they already seemed to be of one mind. The less he had to persuade them, the better.

He exchanged a glance with Ursula, whose thinking seemed to be following the same lines.

"Let's have a look at him now. He's probably cowering in his castle waiting for his little minnows to finish his fight for him." She gestured toward the glistening wall at the opposite end of the room and listened to the murmurs of assent. Stoicese opened a chest that was filled with rows of vials, each with no more than a drop of blood in it. He selected one and handed it to Kaito to confirm that Erov's name was etched across it. Kaito nodded, still dubious, and started to hand it back.

"Oh, no," Stoicese refused the offered vial. "By all means, I think you should have the honor. If everyone is in agreement, that is."

"Just do it, Kaito, so we can get on with this," another answered.

Kaito turned and threw the vial at the crystal wall and they all waited as the blood seeped into the precious and rare stone. As the blood bonded with it, for a brief time images rippled across its glassy surface and they all saw Erov in the cave next to the pool with the imprisoned Miro. Stoicese swallowed the lump in his throat as he saw her face for the first time in centuries and found it drawn in pain. The cavern was definitely not in Realm. The blue flame which burned on the torches gave it away immediately.

"He's broken the Accord!" Ursula announced as the image faded away. "The bastard is hiding in the Wedge while we deal with his monster fish!"

"There's more," Stoicese answered, holding his hands up to quiet the outrage that carried on a dozen voices raised in anger. "Please, listen to me! Erov isn't the only one who didn't heed the call." He held out another vial which contained the blood of the god who was missing.

Avis took it from him and read the name aloud. "Laramak! If you're joking, it's in pretty poor taste. Bell or no bell, he can't come back from Chaos on his own."

"He didn't have to. Erov found a way to bring him back to Aevum."

"What kind of trick are you trying to pull? We all know that's impossible," Kaito said.

Stoicese offered him the vial again and the storm god stood rigidly, obviously afraid to even touch the container that held a part of *him*.

"Oh for crying out loud, just give it to me." Ursula took the vial and waved it smugly under Kaito's nose, smiling when he flinched. She gave it a powerful throw, shattering it against the crystal wall while every god in the room held their breath as though it might somehow open a gate into hell itself.

But they continued to hold their breath when what they saw was as close to the hell they'd feared as possible.

Even Ursula was taken aback when she saw him clearly. It wasn't until the image faded away that anyone found the courage to speak.

"Did you see him? How he's changed?"

"It was horrible! He looks more like a monster than ever."

"He's already creating his berserkers again. There's so many already!"

"And they're bigger than they were before."

"But did you see his *eyes*?"

Stoicese interrupted the din. He'd given it long enough for the effect to soak in. "Where he is now is in the very place where the changes began in Aevum."

"How do you know all of this?" Kaito challenged him.

"The way any one of you would have if Erov hadn't been so busy trying to get you to look in the other direction! Do you see now?"

"We won't be able to trick him a second time," Avis said distantly. Stoicese could see from their faces that they were all filled with the memories of the many failed attempts to stop Laramak. Sylvia was drawn within herself. Her failure had been the worst and had nearly destroyed her mind. Laramak had lured her into her own trap and locked her away with a berserker, only giving her reprieve long enough to heal and turning it loose on her again. The creature had grown fat on her flesh, and deaf from her screams.

"There's nothing else for it. We'll have to enter Aevum again to stop him," Avis finished.

"That would only leave Realm to Erov's horde and end with us destroying Aevum in the process. No," The pain in his voice burned through his solemn voice as Stoicese spoke. "I sent my daughter after him," he said. "I wasn't strong enough to send him far enough away even the last time, and if he survived in the dreams of Chaos for that long then he's going to be stronger now than any of us can imagine. Trotter is our only hope now."

"How can she beat Laramak?" Sylvia asked, her lip trembling and her eyes wide. "She's only half god!"

"No, she's not." Stoicese's grave tone silenced the room once again. "Miro is her mother, not a human. Trotter was conceived before Miro was banished from Realm by Erov."

There had been rumors of infidelity, certainly, but not even Erov had ever confirmed or denied them. Gods tended to be intensely private. Still, the admission was only surprising in one aspect.

"That was over nine centuries ago. She's only a fourteen year old child! How did you hide her?"

"We never had to until about ten years ago. Chaos took her from us before she was born."

*****

"– going?" Prowler finished and then nearly bit his tongue in surprise. "What happened? You just blurred."

"Nothing to worry about." He picked Prowler up.

"Are we going to the Council?"

"No, I just did that. We're going to go get Miro now."

"In the Wedge?" Prowler asked, his feline ears twitching in surprise. "They gave you permission?"

"Let's just say they didn't take too much convincing once I told them that Laramak had returned."

"*What?*"

Stoicese held the cat up to his face and spoke slowly. "Prowler, it's been a thousand years since I've seen her. *One thousand years*," he said slowly. It was all he gave voice to, but his eyes said far more.

"Got it," Prowler answered nervously. "No more questions. Not from me." His ears flattened back against his head as he tried to make himself as small as possible under Stoicese's glare. "Well? What are you waiting for?" He asked meekly, noting on some level that Stoicese wasn't looking at him anymore but the pearl on the ribbon.

"That pearl… I recognize it. The pool I saw Miro in must be filled with water from his sea. That's what's holding her."

"The sea where he cursed her?"

"It's something that no one else knows, but he cursed me there, too. It was his attempt at ensuring that I wouldn't come after him for banishing Miro. Not that I could have without breaking the Accord, anyway." He was thoughtful for a moment. "This means I can't take the pearl to her."

"Why do I think I'm not going to like this?"

"Trotter was right. You worry too much. Besides, a little water never hurt anyone."

"Sure, tell that to the Wendigo," Prowler grumbled.

*****

Trotter tightened her grip around the waist of her rescuer when she heard the first sounds of crashing pursuit behind them. Whether it was Laramak or one of his abominations she didn't know, nor did she care. Whatever it was, one look at it would form the basis of her nightmares for the rest of her, possibly very short, life.

"It's right behind us!" She yelled over the thundering hooves. The pounding behind them sounded like the deep staccato of another horse, but the rhythm was all wrong, and it was accompanied by snorting that was far closer to a growl than anything. She risked a look over her shoulder. And her nightmares crept into the daylight.

It was definitely another horse, or, at least what used to be a horse. And there was a grotesque and twisted rider straddling it, beating it furiously to make it run faster and faster. The growls, she realized, were coming from the rider.

But what made this truly a nightmare was the teeth... *the teeth*. The muzzle of the horse was covered in blood, and the spittle that foamed as

276 ■ Alice Will

it ran single-mindedly was flecked with what could only be bits of flesh. But the teeth... The teeth were no longer the familiar and comical large flat teeth of a horse. They were longer and so haphazardly pointed that they no longer fit within the mouth, nor even pointed in the same direction. It had fangs like daggers, teeth that any predator would envy. And they were so close to her that she could smell the foul breath that pushed out from behind them.

"Pull it now! Pull it now!" The rider screamed as they raced from the edge of the path only just ahead of the dreadful pair behind them. The instant they passed the edge of the wood a rope sprang up across the width of it, waist height for an average man. For a horse, it was enough to tangle its legs and send both it and rider toppling over in a wild somersault.

The crazed horse recovered faster than the rider did and was already on its feet before the soldiers closed in on it with spears. Flailing its head and rearing on its legs it fought, not to escape, but to devour its attackers. The horrible teeth closed on a soldier's shoulder and the hooves, which Trotter now realized had claws extending over them like a bird of prey, ripped a man fully open and further trampled him before they were able to bring it down. The rider had been hindered by a broken neck when the horse rolled over him and had been easier to subdue, despite still trying to attack the soldiers when they approached to stab it.

The soldiers hesitated in killing it once they saw its face. It flopped on the ground miserably trying to turn itself in order to slash out at them with the arm it could still move. The eyes rolled wildly looking for a victim and it hissed and snarled like a trapped animal.

"What are you waiting for? Kill it!" Her rescuer ordered the bewildered soldiers as he dismounted.

"Sir," began one, "it's Vander. Look at the face, and the uniform!" Fear radiated from every face that watched the creature. A horse turned monster, that was one thing. But a friend...

"No," the man answered with a voice that was still learning authority. "It's not Vander anymore. Vander is dead. This creature is something else entirely, something that's using him. If anything of Vander is left in there, then what do you think he'd want? To be trapped inside this creature while it tried to kill his own friends? If this happens to me," he surged ahead, "I want you all to promise that you'll kill the creature that I become, and I'll promise to do the same for you. Now deliver Vander's body from the hell that's holding it!"

The first soldier knelt closer to the face and looked into the black eyes of the creature. Nothing familiar looked back, only murder. "Kill it," he said angrily. "Kill it for Vander!"

Trotter stared in wonder. "I think I get it now. Fear paralyzes, anger mobilizes," she recited.

Her rescuer wheeled around and lifted her from the horse to bring her closer to him and whispered, "Where did you hear that? Tell me!" His blue eyes blazed with both fear and hope.

"Are you Carmony?" She asked him.

He nodded. "Did you see him? Is he alive?" He asked in a whisper.

"If he's still alive, he won't be for long," she answered sadly. "He knew he was dying. He said you were the baron now, and wanted me to tell you to remember about fear and anger. But I think you already do."

"It was the first lesson he taught me, and it was the last thing he whispered to me before he left. He thought Alice was keeping him alive. Where is she now? I saw her with you and then she was gone."

"I'd hoped she escaped, but I've got a bad feeling she went back to the castle to try to find him. I doubt even she can save him now, though. That little demon..."

She broke off as a bigger demon came crashing through the woods with wings that crashed like thunderclaps.

CHAPTER 16

Chaos cradled the tiny world in his mind as he turned it over and over. So much of it had been torn away already by magic, he could see why it had been so easy for the evil dream he'd kept imprisoned outside of it to pierce through. The hole was a blemish infinitely small compared with the immensity of Chaos, but it was enough for him to reach through and search...

*****

"Spears, archers!" Carmony cried over the mingled screams of terror. He'd ordered the soldiers in the village to prepare the defenses while he and the others laid the groundwork for their attack. They were about to return when the first of Arriman's monsters attacked them. Upon seeing Vander, Carmony knew he was the only one who'd returned.

As it stood, the defenses the soldiers had prepared were targeted mostly at the entrances to the village. No one expected an attack to come from the dense tangle of the forest.

They scurried to regroup as the feathered beast blundered into the village, demolishing the first cottage it ran into and slicing through the first soldiers to reach it with razor-edged wings. It paused only to swallow those that it killed whole, tossing them up and into its gullet as easily as field mice. It moved in a lurching gait, neither its wings nor its legs strong enough to support its full weight. It was fully the height of the firs around it and as broad as the cottages it smashed. The erratic way in which it bounded from place to place, flailing with wings and claws alike, made it even more destructive and dangerous.

Carmony watched in horror as the salvo of arrows were absorbed into the creature's feathers and flung away like twigs when it shook and flexed its plumage. The quills, he saw then, made a web as thick as chainmail and probably stronger.

Out of the corner of his eye, he noticed the curling smoke trail rising from the forge.

*****

Sadness was not something Chaos understood. Nor fear, nor anger, nor any other emotion. There was only motion. Action, reaction, momentum. But Chaos was aware of the existence of emotion and he saw the outline of strong emotion pulsing in the mind for which he was searching. This mind burned like a beacon for him to find.

Chaos was momentum, a monolithic embodiment of perfect Brownian motion, and he did not interfere. But this time the momentum of something unwanted was changing something that belonged to him. Something that was part of him.

He reached out for that mind... and touched.

*****

Laramak's owl screeched in frustration as it toppled into a home at the opposite end of the village and struggled to get back to its feet. Stones and wood flew from the building as the creature thrashed.

"Listen to me quickly," Carmony grabbed the sleeve of the first man that ran near enough to reach. The man struggled briefly until he realized that the young man holding him was his new baron.

"Go to the butcher's and gather as much fat as you can carry and bring it back here. Henstrich!" Carmony yelled at the former sergeant. The man had been struggling to lift a spear. By gods, Carmony thought, he still had it in him.

"Yes, sir?"

"Get whatever men are still standing and drag the horse beast over by the forge while that thing is down. We need something to lure him here."

Carmony caught the eye of the Innkeeper who'd been trying desperately to find a place to hide. Frieda had been among those trampled when the owl first blundered into the village.

"I need cloth, in bundles. Wrap it around the end of anything you can find, stick, sword, poker, arrows, it doesn't matter." Earl hurried obediently toward the Inn.

Carmony turned around. "You shouldn't be –" He stopped and scanned the street.

Where was the girl?

*****

Trotter ran as hard as she could up the path toward the castle, ignoring the strange sounds from the forest around her. She wasn't afraid of them anymore. Their hideousness underscored their awkward fragility, and if one tried to chase her she simply made it stop. Stop running, stop chasing, stop breathing, and stop living. She was doing what she knew she had to do now.

Move.

*****

Mounted on his horse, Carmony sprinted back and forth in front of the owl creature as it regained its ever-precarious balance.

"Come on, flea-brain, chase me!" He taunted it as he wheeled the horse and pounded into the village. The creature's muscles bunched as it sprang into the air in its lurching fashion after him, screeching with nerve-shattering volume as it did so. Despite the vast amount of ground it covered with each leap, Carmony was able to outpace the owl on his horse thanks to the amount of time and effort the creature had to expend in order to move forward, and he was out of sight by the time the creature blundered unstably into the square in front of the forge.

The stench of blood saturated the air around the corpse of the berserker horse, and the owl immediately pounced on it and began devouring it in quarters.

"Now!" Carmony ordered from his hiding place behind the forge. A horse was slapped on the rump and driven forward, dragging the end of a rope with it and drawing in the loop which had circled the horse and now the owl. The enraged owl flailed as it fell backward, pulled by its feet. The part of the horse that it still held in its beak fell away as it screeched.

Archers stepped out of the forge with cloth tipped arrows that were drenched in fat. Another soldier ran along in front of them with a torch and, as each began to flame, the archers loosed their arrows at the creature. The arrows might not have pierced the creature's protective quills, but volley after volley of burning arrows were spreading flaming fat over every inch of it. The arrows were followed by spears, sticks, anything that could hurl a wad of burning cloth.

Only when the owl was made a bonfire did Carmony stop bellowing orders and finally dared to breathe. He realized distantly that his men were cheering and chanting his name.

*****

"Grandfather, please wake up. *Please*," Alice begged.

Von Proustich stirred barely, and was aware suddenly of a soft light and the sound of water splashing nearby. He opened his eyes slightly and saw Alice leaning over him, his head cradled in her lap. "Where are we?" He asked weakly.

"I don't know," she sniffed and wiped the spilling blood away from his mouth with the sleeve of her dress. "I came to get you and wished I could go home, and this is where we ended up." She looked around her in wonder. It was beautiful in this place. The grass on which she rested was more like a carpet when compared to the spiky clumps of winter-hardened grass that sprouted briefly between the rocks each summer, and there was a rainbow glinting off of the inexplicable waterfall in the pool beside them. A statue stood silently at the edge of it. Everything was... familiar.

"Is she safe now?" The baron asked.

Alice realized the baron was looking past her, and she turned around to see a very tall man approaching them. His smile was the warmest and most comforting thing she'd ever seen.

"Yes, she is," the tall man answered kindly as he knelt beside them and brushed his hand through Alice's golden hair.

"Then I can rest now?"

"Yes. You've earned it more than most, and I thank you for it." The tall man's voice was soft, but his words were filled with emotion. Von Proustich sighed, the pain finally washing away, and grew still for the last time. The tall man laid his hand against the baron's face and closed his eyes for him

"Grandfather?" Alice blinked as hot tears ran down her cheeks.

"There, there," the man pulled her to him gently by the shoulder and held her while she cried. "He's gone to a better place now, dear child, where none of the pain can reach him."

"Where is this place?" She asked when the sobs finally subsided.

"Can't you feel it? You're home now. You're finally home." Happiness poured from the man, his face awash in his own tears.

Alice stood up on the grass and looked again at the idyllic paradise around her. "Home... yes. It is, isn't it?" She turned around slowly, taking in everything. When she turned back toward the pool she realized that the statue was now staring at her, its mouth open in wonder.

*****

Laramak walked through his castle like a captain inspecting his ship. Everything was exactly as he had left it as though it had never been stricken from the face of Aevum. He stopped when he reached his throne room and laughed, the sound echoing between the walls and swelling there before unfolding in sinister waves into the village below. The reason for his laughter was standing still in front of him, blocking his path to the throne and brandishing a sword she'd taken from the wall on the way in.

"Don't get too comfortable here, Laramak. You won't be staying long." A small voice inside of Trotter was wondering why she wasn't terrified. Actually, that wasn't entirely correct. She *was* terrified. What was strange was that being terrified didn't seem to matter right now.

Laramak towered above her and malevolence poured from him like a pall filling the room. His entire body was as solid as the armor she'd seen on the walls, as though he'd somehow fused with it during his exile. There wasn't a single place where he appeared vulnerable. *But it's still just a body, and bodies can be moved,* the thought, her thought, she supposed, calmed her mounting worries.

"Impressive for something so fragile. You seem to think that you can kill me with a sword you can barely lift." Something glinted where Laramak's eyes would have been. Trotter assumed it was a sign of enjoyment.

"No, I don't really." She threw the sword on the ground. "I just wanted to be sure I had your attention." Before he could react she raised her arms and mentally pushed out at him with all of her strength. The force of her blow nearly knocked her off her own feet and she was surprised to hear Laramak grunt as he slammed into the stone of the wall behind him. He groaned with effort as he extracted himself. As she readied herself to strike him again, Trotter heard the clamor of Laramak's twisted creatures of war racing down the hall toward them and directed her next blow at the huge doorway, collapsing the ceiling around it and blocking his minions out. When she turned her attention back to Laramak he was whispering rage into a family of mice that emerged from the hole he'd made in the wall.

"I can make as many of these as you please," Laramak promised her, laughing. "Kill them all you like, but eventually, you'll be too tired to raise those puny little arms of yours."

Trotter let her arms fall to her side and closed her eyes. As the mice grew in size and menace she pictured them in her mind as changing into something altogether different. Something that would get the point across She opened them again when she heard Laramak snarl.

What would have been his berserker mice now mewed gently as five adorable calico kittens.

"You're a Changer!" Laramak screamed.

"Yeah," Trotter smiled. "They say I take after my dad. He beat you the first time, and don't you know, the apple doesn't fall far from the tree." She raised only one finger this time and pushed, throwing him further into the next wall.

Laramak, blinded by rage and by pain, howled the words he'd only whispered before into the walls of the castle. "MAKE...WAR!!!"

A rumbling began to rise first in the depths of the castle below them, and then grew louder as the stones began to quiver with the weight of the beasts welling up inside of them trying to get out into the world to devour anything in their way. Every mouse, rat, bat, and roach in these walls must be turning, Trotter realized. *Move...* came the thought.

"Enough of this," she said. "You're coming with me."

She raised her arms again, this time pulling Laramak from the wall right into her grasp. As soon as he reached her, he focused all of his strength into turning her into a berserker; the commands he'd howled before now being channeled from the core of his will and nearly boiling from his fingertips into her flesh. He tore at the petite arm grasping him, his armor raking deep gouges in her skin.

"You will be the most grotesque of my creations when I'm finished with you," he promised, ripping another hole in her shoulder while she struggled to maintain her grip on him. Sweat and blood poured from her as she redoubled her effort to subdue him. His voice like thunder in her ear sent electric bolts of fear straight into her heart. "You will crave nothing but blood. You will eat nothing but flesh. You will live forever, rotting from the inside out. *You will make War.*"

She yelled as she felt claws begin to erupt from the tips of her fingers and her grip weaken. The smell of her own blood suddenly seemed disorienting and strong... and delicious.

"No!" She yelled, dispelling a brief and terrible image of herself attacking Prowler, Alice, her father, and everyone she'd ever cared about. She would die before she let that happen. Rather, Laramak would die before she'd let that happen.

She gritted her teeth and dug her new claws into the holes that should have been eyes in Laramak's mask. *"You... will... move!"*

They disappeared, leaving the musk of fear and blood behind.

The castle walls continued to rumble.

*****

Erov sat in a pool of his own blood, and he continued to spill more of it. He could feel the Hostage Crab moving in him, just under the skin, but it moved fast. He sat up straight, grunting with the effort, and slammed his hand down on his thigh just above his knee, cupping his fist as he did so. With his other hand he slid the knife under his skin at the outer edge of the cup and grimaced with pain as he dug with his fingers under the flesh trying to dig the crab out. As always, it was gone before he could grab it. He shook his blood from his fingers and waited to feel it move again. His body was covered with the scars of such wounds in various stages of healing, but the weaker the witch grew, the slower he healed.

And Miro was weakening fast.

"As much fun as I'm having watching you mutilate yourself, Erov, you should know that you can't catch a Hostage Crab."

Miro gasped from the pool and Erov swiveled toward the sound of the voice emanating from the doorway. "You. Of course. At least the wendigo did more damage than I really expected of him," Erov said, eying the sling on Stoicese.

Stoicese walked into the cavern and set Prowler down on the floor. "You don't seem overly surprised to see me, old friend."

"Why should I be? I heard the call of Rostrum, though obviously," he gestured toward Miro in the pool, "I was indisposed. I should have known they would back against me. They are fools, too easy to sway."

"Actually, I didn't really have to do all that much, thanks to you. What did you think was going to happen when you set your mermaids against all of Realm?"

Erov snorted. "Poor timing, I suppose. I thought Arriman would have made your little daughter bring Laramak back by now and everyone in Realm would have flooded into Aevum like lambs to the slaughter."

"Oh, Arriman did succeed. Laramak is back." Stoicese answered disinterestedly, examining his hand as he spoke. He flexed it experimentally a few times in the sling and finally smiled, reaching up to remove the sling from his shoulder. He stretched his healed arm above his head. "Ah, that's better."

"He's back? That's it? Aevum and Realm should both be overrun with terror by now!"

"They are, to a degree." Stoicese leaned closer to him. "But tell me this, Erov. Did you never once suspect that if Trotter was the one god capable of restoring Laramak that she could also be the only one capable of destroying him, too? Did you never once suspect that maybe, *just maybe*, you were getting at her perhaps a little too easily?"

Stoicese took his answer from the fear in Erov's eyes and said to Prowler, "As soon as we're gone, I need you in the water. Get that pearl to Miro."

He grabbed Erov by the throat and vanished from the cavern.

"Crap," said Prowler as he pried the ribbon over his head and took it into his teeth. "Here goesh noshing," he said around the ribbon as he jumped into the water.

Little known fact: despite their famous hatred of water, cats are excellent swimmers. But as he paddled toward Miro he began to feel the pearl growing heavier and heavier, dragging him down. "Miro!" He gasped as he surged below the surface, kicking towards her as furiously as he could. The pearl was swelling as he swam, making it harder and harder to hold onto. Miro reached out toward him as he fell beneath the water again and grabbed him by the scruff.

"Hold on," she said weakly as she reached for the pearl. "This might hurt a bit."

She clasped the pearl in her hand and squeezed until it – and everything else – exploded.

When Prowler reincarnated again, he was lying on the side of what had been the pool with the most terrible case of cottonmouth he'd ever experienced. And Miro was gone.

He had a vague recollection of intense heat, but mostly of evaporation, as though every drop of water had been rung out of his body. He got to his feet a bit unsteadily, feeling thoroughly dehydrated and looked toward the pool. Sure enough, it was bone dry.

"What's a cat got to do to get a drink around here?" He asked irritably.

*****

Erov stumbled, momentarily blinded by the stunning white all around him. Then he realized he was standing on his own again. He looked down at his body and saw that the many slashes he'd made trying to catch the crab were healed.

"You freed her, didn't you?"

"Of course," Stoicese answered. "I wanted you in one piece for what comes next."

Erov's menacing stare turned to one of surprise when he tried to strike out at Stoicese. No magic he knew would work. The god of truth merely laughed at him. "You *are* slow today. Haven't you guessed where we are yet?" He gestured around at the empty expanse of white around them. If there were walls, a floor, or a ceiling, Erov couldn't tell. It was as void of detail as a blank...

Canvas. Erov deflated entirely.

No god could reach the Canvas but Stoicese, and no god had power here with the exception of Stoicese. Erov was, for the first time in an existence that spanned eons, as powerless as a human.

"That's right," Stoicese answered. "And now we're going to visit the world you would have created."

It was easy to recall the place from memory. It was a place to which he had taken Trotter less than a day ago to show her what she would face if Laramak raised his armies once again. As the battlefield sprang up around Erov the sky darkened to a dismal red and the air grew putrid with the stink of fear and death. Not twenty feet from him was a scene of such intense carnage that even Erov looked away in disgust. A pack of wendigos feasted loudly on a dying soldier. When the soldier's screams stopped, one member of the pack heard a whimper from the god watching nearby and slowly, with the precision of a perfect hunter, moved fluidly over the land toward him as Erov turned to run.

"You're going to get your wish, Erov," Stoicese said to him as he stepped out of the memory and began to close the terrified and powerless god into the prison he'd created for him. "Every day for the rest of your existence will be this day in the world you wished for when you decided to bring Laramak back."

Erov's scream as the wendigos pounced on him one after another died away as Stoicese closed his hand on the small loop of reality he had pulled from the Canvas. This small piece, less than a day's worth of memory, would never be opened again but would repeat endlessly.

At least, thought Stoicese grimly, one day of agony for each one of thousands that you cost me in heartbreak.

*****

Darkness.

Tangible, solid, utter darkness swallowed them both here, swirling around them like a shroud.

Trotter released her grip on Laramak and felt him drift slowly away from her, clawing at the unyielding darkness around him.

"What is this?" She asked herself. She wasn't surprised that the words didn't leave her mouth. She was growing less certain that she even had a mouth here to move.

"This is the end," A voice answered her. As it spoke, a tiny pinpoint of light appeared far away from her, spilling just enough light for her to see the shadow of Laramak. He writhed silently in the pool of darkness and appeared to be in great pain.

"The end of what?" She asked the voice silently. The light grew larger as though it were speeding closer to them.

"Of everything. Where nothing else can exist. Not even the great Lord Laramak."

She looked at Laramak again. The light didn't seem to illuminate the shadows so much as push the darkness away from them, much as water washing away a stain. It swirled oddly as it departed, leaving Laramak's figure, what was left of it, in stark contrast to the background.

He was coming apart, crumbling like so much dust. There was no more movement in him, no more recognition of pain. As she watched him flying apart she was reminded of the flood of ants she'd once seen leaving a crushed anthill. So many tiny specks fleeing away... Until there was nothing left.

She looked at her own hands, expecting to see them crumbling away as well.

"Why am I still here, then, if nothing can exist?"

As the point of light grew closer she realized that, if she squinted hard enough into the brightness, it had a shape. It was walking toward her and reached out a slender hand bathed in the light borne of all of the consciousness that had ever existed.

"*Remember*," it said to her as it grasped her hand and shared some of that light with her. The words rang in her ears as she felt completely consumed by the light.

"*Remember* everything."

"Ah," she said. "I see."

*****

The celebration of the victory over the owl came to an abrupt end even as the last flame on the carcass finally expired. It was when the men heard the horses beginning to panic once again that they all realized the ground was trembling.

"Look! The castle!" A soldier yelled, pointing frantically at the dark cloud pouring out of the towers. It was a cloud of individual wings roaring and crackling into the sky. More could be seen flooding from the windows and the great castle gates and climbing down the sides.

"Sire, do you think they made it?" Henstrich asked, fear creeping into his eyes for the first time during that day of horrors.

When the owl was finally brought down, Carmony dispatched ten men to finish the job at the castle. Three to complete the mission, seven to defend them with their lives. It had been a suicide mission, but every man in the village had queued up to volunteer.

"I don't know, Henstrich. All we can do is hope for now. And fight. Kill as many as we can. Kill as many of the bastards as we can!" He repeated, raising his voice and his sword, prompting many of the other soldiers to do the same.

That was when the ground shook so hard that it felt like the entire world had just leapt three feet to the left. It threw several of the men, Carmony included, from their feet and knocked the more damaged of the cottages to the ground with a clatter that went completely unheard over the explosion echoing down from the castle. Carmony regained his feet and stared with hope the mountain. When the second and third explosions came he was more prepared and managed to stay upright, his eyes still glued to the castle. Almost as if in slow motion, the towers began to sink from left to right. They tumbled from the sky slowly, picking up speed as the cascade grew into an avalanche.

Carmony knew many of the monsters must have escaped and would be here soon, but he had good reason to hope that the explosion crushed dozens, if not hundreds of them. "That's one hell of a beer they brew here," he said to no one in particular. Every last barrel of beer had been hauled from the cellars of the now demolished Tarbach Inn and piled at the lowest support walls of the castle, packed along with the dynamite powder that gave it that distinctive flavor. Enough dynamite to move mountains. The ten men who'd returned to ignite it were heroes.

If we survive, I'll make sure every man, woman, and child in Drimbt knows their names, Carmony swore to himself.

"Sire!" A young corporal called as he ran from the southern border of the village. He was winded when he reached them.

"To the southern pass," he panted. "Flags! The army is here!"

Carmony stopped himself from whooping with joy. There will be time to celebrate later, he told himself. Be a leader for now. Be the baron he wanted you to be. He clenched his fist and rubbed his thumb over the band of the signet ring that now felt so heavy on his finger.

"Fall back!" He called, and turned toward Henstrich. "Sergeant, have everyone in the village fall back. We'll meet the army and form up there."

As he climbed back onto his horse to ride out to meet what were now *his* generals, he wondered why he was so certain that Laramak was gone and that the young brown-haired girl had something to do with it.

*****

In Paraben's serene garden there was no indication that a war being fought in Aevum as well as in Realm. Trotter found Miro and Stoicese standing arm in arm next to Paraben watching Alice play with a woman at the edge of the pool. They were both laughing and splashing one another as they raced back and forth in a game of tag. She watched all of them for a peaceful moment, soaking in the details as though she'd never seen anything so beautiful before. The woman's features were familiar, and Trotter realized that she was the same statue Paraben mourned and for whom he had built this paradise. The granite was gone, and her flesh was a soft peach and her face was framed with a mass of golden curls. Curls just like on Alice, she realized.

"She's your daughter, isn't she, Paraben?" Trotter asked, startling them all with her sudden appearance. "That's why she was able to smite Arriman and do all of the amazing things she did. She's a goddess, too. But Laramak made her even stronger, made her a Changer."

Paraben nodded, but didn't take his eyes off of his wife and child. "We had always wanted a child. Always. But by the time Alice came along, Haela was too far gone," a tear rolled down his cheek. "Alice was trapped in her for so many, many years."

"How could she have been trapped in her and survive?"

"It's different for gods than it is for humans, Trotter," Miro said to her hesitantly, almost as though she expected anger from her. "We carry our children in our minds. The souls grow inside of us and when it is ready, sometimes years later, a child comes into existence."

"How did Alice come into being if she was trapped?" She asked.

"We aren't sure. There was a time, a very brief moment, that Haela started to wake up. Alice escaped then, and the loss shocked Haela back into that awful state and made her retreat even further. I could never find her; she was far beyond my reach in Aevum."

"And then Laramak and Erov found a way to use her," Trotter said thoughtfully. "I think that must be why Chaos brought me back when he did. He knew that it was going to happen."

Miro exchanged a nervous look with Stoicese. "Trotter," she began. "I don't know if you can ever forgive us. But –"

"Mom," Trotter savored the word in her mouth, "stop." She smiled and began to let the flood of emotion that she'd been holding at bay soak over her. "Mom, I understand. I understand everything." She let herself go to her parents and be folded into their arms. "It had to happen just as it did. If you'd told me you were my mother, the Watcher would have found me out and I'd never have been safe. Even if you'd been able to teach me how to use all of my powers and helped me destroy Laramak before any of this happened, Erov still would have found another way to start a war in Realm and eventually the gods would have spilled back into Aevum. He had to be exposed or he never would have stopped. And without Laramak, without letting Erov believe he was winning, you didn't have enough rope for him to hang himself."

"In order to protect both of our worlds, we had to let them nearly be destroyed." Stoicese said. "And we had to be prepared to sacrifice everything we loved," he added, his face a mingling of apology, pride, and sorrow.

"I know why you didn't tell me. I never would have gone along with it before."

"How did you destroy Laramak?" Paraben asked her.

"I took him to the end, where even he couldn't exist. Back to where I was born," she added quietly.

Alice looked up from her play with her own mother and saw Trotter. She waved happily before giving over to fits of laughter under Haela's tickling.

"I'm going to put it all back just the way it was," Trotter announced. "Every stone, every grain of sand."

"Realm won't be as easy. It's not a part of the Canvas like Aevum," Stoicese said.

"That's where you're wrong."

He looked at her in surprise. "But it's built from our own minds, not Chaos," he argued.

"And you're built from Chaos. How could anything you build not also be a part of the Canvas? But I think I shouldn't help with Realm," she said thoughtfully. "I think if the world they destroyed in their own jealousy is simply handed back to them then they still wouldn't learn from their mistakes."

"I'm not so sure any more that gods ever *do* learn from their mistakes," Miro said sadly.

"It's not that simple. What Chaos gave you was the ability to *choose* to learn from your own mistakes. It's the same choice you gave humanity. But, human or god, choosing to learn from it also means admitting that you were wrong. Chaos also believes that the more powerful the creature, the more difficult that admission will be. Mastering that ability, if anything, should be the meaning you have all been seeking for so long."

"Chaos – Chaos actually talked to you?" Miro asked, fear and awe in her voice.

"Sort of," she answered, looking at her hand and remembering the light that filled her. It was the same light in which her soul had grown and changed for centuries before Chaos sent her back to Aevum with Miro. She'd always wondered why she had no real memories before she was about four years old. Now she knew that she had many lifetimes' worth of memories that she just hadn't been able to reach before now.

"I think I suspected that you were my mother first because of something Cronus said to me. He told me that my mother's gift would save me, and after I met Paraben all I could think of was you and the staff. Then I learned something more. He didn't mean my mother in the traditional way. He meant the mother who gave me most of my power." She sighed softly, a faraway look in her eyes.

"So, in a way Chaos talked to me, and in another way, I'm a part of Chaos," she finished.

*****

This time as Trotter walked across the surface of the Canvas it no longer felt blank to her. It was only blank to eyes that couldn't see it for what it was. Every step she took showed her a vast world from a different point of view in space or in time. It was as though the fabric surged with an infinite number of maps that were all at her fingertips for the asking.

This time, she didn't even have to raise her arms. The baroque dance that her father had performed was a fugue to her lament as she stood silently, mourning the world she'd lost with her wishes and memories. And her memories stretched far…

The first memory that she completed left her standing barefoot on the warm sand of Sarano's bay, the salt air tickling her face and the crying of the gulls which, for the first time ever, was music to her ears. When she could hear the hammers and bells from the shipyard and see the smoke rising from the blacksmiths' fires on Bellows Street she allowed the dream to shift from Sarano over the Prawn Mountains to the tropical forests of Ostano, where she'd never been.

It rose around her in a chorus of bird song and the rustling of leaves before moving past the Soggy Desert and forward to the far-flung reaches of the powerful kingdom of Tier Aní, of which Sarano was only a small part. She spun her memories forward to the rolling pastures and cliffs of Abellan and even brought back the notorious Gulf of Quisquiliae, the gulf at the shallowest edge of the Revolving Sea where the debris of an entire world collected on the shores. Pirates and scavengers battled each other for the right to pull treasures, trash, and bodies alike from the water, because anything could be sold somewhere.

As Aevum grew on the Canvas and her memories built faster and faster, she drew the world down to see it in all its splendor. It hung in front of her, the oceans glittering like jewels and the flocks of birds drifting like mist from the trees, and turned gently so that she could inspect it from every angle. Everything that had been boiled away by magic was here at her fingertips. This world, created as an act of love and also destroyed as an act of love, would be reborn of her own heart.

Satisfied that everything was there, she pushed. She pushed the missing parts of the world back into place where it encircled the tiny valley in which Klempt sat once again. And no one would remember that there was ever a time during which they had not existed.

Klempt alone sat untouched by her hand. She could restore those whom magic slipped out of reality, but the one thing still beyond her power was to bring back those who'd died. Death was final. Even while she was still drunk with the power of Chaos, however, something held her back from reaching in to destroy the creatures that escaped Laramak's castle. That part of her mind that was unstuck in time recognized the challenge ahead of Carmony to hold the barony, and it recognized that without a charge to lead it would fall to another squabbling noble who would tear it apart. She felt she owed it to von Proustich, for herself and for Alice, to see that Carmony had a fighting chance. *I could put it back together,* she thought, *but he'll rebuild it stronger than ever.*

Here, on the Canvas, she had pulled everything that had existed, good and bad, and replaced it in the world. Still, the temptation had been there to make changes. Changes that would have been intended for the better, of course, but she remembered what her father taught her and why the gods left Aevum to its own devices. For better or worse, the mortals had the exact world that they had built on their own after the gods finally left them alone. The pains, the joys, the justice and the injustice, and she wouldn't have dared to alter it a bit.

But there was still another debt she owed that she couldn't repay from here. Her father had been wrong about the Canvas when he told her it was the bedrock of everything. The Canvas was only the bedrock of the reality that *he* knew.

Truthfully, it was only the tip of the iceberg.

Trotter focused and left the Canvas for the place that she remembered from her centuries in Chaos. Where she had left Laramak was the end of everything, where all of the potential and all that existed had collapsed back into the fierce radiance of Chaos. But where she was going now was the exact opposite. Here, when she opened her eyes and gasped at the beauty and excitement of the galaxies and universes dancing and glittering in the darkness like densely scattered jewels, was the beginning of *everything*. Everything that might ever be could and did exist here, and she had only to search to find the right universe from which to borrow it.

She figured that there was a low probability of what she was looking for ever happening anywhere and had assumed that she'd have to search for a long time to find it, but in this she was wrong. She laughed when she discovered it so quickly and found that it happened in far more places than she'd ever expected.

There we go, she thought as she pushed her gift out into the world. *Her* world. One debt repaid.

She smiled as she went back to the garden to spend more time getting to know her parents. It was nice to know that they would have all the time in the world. In the universe, for that matter.

EPILOGUE

Not for the first time that day, Prowler was muttering sullenly to himself as he limped out of the wendigo's former prison and into the Wedge. Reincarnation might work, but it certainly wasn't gentle. He was tired, he was sore, he felt completely put upon and, most of all, he was *starving.*

Fighting the urge to lie down and sleep, he trudged miserably toward the Night Market hoping to find a dish of cheddar rat soufflé with his name on it. Then he heard a familiar voice behind him.

"Hey, Lap Cat." Felicia purred as she sauntered up beside him. "You look like death warmed over."

"Twice, in fact," he answered bitterly.

"What?" Her head cocked curiously.

"Nothing," he sighed. "Listen, I'd love to stay and chat, but I've got to get something to eat before I fall over."

He jumped slightly as something heavy thudded next to him, and then something else beside it, and then something else. They were silvery and smelled... heavenly. The patter came faster and faster in the alley until it was piled heavy and the aroma spread over him like a mouth-watering blanket.

"I must be dreaming. It looks like it's raining fish!" Felicia exclaimed, her tail twitching nervously.

"No," Prowler said, his eyes wide. "You know what this looks like to me?"

"What?"

He licked his lips as he plunged into the nearest pile. "A seafood buffet!"

THE END

Author's Note

If you have enjoyed this first installment in the Dreams of Chaos Series (and if you made it this far you probably have unless you have latent masochistic tendencies), I would be eternally grateful if you would help other fantasy readers discover the world of Aevum by leaving a review and telling them why you enjoyed it. If you do leave a review, please send me an email at ash@ashleychappell.com and I will send you a free electronic copy of *Tilt: Dreams of Chaos #2* as a way of saying thanks.

Until then, remember...

We are all just dreams of Chaos.

THE PANTHEON OF REALM

Name	Dominion
Aliel	Goddess of the Sun (Diminished)
Avis	God of Birds
Bidel	God of Rivers (Diminished)
Brino	Goddess of Love
Cronus	God of History
Erov	God of the Sea
Gale	God of Winds (Diminished)
Glacier	God of Ice (Diminished)
Grandol	God of Justice
Haela	Goddess of Fertility; Wife of Paraben
Harpicides	God of Music
Kaito	God of Storms
Laramak	God of War
Lepru	God of the Moon (Diminished)
Melodramus	Goddess of Theater
Miro	Goddess of Sea Creatures; Wife of Stoicese
Pak	God of the Songs of War
Paraben	God of the Field; Husband of Haela
Rhombus	Patron god of Jewelers
Stoicese	God of Truth and Reality; Husband of Miro
Sylvia	Goddess of the Forests
Tercius	God of Tactics (Diminished)
Thorium	Patron God of Blacksmiths
Topus	Patron God of Cartographers (Diminished)
Ursula	Goddess of Bears
Wymbala	Goddess of Courage and Bravery

Find more resources about the Chaos Universe including maps, glossaries, music, and character extras at www.AshleyChappellBooks.com.

Made in the USA
San Bernardino, CA
21 June 2018